WHEN I FALL IN LOVE

Sean glared at Logan, who stared out the windshield at the darkness. She said through clenched teeth, "This is not the house. Where are we?"

His grin, visible in the light of the moon glowing through the windows, made her momentarily forget her anger. "Your dad told me this morning when we drove by this place on our way to hang . . . to the golf course, that high school kids come here to make out. Now I know what you didn't do when you spent your summers here."

She refused to be embarrassed and snapped, "You're not cute, Riley."

"Yes, I am."

"Why did you bring me here? Is this part of the challenge?"

"I want to talk."

"I want to talk, too," Sean said emphatically. "I want to talk about why you think that you can kiss me anytime you feel like it."

BOOK YOUR PLACE ON OUR WEBSITE AND MAKE THE ARABESQUE ROMANCE CONNECTION!

We've created a customized website just for our very special Arabesque readers, where you can get the inside scoop on everything that's going on with Arabesque romance novels.

When you come online, you'll have the exciting opportunity to:

- View covers of upcoming books

- Learn about our future publishing schedule (listed by publication month and author)

- Find out when your favorite authors will be visiting a city near you

- Search for and order backlist books

- Check out author bios and background information

- Send e-mail to your favorite authors

- Join us in weekly chats with authors, readers and other guests

- Get writing guidelines

- AND MUCH MORE!

Visit our website at
http://www.arabesquebooks.com

WHEN I FALL IN LOVE

Tamara Sneed

ARABESQUE

★BET BOOKS

BET Publications LLC
http://www.bet.com
http://www.arabesquebooks.com

ARABESQUE BOOKS are published by

BET Publications, LLC
c/o BET BOOKS
One BET Plaza
1900 W Place NE
Washington, DC 20018-1211

All Kensington Titles, Imprints, and Distributed Lines are available at special quantity discounts for bulk purchases for sales promotions, premiums, fund-raising, and educational or institutional use. Special book excerpts or customized printings can also be created to fit specific needs. For details, write or phone the office of the Kensington special sales manager: Kensington Publishing Corp., 850 Third Avenue, New York, NY 10022, attn: Special Sales Department, Phone: 1-800-221-2647.

First Printing: February 2002
10 9 8 7 6 5 4 3 2 1

Printed in the United States of America

One

Logan Riley repeatedly pressed the television remote control buttons until he had passed through all two hundred cable channels. Nothing was on television that would remotely interest a twenty-eight-year-old single man. He wasn't surprised. It was Saturday night. Television programmers figured that most men his age were on dates, or hanging with their single friends, out having fun. Single men his age definitely did not sit at home alone in front of the television on a Saturday night restraining the urge to throw the remote control across the room.

Logan glanced at the silent telephone that innocently rested on the sofa cushion next to him. It hadn't rung all night. He knew that meant that he was once more in trouble with the various women in his life. Jennifer had been angry with him because he hadn't called when he said he would. Sheila had been angry with him because he had accidentally called her Liz. And Liz had been angry with him because she had seen him on a date with Jennifer.

Logan finally flipped off the television, then roamed around his apartment. He ignored the view of Golden Gate Park outside his living room windows. He definitely ignored the men and women walking on the street below his third-floor apartment heading toward the various restaurants and bars only a few blocks away. Judging from the noise and traffic on the street that drifted through his open window, everyone in San Francisco was doing something except him.

He strolled into the kitchen and opened the refrigerator door. He stared at the half-empty contents, which he had memorized twenty minutes ago when he last looked in the refrigerator. He slammed the door and prayed for the telephone to ring. He would talk to a telemarketer, a bill collector, anything to relieve the boring stillness of his apartment.

Suddenly a loud female scream ripped through the air. Another ear-piercing scream immediately followed, and Logan identified the noises as coming from his next-door neighbor's apartment. Adrenaline raced through his body as he sprinted into his bedroom and grabbed his off-duty gun from the nightstand drawer. He ran out the front door and down the building hallway, where he pounded on the door of Sean Weston's apartment.

He didn't expect or wait for an answer; he kicked the door open. Wood from the door splintered one way as the door swung in the other. In one smooth motion that was worthy of the silver screen, Logan dropped to the ground and rolled into the apartment, coming to one knee with his gun pointed directly at the figure who stood in the cluttered living room.

With wide eyes and an open mouth, Sean Weston gaped at Logan's commando entrance. He noticed the large red boxing gloves on her hands and a newly installed punching bag that hung in the middle of the living room. Sweat glistened on Sean's forehead, and her usual messy shoulder-length ponytail was in an even wilder state than normal as a result of her workout. She wore her usual after-work and weekend uniform of dark exercise pants and a food-stained tank top that molded to her tall, athletic frame. With disappointment, he realized that she was alone.

He reluctantly engaged the safety on the gun and stood as he stuffed it into the waistband of his pants. The idea of pounding some sense into an intruder had almost made him forget how bored he was.

"What are you doing?" Sean finally spoke, sounding to Logan more irritated than grateful.

"I heard you scream and, even though it was you, I came to help," Logan muttered. He walked into the kitchen that, as in his own apartment, was separated from the living room by a counter. "Do you have any beer?"

She ignored his question and tore off her gloves as she ran to the door. "You ruined my door."

"It's all right," Logan dismissed her as he found a bottle of beer in the refrigerator. He smiled in victory when he spied Chinese take-out containers that had not been in her refrigerator the night before. It was just like Sean to try to sneak food past him. He shook his head in amusement because, although they had been neighbors for two years, Sean still had not learned that she could not hide food from him.

"What did you think you were doing, Logan?" she demanded, glaring at him from across the room. "Starring in your own private action-adventure movie?"

"I heard you screaming. You can thank me later," Logan said as he forked noodles into his mouth. He walked across the apartment to stand near the punching bag. "Did anyone ever teach you how to use one of these things? You're not supposed to scream at the top of your lungs every time you hit the bag."

"I know how to use it," Sean protested, sounding like a petulant child as she crossed her arms over her chest. "I'm a law enforcement officer, just like you."

"I'm a cop, Sean. You're an FBI agent," he pointedly corrected her.

"We're both law enforcement officers," she insisted.

Logan rolled his eyes, then sighed in resignation. Sean would never understand the fundamental difference between being a homicide inspector for the San Francisco Police Department and being an agent who sat behind a desk staring at a computer all day for the Federal Bureau of Investigation. Logan's brother worked for the Bureau, and even Cary admitted the dull routine of his work. Of course, anything would be dull to Cary after being an undercover agent for the National Intelligence Group, a covert section of the FBI.

"I wonder how much you're going to have to pay to fix my door," Sean mused.

"You're good with stuff like that. I'm sure that you can fix it yourself," he said dismissively, then leaned against the counter to watch Sean study the door as if he had destroyed a priceless work of art.

As he studied her, Logan was surprised to suddenly notice the fullness of her breasts underneath the tank top she wore. Most days she wore shapeless suit jackets and blouses that hid any hint of her having breasts or femininity, or the more likely explanation was that she didn't have any femininity. But he could admit that Sean had all the right equipment.

She had long legs, full-sized breasts, smooth, walnut-colored brown skin, and shoulder-length black curls that could have been sexy in a just-got-out-of-bed way if she ever ran a comb through her hair and didn't just throw it in a ponytail. Instead of being small and compact or tall and hulking like most of the female cops at his job, Sean was long and supple.

He didn't doubt that she could handle herself in a dark alley with a suspect, but there was also a softness that Logan knew she probably cursed each day she looked in the mirror. Because regardless of all the equipment, the equipment belonged to Sean Weston.

Logan had never noticed her breasts. That was almost unthinkable for a man like him, who prided himself on noticing every aspect of any nearby woman. Although he wasn't certain if Sean considered herself a woman. However, as neighbors went, Logan couldn't have asked for a better one. She always had beer in her refrigerator, and she protested for only a few seconds when he took one.

"What are you staring at?" Sean demanded as she closed the door. She groaned when she noticed the small hole near the knob.

"You know what, Sean? You're not half bad," Logan said suddenly.

She directed her full attention to him, and Logan smiled at the anger that sparked in her eyes. Maybe his weekend was shaping up better than he thought. Sometimes Logan actually thought that he would rather trade witticisms with Sean than walk into another dark bar to meet another woman, who would become angry with him and not want to go out on a Saturday night when he was bored out of his mind.

"I must be going half-insane, but I'm going to ask. . . . What is that supposed to mean?"

"With makeup . . . If you actually combed your hair once in a while, maybe one Saturday night you could be on a date instead of sitting around your apartment screaming at a poor, defenseless punching bag."

"Don't make me hit you," Sean muttered as she stalked across the room to grab a bottle of water from the counter.

"I'm just saying you have about as much to offer as any woman out there," Logan said with another shrug.

"You are such a chauvinist pig," she said matter-of-factly. "Why do I have to offer a man anything? Maybe he should offer me something."

Logan suddenly snapped his fingers, as if he had reached a startling revelation; then he said, "Now I understand why you're always home alone on Saturday nights."

She rolled her eyes and plopped onto the sofa. Logan laughed, then threw the empty carton of food into the overflowing trash can in the kitchen. He surveyed the living room and shook his head in hopelessness at the clothes, papers, and law enforcement magazines littering the room.

Before Logan realized what he did, he went around the room picking up clothes and stacking the magazines on the coffee table. He balled the clothes into a bundle then stuffed them into a clothes basket that had never quite made it to the laundry room. He shook his head at the pile of dirty clothes. His hands itched to transfer the pile to the washing machine and dryer in the basement. At the last minute he talked himself out of it. Sean already teased him for being a neat freak. If he started cleaning her apartment on a Saturday night, she would never allow him to live it down.

Logan heard Sean's chuckle and he turned to see her watching him with an amused expression.

"You're itching to clean this apartment from top to bottom, aren't you?"

Logan ignored her question and grabbed his bottle of beer from the counter before he sat next to her on the sofa. "There's a fight on pay-per-view tonight. Do you want to watch it?"

"Of course; I already ordered it. . . ." The excitement vanished from her face, replaced by suspicion as she studied him. "As you've mentioned, it's Saturday night. What are you doing here? Shouldn't you be taking one of your brain-dead dates to an expensive restaurant so they won't eat?"

"I'm having women problems," Logan reluctantly admitted.

"When are you not having women problems?"

"Yeah . . . Too bad I don't have a woman to talk to who can translate women to me," Logan said then laughed at Sean's offended expression. He stood as he said, "I have to lock up my apartment; then I'll be back."

"I'll call for pizza."

"If you were a woman, Sean, I think I'd be in love." Logan winked at her, then sauntered from the apartment.

Sean groaned as soon as Logan closed the door to her apartment. She had just told herself that morning that she would not allow herself any more Logan fixes. He was hazardous to her health. She was a twenty-seven-year-old woman with a crush on her next-door neighbor. It was almost embarrassing. When she didn't want to knock him senseless for some of the things he said to purposely annoy her, she wanted to throw her arms around him and taste the lips that she had dreamed about for the last two years. How could a woman not love a man who didn't even question the fact that she had installed a punching bag in the middle of her living room?

But Sean's "relationship" with Logan was strictly confined to her dreams and fantasies. Besides the insurmountable obstacle that Logan would never see her as anything but one of the guys, Sean wanted a man who would love her, and only her, and she hadn't seen Logan with the same woman more than three times in the last two years—not that she paid attention to his dates.

She vowed that when she fell in love, it would happen once, and it would last forever. She had never admitted her vow to anyone, because then she would have to admit that she liked perfume, fingernail polish, and that she occasionally leafed through *Cosmopolitan* at the supermarket. Sean wanted a one-woman man who would accept her for who she was—a woman who loved watching the WWF more than *Days of Our Lives*—and she knew that Logan Riley was not that man. Logan's women were gorgeous, sophisticated, and the epitome of everything female that Sean proclaimed to dislike; but sometimes, late at night, she wondered if she didn't like it because she didn't understand it.

Sean reached for the cordless telephone on the floor to call her favorite pizza restaurant just as it began to ring.

"Hello," Sean said, trying not to sound surprised that her phone had actually rung on a Saturday night. Only her mother usually called her, but this weekend Sheriff Sandra Weston was hunting with some of her deputies.

"Sean, darling, it's Tina."

Sean silently groaned at the sound of her stepmother's high-pitched, cultured voice. She rolled her eyes toward the ceiling and fell onto the sofa with a long-suffering sigh before she said through clenched teeth, "Tina . . . How are you?"

"I'm as good as I can be, considering my youngest daughter is getting married in less than a week and two hundred guests will be coming to town for the wedding," Tina gushed, the excitement more than evident in her voice over the impending marriage of her beautiful and equally bubbly daughter Tracie. "We're all having such a wonderful time celebrating the wedding, Sean. We've missed you so much, but I guess that work comes first."

"It sure does," Sean muttered, as she mimicked Tina's words in her head. Sean had used work as an excuse for every invitation that she had received from her stepsister during the months preceding the wedding. Neither Tina nor Tracie seemed to see through her ruse, but Sean's father had called her the week before when she had canceled on the final gown-fitting party to tell her that he knew what she was doing.

Sean loved her father, but not even for him would she spend a whole day with her twenty-two-year-old stepsister and her giggling college friends, who stared at Sean as if she were an alien.

"I know that you have to work, sweetie. Your dad told me how important your career is, but you absolutely must be in Santa Barbara by Wednesday. We have receptions and cocktail parties and, of course, the wedding rehearsal Friday afternoon and the rehearsal dinner to follow," Tina continued, and Sean could practically envision Tina ticking one manicured nail after another at the activities that she listed. "Then Friday is the bachelorette party, which Terri is planning—"

"Bachelorette party." Sean moaned at the idea of her other stepsister planning the event. Terri was twenty-four years old and, of course, she was as drop-dead gorgeous as her mother and sister. Sean envisioned the bachelorette party taking place in a bar that played eighties music with a bunch of wealthy young women forcing Tracie to drain drinks like

Sex on the Beach and Blowjobs. In other words, Sean's own private version of torture.

"And then Saturday morning, of course, is the wedding," Tina finished with a dramatic sigh.

"And there's one last thing. . . ." Sean heard Tina's hesitation over the receiver, and she instantly straightened on the sofa and gripped the telephone to her ear. Sean knew what was coming. Every time she spoke to her stepmother since Tracie had announced her upcoming marriage, Tina broached the subject. "You haven't told us if you'll be bringing a date to any of the events."

"A date?"

"I know you will, because no one goes to a wedding alone—not even an FBI agent—but your father thought that I should still ask you."

"A date . . . as in a man? For a whole weekend?"

Tina suddenly sounded nervous as she said, "I'll just reserve space for your date at all of the events. And, of course, he can stay here with us at the house. I'm sure that he can take a vacation from work—I'm certain that he works—to come to Santa Barbara."

As if the matter were settled, Tina continued, almost speaking to herself. "I have to call the florist, then the caterer, and the seamstress, and . . . and a mother's work is never done. I'll see you Wednesday, sweetie."

Sean viciously jabbed the disconnect button and jumped to her feet to throw the telephone across the room just as Logan walked into the apartment. Even in the midst of the usual anger and frustration that resulted when she finished a conversation with her stepmother, her heart skipped a beat when she saw his dimpled grin.

He was tall and lean, with caramel brown skin and just enough muscles to make her drool, but not enough to scare small children. He had black curls that though cut short were still unruly enough to make Sean want to run her fingers through them. But the feature that she dreamed about, besides his luscious mouth, was his piercing amber-colored eyes that seemed to stare directly through to her soul when he wasn't laughing at her. Sometimes when she stared into his beautiful eyes, she became completely oblivious to whatever he rambled about. Then she would have to insult him just so he wouldn't notice how lost in his eyes she had been.

She had lived next door to him for such a long time that Sean had seen Logan in suits, shorts, and sweats, but she knew that her favorite outfit he wore was wrinkled khakis and a wrinkled T-shirt. For some reason, the idea of him looking wrinkled and rumpled, and not as immaculate and impeccable as he always did, made her think of lazy Sunday afternoons and reading newspapers in bed. Except she knew that she and Logan would never read newspapers in bed together. Logan would probably hit her with a newspaper, but that would be as close to her fantasy as she would ever get.

She turned in to Logan's solid chest, surprised to find that he had moved across the room to stand close to her. Laughter rumbled deep in Logan's chest as Sean rubbed her sore nose, which had bumped against the unyielding wall of human flesh. At five-foot-nine, she was not a short woman, and it always made her heart beat a little faster that her head barely reached Logan's shoulders. If she could ever feel feminine or dainty, Sean felt something akin to that around Logan.

"Is the pizza on the way?" Logan asked as he fell on the sofa and picked up the television remote control. As usual, he was completely oblivious to her inner conflict over her feelings for him. That was reason number 2,031 why Sean could not allow herself to be attracted to him.

"I haven't ordered it yet."

"Who were you talking to on the phone?"

"Tina," Sean spat out, then plopped onto the sofa next to him and wailed, "Why can't I have a wicked stepmother like everyone else? Why do I have to have the cheerful stepmother who wants to be one of my best girlfriends?"

Logan laughed as he said, "There are worse things in life than a stepmother who likes you."

"She only likes me because she knows how much it irritates me."

"Face it, Sean, you're just lovable," he said as he pinched her right cheek. Sean grabbed his thumb and used it to pull his entire hand from her face. Logan laughed even as he winced in pain.

Even though it didn't hurt, Sean rubbed her cheek to attempt to rid herself of the feelings the heat of his fingers sparked. She stood from the sofa to grab a bottle of beer from the refrigerator, but it was only a pretense to put distance between them.

"How are you going to survive next weekend, Sean?" Logan mused as he watched the images on the television screen. "A whole week around the Three Ts—Tina, Tracie, and Terri. At a wedding, with happy people. And you'll have to wear a dress. I don't think I've ever seen you in a dress."

Sean's retort faded from her brain as she realized that Logan was staring at her. He took a slow perusal of her body, as if picturing her in a dress. In an instant her skin began to tingle with strange bursts of lightning and an explosion of heat soaked her body. She resisted the urge to cover her suddenly flaming hot face with her hands.

His gaze finally rose to her eyes and Sean tried to speak, but her throat was suddenly dry. For the first time in their friendship, Sean could not discern the expression on Logan's face. His golden eyes had darkened and he seemed completely still, as if he waited for her to move.

Almost in unison they both moved, breaking the strange moment in the room. Sean grabbed the telephone on the kitchen wall, mumbling about pizza, while at the same time Logan turned to the television screen.

Two

Sean bit into the Snickers bar, then set it on her desk before her fingers flew over the computer keyboard. After a restless weekend during which Logan had forced her to clean every inch of her apartment—although she admitted that he had done most of the cleaning while she had done all of the complaining—Sean had been relieved to return to work that Monday morning. She had been relieved to return to the barely controlled chaos of the FBI offices—the ringing telephones, the jumble of human voices, and the smell of active brainpower. Burying herself in her work was the exact counterresponse she needed after a weekend spent with the soapy scent of Logan in the air and with his teasing laughter ringing in her ears.

The telephone on her desk rang, blending with the other ringing telephones in the background, and Sean reached for it just as she remembered the chocolate on the tips of her fingers. She groaned at the smudges on her keyboard and the smear on the beige telephone. Sean yanked open the top drawer of her desk and, amid the mess of pens and papers, she found a balled-up tissue. She quickly wiped off her fingers and the telephone, then grabbed the receiver.

"Agent Weston," she snapped into the receiver.

"Sean, it's your mother." Sean heard the familiar din of the Santa Cruz County sheriff's office in the background.

Sandra Weston was the sheriff of Santa Cruz, a small beach community an hour south of San Francisco, and she was one of the most legendary female police officers in California. Sean admired her mother more than any superior she ever had at the FBI, but she also felt the awesome responsibility of having to live up to being the daughter of Sandra Weston in the northern California law enforcement community.

"After twenty-seven years I know your voice by now, Mother." Sandra's answering silence made Sean sigh and mutter, "I'm sorry."

"Are you having trouble at work?" Sandra finally spoke.

Sean raked a hand through her hair, not caring that she dislodged her ponytail and scattered curls across her head. "Nothing that I can't handle. Was there a specific reason why you called?"

"I want to talk to you about Tracie's wedding." Sean groaned, sensing the impending lecture. "Your father and I talked last night about your less-than-enthusiastic response to your part in the wedding."

Not for the first time in her life, Sean wished that her divorced parents were not such good friends. Their relationship had improved once they divorced when Sean had been eight years old and she and her mother had moved to Santa Cruz from San Francisco. Her father had moved to Santa Barbara, where he met Tina, and married her two years later.

"I know you think the Three Ts—" Sandra sighed in disgust at her own use of the nickname that Sean had given the three women. She continued in a firmer voice, "I know that you think Tina, Tracie, and Terri are beneath you and all of your feminist ideology, but they are your family and you have a responsibility to be a part of this wedding."

"I don't think that they're beneath me, Mom."

Sandra continued her lecture as if Sean had never spoken. "I want you to show some excitement for this wedding. I want you to be the happiest bridesmaid at the festivities.

And I want you to smile. Tina is very excited about this wedding, as are your father, Tracie, and Terri. I don't want to hear any of your sarcastic comments. Do you understand me?"

"Yes," Sean grumbled, feeling like a suspect who had been given no option—talk and go to jail or don't talk and go to jail. Sean rallied for one last protest of innocence: "I still don't know why Tracie asked me to be a bridesmaid."

"Because she thinks of you as her second big sister, even if you see her only as an inconvenience."

Sean rolled her eyes in disgust at herself. Even as an adult, it took one lecture from her mother to make her feel like an ungrateful brat. Sean suddenly grinned when she saw the light flashing on the telephone console to indicate another call.

"I have to go, Mom; I have another call." She hoped that her mother didn't hear the relief in her voice.

"The next time I speak to your father, I want to hear that there has been some improvement in your attitude."

"Yes, ma'am."

"When are you leaving for Santa Barbara?"

"In two days."

"I probably won't see you until the day of the wedding. Drive safely."

Sean didn't respond but switched to the next call. She almost wished that she had listened to more of her mother's lecture when she heard the greeting giggle of her stepsister Terri.

Sean found herself patting down errant strands of hair at the sound of Terri's voice. There was something about the Three Ts that made Sean feel like a rumpled, unwanted child. As children, Terri and Tracie had never gotten their clothes dirty, never had a hair out of place, while Sean hadn't been able to wear clean clothes for more than thirty seconds without dirt attaching to her like a parasite. It drove Sean particularly insane because she didn't normally care about things like her hair and the state of her clothes until she ran into the perfect, immovable wall of the Three Ts.

"Hi, Sean," Terri greeted, her enthusiasm practically bubbling over the telephone to strangle Sean.

"Hi, Terri." She forced a smile into her voice, remembering her mother's warning. "Is there a problem? I just spoke to your mother last night."

"Of course not," Terri responded. "I just wanted to tell you how much I'm looking forward to seeing you again. I can't remember the last time we saw each other."

"Nine months ago at Dad and Tina's anniversary party," Sean instantly replied. Nine glorious and free months when she had carefully avoided most telephone conversations with her stepsisters and had kept the ones that she'd been forced to have to a polite minimum.

"You left as soon as the party was over. You and I never got a chance to talk. This time you'll be here for the whole weekend," Terri reminded Sean. "Did you receive the bridesmaid dress?"

"A few days ago." Sean didn't respond that the expensive dress still sat in the box that it had been delivered in. She prayed that it fit the day of the wedding, because she could not force herself to look at whatever pastel chiffon creation Tracie had envisioned Sean in.

"You probably noticed that it's strapless and anklelength." Terri audibly hesitated, then added, "You should shave under your arms. Just to be safe, you should shave your legs, too. We never know when a breeze may come and lift up the dress."

"I shave under my arms," Sean grumbled. She didn't add that a razor hadn't touched her legs in almost three weeks. What was the point? All of her suits included pants, not skirts.

Terri continued in the same nervous voice. "There was another reason why I called. I know that you don't like . . . I know you're . . . If you need help with your hair or makeup for any of the events, I'll be more than happy to assist, Sean."

"That won't be necessary, Terri," Sean coldly replied, feeling once more like the rumpled little girl of her youth.

"Not for the rehearsal or the bachelorette party, but the wedding . . . We can discuss this later." Terri's nervous laughter filled the charged silence as Sean took a big chunk out of the Snickers bar. Terri cheerfully said, "Mother told me that you're bringing a date here for the whole weekend. Who is he, Sean? I didn't even know that you were dating someone. I told Mom that it would happen sooner or later."

"A date." Sean nearly choked on her mouthful of chocolate.

Terri giggled as she said, "There's someone for everyone, right, Sean? I'm just glad that you have a date. It would have been a little uncomfortable for you to be the only person at the wedding without one. Even your mother is bringing someone."

"My mother is bringing a date?"

"Didn't she tell you?" Terri asked cheerfully. "She said that you know him. Phil Howell."

"Deputy Howell." Sean quickly gulped from the bottled water on her desk. Her mother was dating her deputy, the deputy whom she always complained about because Sandra thought that he resented her authority. Sean felt betrayed— not because Sandra was bringing a date to the wedding, but because Terri had known and Sean had not.

"Sean, my assistant just walked into the office," Terri said, appearing completely oblivious to Sean's shock. "I'll see you Wednesday afternoon, right?"

"Right."

"And tell your escort not to worry. If he wants to go to Sheldon's bachelor party while you're at the bachelorette party, he's more than welcome. Sheldon has always liked you. He'd love the chance to meet your boyfriend."

Sean wordlessly hung up the telephone, feeling unable to

move except to lift the chocolate bar to her mouth for another bite. Besides, who the hell was Sheldon? Sean's eyes moved to Tracie's wedding invitation that Sean had pinned to her cubicle wall. Tracie Harrison-Weston and Sheldon Cameron. Sheldon was the groom. At least one mystery had been solved. Now for the next problem. Where was she going to find a man willing to go to Santa Barbara with her for four days?

Sean dropped her briefcase and purse in the middle of the hallway of her apartment building; then she pounded on Logan's apartment door. She glanced at her watch. It was almost nine o'clock. She had just gotten home from work and she needed to talk to him. As infuriating as Logan could be, he was also the only person Sean knew who could make her feel better.

She needed to talk to him. He had to help her. She had spent the entire day fuming over the telephone call with Terri. Sean knew how to shave. She could wear makeup with the best of them. She didn't need help from her stepsister. But she did need help from Logan.

Sean kicked the door in frustration just as Logan reached the top of the staircase of the apartment building. He automatically smiled when he saw her, and Sean's heart did the normal Logan Riley flip. Did he have to be so beautiful? In the charcoal gray suit and matching tie that he wore, he exuded as much sex appeal as some men would in a tuxedo or nude. Sean's dreamlike thoughts of Logan instantly stopped when she noticed a woman walking behind him.

As was the case with all of Logan Riley's dates, she was not just beautiful: the woman was stunning. She was tall and thin, and wore a shimmering, cleavage-baring, thigh-skimming dress that would have showed body flaws on any other woman, but only emphasized her chocolate brown perfection. Sean would have probably fallen flat on her face if she had worn the three-inch spiked heels the woman wore, instead of floating down the hallway as this woman did. And the most offensive thing about her as far as Sean was concerned was that woman's shoulder-length black hair hung like a sea of glass around her shoulders, not one stray curl rearing its ugly head. The woman smiled at her, and Sean barely resisted the urge to snarl.

"Are you attempting to give my door the same treatment that I gave yours?" Logan asked, glancing at the dark mark from her shoe on the bottom of his white door.

"Terri told me to shave," Sean practically exploded, her pent-up anger making her momentarily forget the African goddess standing behind him. She bitterly laughed, then snorted. "As if I don't shave."

Logan didn't blink as he pointed out, "You don't shave."

"Why does everyone think that? I shave. Not every day, but I shave. And why should I shave my legs when I never wear a skirt? What's the point of shaved legs underneath pants . . . ?" She waved her hands dismissively as her anger only increased. She took several deep breaths, then said in what she hoped was a calm voice, "I need your help, Logan."

"I didn't think that I'd ever hear those words from your mouth," Logan said, laughing. "What can I possibly do? Have you forgotten how to shave and you need me to give you a refresher course? I've never shaved my legs or under my arms, but it can't be that different from when I shave my face—"

Sean landed a not-so-playful fist on his arm, and Logan grunted in pain even as he laughed. He rubbed his biceps and pretended soreness. Sean knew that her hand probably hurt more than his biceps, which felt like chiseled granite.

"I'm serious, Logan. I need your help," she said more firmly.

"Logan, maybe I should wait inside while you two talk."

The woman spoke in a soft, husky voice that Sean instantly knew would cause men to drool.

Logan turned to the woman and offered a smile that forced Sean to remind herself that she was not jealous of Logan's latest conquest. The woman was gorgeous, but she was also probably as dumb as a doorknob—too dumb to pass the rigorous FBI admission exams.

"I apologize for my rudeness," Logan practically purred to his date as he guided one of her delicate and no-doubt soft hands to his mouth for a kiss that made Sean clench her callused hands into fists. "Jennifer, this is my next-door neighbor, Sean Weston. Sean, this is Dr. Jennifer Gridley. She teaches nuclear physics at UCSF."

Sean tried not to cringe as she shook hands with the nuclear physicist. So Jennifer was smart. Sean still would bet that the nerd could not do sixty sit-ups in thirty seconds.

"Logan has told me so much about you. It's so wonderful to meet women like you, women who make little girls believe that they can be anything they want, even an FBI agent."

"You, too," Sean mumbled, cursing Logan for dating not only beautiful but smart and nice women. No matter how much she wanted to, she could not intrude on his date, even if he would allow it, which Sean knew he would not. She swallowed the thick lump in her throat even as she forced a smile. "I'm sorry to interrupt your evening. I'll talk to you tomorrow, Logan."

Sean turned toward her apartment, but Logan grabbed her arm. She was surprised by the concern on his face. She shouldn't have been. Logan was a caring person . . . even for his not-quite friends.

"Jennifer and I have some time before we have to make our dinner reservation. We can talk," Logan said, then glanced at Jennifer and sweetly cooed, "if that's all right with you?"

"Of course. I'll freshen up." Logan unlocked the door to

his apartment. After another kiss on the back of Jennifer's hand, Jennifer walked into the apartment.

"A nuclear physicist, Logan?" Sean said in a hiss as soon as the door closed. "Where do you find these women?"

"What do you mean?"

Sean rolled her eyes in frustration at his blank expression. She forgot that model-beautiful nuclear physicists were everyday occurrences in Logan Riley's world.

He ignored her outburst and asked, "What's wrong, Sean? I haven't seen you this upset since you found out that professional wrestling is fake."

It took Sean several deep breaths to calm herself again; then she asked seriously, "Do you know the story of Cinderella?"

Logan frowned as he answered, "Neglected stepdaughter treated like dirt. Can't go to the ball because she doesn't have a dress. Then magical fairy godmother appears, creates a dress and car with a wave of her wand. The hapless prince can't take his eyes off Cinderella when she gets to the ball. And in a strong case of why lust is the most dangerous emotion known to man, they wed and she gets half of his kingdom when they divorce three years later."

Sean only glared at him while Logan laughed hysterically at his own joke. She said through clenched teeth, "Are you finished?"

Logan laughed a few seconds more, then struck a pose of mock seriousness as he stared at Sean. "Please, Sean, continue."

Sean knew that she should have stormed away that second, but instead she blurted out, "I always pictured the Three Ts as my own wicked stepmother and wicked stepsisters . . . without the wicked part. Anyway, in the story Cinderella goes to the ball. I'm still waiting."

Logan paused, then asked in a patient tone, as if he spoke to a child, "What are you talking about, Sean?"

She paced for a few feet, then stopped and looked at him before she cried, "I want to go to the ball, Logan!"

"Maybe I'm the problem, but you're still not making sense."

"Cinderella becomes beautiful and goes to the ball, proving her stepsisters and stepmother wrong about her. She can wear the makeup and the clothes and look just as beautiful as they do. I want that, too."

"You've never cared about that stuff before," Logan said, surprised. "You're the first one to make fun of my dates when they run to the bathroom to do their makeup and come back half an hour later. And you obviously don't care about clothes or you wouldn't wear half of the things that you do."

"What's wrong with my clothes? Don't answer that . . . I know how hypocritical I sound," Seàn snapped. She sighed in frustration as she muttered, "There's just something about the Three Ts. . . . Just once, I don't want to disappear when I'm around them, or if people notice me I don't want it to be to note how strange it is to meet a female FBI agent. I want to look as beautiful and sexy as the Three Ts."

"I think I understand," Logan said in a confused tone that made Sean realize that he didn't understand anything. "But I don't understand what you want from me."

"Cinderella always has a Prince Charming."

Comprehension dawned in his eyes, and Logan grinned in that cocky way that made Sean want to hit him or kiss him—after two years, she still didn't know which. "And I'm your Prince Charming."

"You're not Prince Charming, but you'll do."

"This is a day for the history books," Logan announced, ignoring her retort. "First you ask for my help. Now you're admitting that I'm every woman's fantasy."

"Every woman's fantasy? How did you get that from—"

"Prince Charming always helps the poor and needy. Maybe I should help you," he mused.

He eyed her from head to toe, then back again. Sean

wanted to respond to his "poor and needy" comment, but her breath caught in her throat as his eyes lingered a second too long on her breasts. Men had looked at her breasts before. A lot of men. She never understood their fascination. They were two large lumps of flesh, created for the sustenance of babies, that got in her way when she exercised. That thought had always swarmed through Sean's head when some man leered at her breasts—until Logan. He made her think of lingerie and candlelight. She imagined him, not a baby, suckling her breasts.

She quickly crossed her arms over her chest, which made him smile at some unspoken victory. She gruffly told him, "I need you to take off from work Wednesday and come with me to Santa Barbara for the rest of the week."

Logan laughed in shock and disbelief. "What?"

"I know it's short notice and I know that I'm asking a lot—"

"You're asking the impossible, Sean. I have open cases at work and meetings and appointments and . . . dates. I can't give a one-day notice that I'm taking a vacation."

Sean glared at him for a moment, then averted her gaze to stare at the door behind which Miss America had disappeared. She shouldn't have asked him. She didn't know what had possessed her. She should have known from years of practice that she needed to think over any decisions she made after speaking to one of the Three Ts. If she were Logan, she wouldn't have left a woman like Jennifer to spend a weekend with her either.

"Assuming I would do this, what would I get in return for all of my hard work?" Logan suddenly asked, arching one eyebrow that was perfectly and naturally arched.

"My gratitude," Sean warned through clenched teeth.

She knew snapping at him would not make him change his mind, but all of his gloating "Prince Charming" comments made her barely restrain the desire to use him as her punching bag. Besides, Logan wouldn't help her anyway.

Why would he? She would have to face her family the same as always, as tomboy Sean, the one whom everyone shook their heads at while making certain that expensive objects in the house were safe from her hiking boots.

"Just come the day of the wedding," Sean tried again, her voice cracking in desperation. She hated the long silence that followed her plea as the laughter slowly drained from Logan's face.

"You're serious . . . I didn't think that you were serious. I wish that I could help you, Sean, but I can't take the time from work," Logan finally said. She saw the pity in his eyes and began to plan her escape. She could take the teasing, and even the distaste, but never the pity.

"I understand, Logan; don't worry about it. Attribute this entire conversation to Three Ts syndrome," she quickly said, not meeting his eyes. "I hope that you and Jennifer have fun tonight. She's really beautiful, Logan. . . . She's a nuclear physicist, for God's sake. What more can a man ask for?"

She headed for her door, horrified that he might notice that she trembled. She wanted to cry. She wanted to sit in the shower and cry at the idiot she had made of herself tonight. Before tonight, Logan might have thought that she was an annoyance, but he had never thought that she was pitiful until now.

"Sean, I'm sorry—"

Sean didn't hear the remainder of his apology because she walked into her apartment and softly closed the door behind her. As the first tear fell, she wondered how she could live next door to him and never speak to him again.

Three

"Foul!" Logan cried as his older brother roughly pushed past him and, like an NBA point guard, dribbled the basketball toward the basket on the opposite end of the court. Logan screamed in protest as Cary soared through the air and slammed the basketball through the netless outdoor hoop. Like a cat, Cary landed gracefully on the hard pavement, then stared at Logan.

Logan rolled his eyes at his brother's dramatics. "Do you remember what the word 'foul' means? It means that Cary Riley has once more turned the basketball court into his own private search-and-destroy mission."

"I don't recognize fouls, little brother," Cary casually commented. He added as an afterthought, "And I won."

Cary broke into a wide grin as he jogged across the court to his water bottle and towel. For the last four years since Cary had moved to San Francisco, the two brothers played basketball twice a week before work. Logan was definitely not a morning person, but after five years apart from his brother, he welcomed the chance to know Cary again not only as a brother, but also as his friend. So Logan dragged himself to the court, and surprisingly these quiet early mornings with his brother now seemed as natural as breathing.

Logan grumbled as he walked toward a bench and dropped next to Cary. Even though the brothers had been playing for an hour and Logan could feel the sweat pouring down his face, his back, and his chest, Cary seemed as composed and cool as a statue. The only sign that Cary expressed of his recent exertion was the heavier than usual rise and fall of his chest.

The two brothers sat in companionable silence, watching the sun naturally light the nearby trees and apartment buildings. More cars began to filter onto the streets, and more people began to hurry by on the sidewalk. Another day in the city was beginning to play.

"What's on your mind?" Cary asked, breaking the silence. "I know I usually crush you on the court, but you usually put up a better fight."

Logan laughed at the teasing smile on Cary's lips. Logan didn't think that he would ever completely get over the fact that the man sitting next to him was the same silent stranger whom he had surprisingly encountered on the streets of San Francisco four years ago. Cary still could probably win a silent contest with a mute, but he was not the same Cary Riley who had moved with the shadows as an operative for the Group. Logan knew that Cary's wife, Jessica, who was pregnant with their first child, had a lot to do with the difference in Cary. And hopefully Logan could claim a little credit, too. Whatever the reason, he was glad to have his brother back.

"Nothing's wrong," Logan finally answered.

"Women problems?" Cary pressed.

"Not exactly. Sean problems."

For some reason Cary sighed and took a long gulp of water before he said, "What did she do now?"

"She wants me to go with her to Santa Barbara tomorrow. She wants me to pretend to be her boyfriend at her stepsister's wedding," Logan said, then laughed in disbelief at the insanity of the plan.

Cary didn't respond but continued to watch Logan. Logan

rolled his eyes in irritation as he pointedly said, "Isn't that the most ridiculous thing you've ever heard?"

"It's dramatic," Cary finally said.

"That's all you have to say? It's dramatic? What about stupid and dumb and . . . It's lying. We're the law. We're not supposed to lie."

"She specifically asked you to lie to her family?"

"No, she just said that she wanted me to go with her," Logan reluctantly admitted, then added, "But why else would she want me there except for me to pretend to be her boyfriend?"

"Maybe she wants a friend to be with her," Cary said with a shrug. The simplicity of his statement made Logan pause. He had to admit to himself that he had never thought of that. Sean needed something? Sean thought of him as a friend? Both possibilities seemed strange and very un-Sean-like to Logan. Cary asked, "What's wrong with her family?"

"Don't you mean what's wrong with Sean?" Logan said, for some unknown reason annoyed with him. Cary never responded the way Logan wanted him to, when and if Cary did respond. That was one of many problems with having an ex-spy as a brother.

"What's wrong with Sean?" Cary asked neutrally as he handed Logan a bottle of water.

"She has some inferiority complex when it comes to her stepmother and two stepsisters. She sees them as the wicked stepmother and stepsisters from *Cinderella;* although she says they're not wicked."

"Is she jealous of them?"

"I don't think Sean could be jealous of any woman. The only time I ever saw her jealous was when a guy from work stopped by the apartment to show me an antique Winchester rifle he found at a garage sale. Sean practically turned green." Logan laughed at the memory of the pure, unsheltered want that had been in Sean's eyes when she had gazed at the gun.

He stopped laughing when he remembered his friend watching Sean during the visit, and later asking Logan if he should ask Sean out. Logan hadn't told him no, but he must have conveyed his silent objection to the notion, because Hugh had quickly dropped the subject. Logan never tried to figure out why he had cared if a nice brother like Hugh dated Sean.

"If she's not jealous of her stepsisters, then—"

"I think she's intimidated by them," Logan mused. "And I think the fact that someone can intimidate her scares her. Sean likes to win. And in this case winning would be to arrive at the wedding with a date—a handsome, sophisticated, Prince Charming type date like myself."

"I'll allow that Prince Charming comment to slide. Are you going to help her?"

Shocked that Cary would even entertain the notion, Logan stared at his brother. As usual, Cary didn't blink but simply returned Logan's gaze.

"Of course not," he sputtered. "I can't just leave work in the middle of the week."

"Maggie told me that you haven't taken a vacation since . . . since Mom and Dad's death."

Logan saw the conflict of emotions and guilt briefly flash across Cary's face at the thought of their parents. Even nine years after the car accident that had taken their parents' lives, Cary still could not completely forgive himself for having survived the accident. Logan knew his brother had come far from when he had extracted himself from Logan's and their sister Maggie's lives because of his guilt, but Cary obviously had much farther to go before he truly came to peace with the accident. It had taken Logan a long time himself to accept the fact that death was as much a part of life as the love his parents had given him while they were alive.

"I've never taken a vacation because I'm a cop living on a cop's salary. Where am I supposed to go?"

"Santa Barbara.

"Cary, you're not suggesting that I should . . . You actually think that I . . . That's stupid. I can't go to Santa Barbara."

"Why would you do it?" Cary agreed, then took a long gulp of water and added, "You don't even like Sean."

"I like Sean," Logan quickly protested.

"Do you consider her your friend?"

"Sure," Logan replied uncertainly. "Since I eat dinner at her place more than mine, she can't be just an acquaintance, right?"

"Will you spend the rest of the week wishing that you were in Santa Barbara helping her through an ordeal that might not be painful for you and me, but could be painful for her, no matter how harmless we think it is?"

"I think I liked you better as the nontalking sphinx than as the guilt-tripping older brother."

Cary smiled, then said, "I'm not trying to make you feel guilty."

"You think that I should go with Sean."

"I think that you should do what you want to do."

"And I think that you should stop talking in riddles and just tell me to go or not to go," Logan snapped, glaring at Cary, who only laughed at him.

"I can't give you answers, Logan."

"Try."

"You need a vacation. Santa Barbara is a beautiful city. Put two and two together." Cary rolled his eyes in frustration as Logan continued to watch him doubtfully. "Sean will introduce you as her friend, and if her family wants to think there's something more to the friendship then you won't correct them. Either way, I can't see Sean expecting kisses from a boyfriend—real or imagined. While she's being herded around from one wedding event to the next—and take it from a man who knows, there will be a lot of events—you can go to the beach, hike, ride horses. . . . Do all of those things that people do when they go on vacations."

Logan was surprised by the jump in his stomach at the thought of kissing and caressing Sean. She did have nice skin. She had nice skin and nice teeth. It wouldn't be completely terrible to spend a week with her in a southern California beach city as beautiful as Santa Barbara. As much as Logan loved his adopted city of San Francisco, there were times when he missed the slower pace of Arizona. Santa Barbara could provide the temporary respite that he needed from city living.

"There's not anything too pressing at work right now," Logan reluctantly admitted.

"Maybe you can help Sean with something else," Cary suddenly said. "It sounds like she feels invisible around her stepsisters. Jess always teases me that after she leaves the beauty salon, every man she encounters on the street flirts with her. Maybe that's what Sean needs."

"A beauty salon?" Logan asked dumbly.

"Have her hair done, pedicure, manicure, massage, waxing—the works."

"You have been married for too long. What the hell do you know about female waxing?"

Logan laughed when he noticed a flush cover Cary's caramel brown face. Cary pinned him with a hard glare and said, "I don't know the specifics, but I know that after Jessica leaves the salon, she feels sexy. She's always sexy to me, but when she feels sexy, things get a little more interesting. . . ." Cary's voice trailed off and he grinned, a grin that told the whole world he was exactly where he wanted to be.

"How do you propose that I get Sean Weston into a beauty salon?" Logan asked dryly. "This is a woman who pulled a gun on her date when he suddenly reached into his coat pocket to pull out a handkerchief. Could you imagine her reaction if someone came near her with a pair of scissors?"

"Ask her if she'd like to do it. I bet you'll be surprised by the answer."

Logan didn't want to break it to his brother that he made it a habit to never to ask Sean anything because the answer would always be no. Still, Logan remembered the look in her eyes the night before outside his apartment. He had never seen her look so hopeless before. In fact, he had spent his entire date with Jennifer remembering the look on Sean's face. As a result, Jennifer was once more angry with him. Logan didn't know when he had decided to help Sean, but he did know that since he suffered on his date because of her, she would now have to suffer. And he couldn't imagine a worse punishment than sentencing her to a day in a beauty salon.

"Do you think that Jessica could go with her to make certain that she doesn't shoot anyone at the spa?"

Cary burst into loud laughter. Logan knew that Cary thought Logan was only joking, but Logan shuddered because the possibility of Sean blowing off some poor hairstylist's head because he gave her a bad haircut was more real than even Logan wanted to think about.

After jogging the mile from the basketball court, Logan sprinted up the stairs of his apartment building to the third level. He ran down the hall to Sean's apartment and pounded on the door. It was barely seven-thirty in the morning. He knew that Sean, who hated mornings almost as much as he did, would be hitting her snooze button for the second time around seven-thirty. Logan patiently waited, then knocked louder, almost rattling the new door on its hinges.

He smiled as he heard Sean's loud and colorful curses before he heard the sound of many locks being disengaged. Sean swung open the door, and Logan couldn't prevent the larger grin that worked its way onto his face. One part of her hair had become stuck to her face during sleep, and the remaining curls stood in a variety of directions. The robe that she had thrown around her body was inside out and twisted almost into a knot, revealing more than it hid, including her long brown legs that Logan noticed were smooth in the early morning light that shone through the living rooms. So Sean did shave her legs.

Logan saw the threatening glare in her eyes, but he took his chances and walked into the apartment. As a peace offering, he held up a wrinkled bag filled with bagels and various containers of cream cheese and two cups of coffee.

"Only because I smell coffee, I haven't shot you," Sean greeted him as she closed the door. She engaged the safety on the nine-millimeter Beretta that she held in one hand, which Logan hadn't noticed. She set the gun on the table near the front door then practically fell onto the sofa. "What time is it?"

"Do you always answer the door with a gun in the morning?"

"Only when the idiot pounds on my door, waking me out of a peaceful sleep at the crack of dawn."

Logan sat beside her on the sofa and began to spread out the food. He knew that Sean could eat two bagels at a time. And he had made certain to purchase her favorites—blueberry and cinnamon raisin. It had surprised Logan that he knew what Sean's favorite flavors of bagel were. It had surprised him how much he knew about her. Logan had spent the fifteen minutes that he stood in line at the coffee shop realizing that he knew more about Sean Weston than he knew about the various women he had dated over the last four years.

"Maybe I should still shoot you; it's too early even for coffee." Sean groaned as she buried a sofa pillow over her face as if the sunlight were too painful.

"It's almost eight o'clock," Logan cheerfully replied. He offered her a bagel that he had slathered with honey cream cheese. When she didn't reach for it, Logan tore the pillow from her hands and held the bagel up higher.

"It's too early," Sean grumbled, even as her stomach loudly protested and she snatched the bagel from him.

Logan laughed, then said, "You're going to need all of your energy this morning. You have an appointment at nine-thirty."

"No, I don't."

"Yes, you do. At a beauty salon. My sister-in-law, Jessica, will meet you there."

Sean's eyebrows scrunched together as she slowly sat up and, unfortunately, pulled the lapels of the robe closer together. Logan had begun to notice a small expanse of cleavage in the tank top she wore—beautiful brown cleavage that hinted at full breasts underneath the thin cotton robe. Logan was horrified at his thoughts. Was he really ogling Sean's breasts?

"What are you talking about, Riley?" Sean demanded.

"I already told my partner and my lieutenant that I'm taking the rest of the week off. My lieutenant would have liked more notice, but since I haven't taken a vacation or a sick day in the seven years that I've worked for SFPD, he couldn't complain too much."

"You're going with me to Santa Barbara?"

"One Prince Charming at your service."

Logan hadn't known what he expected Sean to do in response to his agreement to help her, but none of his imagined scenarios included her staring at him as if he had sprouted a second head.

"Why?" she finally demanded, narrowing her eyes.

"Don't fall all over yourself thanking me," he muttered dryly.

Avoiding his eyes, she suddenly became interested in the bagel in her hands. Logan was not fooled, but he was intrigued. Sean didn't avoid anything. She faced everything head-on: suspects, convicted criminals, him. He didn't think she knew how to suppress her feelings.

"Sean, I'm going to help you," Logan tried again.

She glared at him and angrily snapped, "I'm not a charity case."

"I never said that you were. Do you not want me to go with you anymore?"

"I'm not going anymore," Sean announced as she surged to her feet, knocking bagels to the floor and almost tipping over the cup of coffee, which Logan barely managed to catch. She didn't appear to notice the calamity as she stalked to the windows.

"You're not going to your sister's wedding?" Logan asked incredulously as he picked up bagels from the hardwood floor.

"Stepsister," Sean immediately corrected. She turned to face him as she said, "No one will miss me. Tracie asked me to be in the wedding only to please my dad. The Three Ts would do anything to please him."

Logan suddenly grinned when he saw the indecision on Sean's face. She noticed his smile and suspiciously glared at him.

"You're scared, aren't you?" Logan guessed.

"What would I possibly be scared of?"

"Your family. The Three Ts."

"Don't tell me; let me guess. The ball hit your head during your morning basketball game with your brother and it's affected your thought processes," Sean dryly retorted. "I'm not scared of the Three Ts."

"Yesterday you were going off about Cinderella and Prince Charming, and this morning you're not going to the wedding? What happened?"

"I used my brain. Who am I kidding? I can't sweep into my father's house and pretend that I'm . . . that I'm anything but me."

Logan would have laughed except that he saw the dejected slump of Sean's shoulders before she suddenly remembered that he watched her. She quickly straightened up but stood motionlessly across the room, holding his gaze.

"Don't you want to see your sis—your stepsister get married?"

"It's actually surprising how much I do want to see it. Tracie is the least irritating of the Three Ts."

Logan laughed at her flippant response. He wondered why Sean didn't want anyone to know that she had the capacity to care for anyone. For some unknown reason, just once he wanted her to lower her shield for him.

"You're going to the wedding, Sean, and you're going to knock 'em dead just like ol' Cindy."

"Cindy?" she questioned, confused.

"Cinderella," Logan said with a dramatic and frustrated sigh at her missing the reference. "She was scared at first, but she went to the ball."

"Stop implying that I'm scared," Sean said in a snarl, while clenching her hands into fists.

Logan grinned, because for some reason he liked her angry and combative—anything but the sad way she had made the notion of being her seem repulsive. He didn't like seeing Sean sad. It was a realization that had taken him a long time to understand, but he had accepted it a few months ago when he had allowed her to insult him for a full twenty minutes after he found her almost crying over a botched operation at work.

He couldn't explain why, but he wanted her to live her fairy tale. He wanted her to go to the ball, to be the envy of everyone in the room. And even though he knew she didn't need him or anyone else to do that, she thought that she did. And, as always, he would do whatever she wanted. But not without a fight.

Logan walked across the living room to hand her the coffee cup. Over the rim of the cup, she continued to regard him as if he were a suspect she was questioning in the bowels of the Bureau. He would bet that Agent Sean Weston was a very intimidating interviewer. Even while she was wearing a ridiculous robe that had bright yellow suns and clouds on it, he knew that most men would proceed carefully when Sean was involved. Logan wasn't most men.

"If we do this, we're going to do it my way," Logan quietly told her.

"What does that mean?"

"It means that in this fairy tale, I'm going to play a dual role. I'm going to be your Prince Charming and your fairy godmother." Logan paused for a moment, then quickly added, "And, yes, I'm secure enough in my masculinity to equate myself to a fairy godmother."

"I think you're taking our five-minute discussion of *Cinderella* a little too far."

"You want to be Cinderella, and I'm going to give it to you."

"I'm scared," Sean told him, while shaking her head in irritation.

Logan grinned as he responded, "You should be."

"What if I don't agree to your way?"

"You will, because I think deep down inside you really wonder what it'd be like to be a princess for a week."

Sean held his gaze for a long, silent second, and for the first time Logan noticed the rich color of her eyes. He always thought that her eyes were a plain brown. And he had been partially right—her eyes were brown, but there was nothing plain about them.

The rich, deep brown of her eyes shone in the bright morning sun, ensnaring him in their depths. His eyes drifted to her wide mouth, the thick lips, the pink tongue that suddenly darted across her lower lip. Logan had the insane urge to grab her so that his tongue could follow hers. He wondered if her lips would taste like the coffee she had sipped or sweet like the honey cream cheese.

"Are you sure that you want to play this game, Riley?" Sean's hard voice interrupted his suddenly vivid fantasies that included untying her robe and seeing what was underneath. Logan shook his head and mentally kicked himself.

"The question is—are you sure?" Logan finally shot back. "You don't have to do this their way."

She licked her lips again, causing Logan to silently groan as he felt a strange flutter in his groin at the movement. He refused to believe that Sean Weston was the reason that certain parts of him now hardened. He blamed it on the coffee. Good coffee always excited him. She said in a quiet voice, "Yes, I do . . . this once."

He abruptly walked to the door, not stopping long enough to grab his own breakfast, because he had to get away from her as fast as possible. Not even coffee could be that good.

He stiffly told her, "Your appointment is for nine-thirty at City Salon. I've already taken care of the payment—"

"That's stupid, Logan; I can pay for the torture myself."

Logan turned to face her once more, making certain to keep his eyes away from her breasts, away from her mouth, away from her eyes. He concentrated on her right ear.

"I've taken enough of your beer and food to owe you a few trips to a beauty salon.

"You have a point," she replied seriously, but Logan heard the teasing in her voice, and he was glad that his shirt hung over the front of his shorts. She cleared her throat, then grumbled, "I guess I can take an hour from work."

"An hour?" Logan laughed at her misunderstanding. "Guess again, Weston. You'll be lucky to get out of the spa before six o'clock tonight."

"Are you kidding?" Sean practically pleaded. "What could they possibly do to me for that long?"

"You'll find out." Logan opened the door before he leaped across the room, tore off her ridiculous robe, and wrapped her long brown legs around his waist. Of course, he would never get that far with his fantasies because she would pile-drive him to the floor first, but he almost thought the pain would be worth it. "I have loose ends to tie up at work, so I'll probably be late tonight. I'll see you tomorrow morning. We leave at six."

Before she could respond, he walked out of the apartment and closed the door. Logan ran his hands over his face, suddenly feeling much older than his twenty-eight years. After he returned from Santa Barbara, he was making a doctor's appointment. Coffee should not cause a man's body to respond like that.

Four

Sean refused to be scared of a place that had pink and beige walls. Even as she told herself that, she had to resist the urge to caress her gun, which rested against her thigh underneath the pink smock the drill master—also known as a receptionist—had ordered Sean to change into at City Salon. Sean sat in the plush and quiet lounge area, mentally devising the types of torture methods she was about to endure all in a juvenile attempt to fit in with Tracie and Terri.

It wasn't that Sean had never been to the hairdresser. When she was little she had been forced a few times to suffer under the not-so-gentle ministrations of her mother's various hairdressers, but she had not been since her last trim six months ago. But Sean also knew that she could attribute her disdain for hairdressers to her mother, who had treated each visit as if she faced an execution squad. When she was little, Sean sometimes had to sit for what seemed like interminable hours waiting for her mother to have her hair done. Sandra Weston had finally given up her once-every-two-weeks appointment and now went once every few months to have her closely shaven hair neatly trimmed.

Now Sean found herself willingly putting herself through the same experience. And for what? To impress Tina, Tracie, and Terri . . . and her father and all of their friends in Santa Barbara who thought Sean had come from another planet because she didn't fit in with the new Weston family. She was a part of Weston family number one, with a cop for a mother, nothing like Weston family number two, in which Tina had probably never cursed in her life, much less handled a police station, where cursing was better understood than plain English.

Sean had just talked herself into a rage to leave when the door opened and a tall, slender woman walked into the room. The woman wore the same pink smock as Sean, except that, unlike Sean, she didn't look uncomfortable or the least bit frightened. Even though she wore no makeup, her cinnamon-colored brown skin was flawless, and her thick brown hair was neatly swept into a ball at the nape of her neck.

The woman smiled at Sean, and Sean found herself smiling back, even though normally she thought strangers who smiled at her either were criminals who recognized her from the Bureau or people who laughed at her because of food on her clothes.

"You must be Sean," the woman said warmly, while extending her hand. "I'm Jessica Larson Riley, Logan's sister-in-law. I'm sorry that I'm late, but an early morning meeting ran a little longer than I planned."

Sean couldn't withhold the sigh of relief as the woman introduced herself. She hadn't known what to expect when Logan told her that she would meet the woman who was married to his brother. Sean had seen Cary Riley a few times at Logan's apartment, but she had never spoken to him. He was a legend around the San Francisco Bureau. None of the agents knew how Cary Riley had achieved such a prominent position in the Bureau at such a young age, but his hard, expressionless brown eyes scared anyone away from asking. Sean had even heard rumors that Cary once worked for the rumored intelligence section of the Bureau that none of the rank-and-file agents were certain existed.

"It's nice to meet you," Sean said, standing to shake Jessica's hand. Jessica's eyes widened slightly at the exuberant shake Sean gave her hand. Sean cringed as she said, "I'm sorry . . . I'm a little nervous, not scared, but nervous about this."

"Don't be nervous. Celeste is one of the best stylists in the city, and the staff here will make you feel like a queen. If there's anything that makes you feel uncomfortable, just tell them to stop."

Sean unconsciously patted the familiar weight of her gun. She noticed that Jessica's eyes were drawn to the bulge on the side of Sean's robe. Jessica appeared unfazed by the obvious outline of the gun as she pulled a card from her robe pocket. Sean reminded herself that Jessica was the wife of an FBI agent and the sister-in-law of a cop. She probably had seen her share of guns.

Jessica excitedly read from the card, "First, we have a thirty-minute neck and back massage. Then a facial, manicure, and pedicure, and then the real fun will begin—hair and makeup."

"We're going to be together the entire time, right?" Sean asked hopefully.

"Not the whole time." Jessica lovingly rubbed her lower abdomen as she explained, "My doctor recommends staying away from the fumes in the nail room."

"Are you pregnant?"

Jessica's answering grin was bright enough to give the sun a run for its money. "I'm four months pregnant," Jessica confirmed.

"Congratulations."

"Cary and I have been married for four years. For career reasons, I thought that I wanted to wait until the five-year mark of our marriage to have children, but I couldn't wait another year. I want to have our baby."

Sean, who had prided herself on being as unsentimental as the next guy, actually felt her heart speed up at Jessica's words, because Sean pictured a little brown baby with Logan's hypnotic, amber-colored eyes, his dimple, and his uncontrollable black curls. Sean instantly cringed at the thought. She had been in the pink room less than twenty minutes and already she was planning kids with Logan Riley.

Jessica glanced at the clock on the wall, then said, "It's time for our massage. You're going to love this, Sean."

Jessica surprised Sean by linking arms with her before leading her out a door that led to the massive three-level salon. As the mixed scent of hair products and perfume filled Sean's senses, Sean realized that she had entered another world—a world where women wore only pink-and-white robes, where other people dressed in all-white clothes lived to serve the robed women, and there was no such thing as dead plants or a bad joke.

There were no windows on the first floor, but as bright as the room was, the sun itself must have somehow provided illumination. There were only white walls, calm, serene landscape paintings, and the soft whir of machinery that made women feel beautiful. Everywhere Sean looked, women glowed with contentment and relaxation, seemingly unaware that on the other side of the door the big, bad world awaited. And Sean realized that she belonged on the other side of the door. She could not go through with this. Any of this.

"Are you all right?" Jessica asked, noticing that Sean had stopped in the middle of the room.

Sean stared at Jessica and demanded, "Did Logan tell you why I'm here?"

"He said that you were going to your sister's wedding in Santa Barbara."

"Stepsister," Sean automatically corrected. She grabbed Jessica's hands, not surprised by the instant concern that crossed Jessica's face. Jessica probably wondered how soon she could slip away from Sean to call her husband to save her from the Bureau loon. "I want to look drop-dead gorgeous. For once, I want to blend in with my stepsisters and my stepmother. I want men to stare at me. I want men to lose the ability to speak around me. I want men to offer me dinner and dancing and champagne. I want all of the things that I've seen happen to my stepsisters. Do you think these people can make that happen?"

"You are beautiful, Sean," Jessica said with enough conviction that Sean believed she was sincere. "These people here can style your hair and give you makeup, but that's all they can do for you. The qualities in a woman that drive men crazy are her confidence, her carriage, her attitude. The makeup, the clothes, the hair . . . that's all wrapping paper."

"And I want that wrapping paper to be the most gorgeous in the store," Sean immediately responded.

Jessica wordlessly opened her mouth, then laughed. She finally told Sean, "This place could have turned the Hunchback of Notre Dame into a French version of Taye Diggs."

Sean laughed as she said, "I hope that I don't have that far to go."

Jessica didn't answer but grabbed Sean's hand and led her deeper into hell—or, as Sean figured every other woman on the planet would call it, heaven.

Six hours later, after being groomed, polished, and poked enough to last a few lifetimes, Sean walked out of the building feeling . . . feeling like a woman. Growing up with Sandra Weston as a mother, Sean had known from an early age that feminine beauty came in many shapes and guises. Sandra had always retained that core of femininity that still made men jump to open doors for her, while Sean had to be careful that the swinging door didn't slam in her face. Sean took a deep breath and decided to look at herself for the first time since leaving the flattering mirrors and lights in the salon.

From a canvas bag the salon had supplied her, Sean pulled out a compact mirror. She had bought the compact, and about three hundred dollars of makeup, in the salon, hoping to replicate the exact movements and color choices of the makeup artist who had worked on her. Sean stared at her reflection and reluctantly admitted that she didn't look as if a clown had scribbled on her face. In fact, she looked like a completely different woman—a woman who wore foundation, mascara, and lipstick. A woman who had hair that fell to her shoulders in gleaming waves, and didn't look as though she had just stuck her hand in an electrical socket.

"You look gorgeous, Sean." Jessica sighed as she stepped out of the salon.

Jessica looked even more composed and beautiful than when Sean had first seen her. Sean squinted to see if she could distinguish Jessica's makeup, but whatever cosmetics Jessica wore, Sean couldn't make out. Jessica was one of those women who needed little makeup to look naturally beautiful, while the makeup artist, Collette, had told Sean that it would take an hour to achieve that natural look.

"I can barely move my mouth. The makeup is weighing down my facial muscles," Sean murmured, while being careful not to open her mouth too wide. Collette had also told her that whenever women opened their mouths, they invariably ruined their makeup. Sean wanted to ask then when were women supposed to talk if they were always supposed to wear makeup, but Collette had told Sean to stop ruining her makeup.

"Did Collette teach you how to apply the makeup?"

"For an excruciating forty-five minutes. I thought that my instructors at the Bureau were tough."

Jessica laughed, then squeezed Sean's hands as she said, "You look beautiful, Sean. You're going to knock them dead."

"So do you," Sean said sincerely. Sean raised a hand to touch her hair, almost afraid to muss the perfect curtain that had been whipped into place by the stylists and blow-dryers and hair spray. She uncertainly asked Jessica, "Do you really think that I'm . . . that I'm all right?"

"You're better than all right." Jessica motioned around the street as she laughed. "If you hadn't noticed, you're causing a traffic jam."

Sean glanced toward the street and noticed cars slowing to a crawl as men hung from windows to stare at her. Men were staring at her, leering at her. All because she had put on a little makeup and actually combed her hair. Sean wanted to be offended at the rudeness of the men. She wanted to roll her eyes and ignore them, but she could barely restrain the smile that threatened to break out on her face. It worked!

"What are you going to do now?" Jessica asked, her eyes twinkling as she obviously noticed Sean's attempt not to smile at the attention.

"Eat," Sean instantly responded. "I can't believe lunch to those people was a tuna sandwich and fruit. I haven't eaten a lunch that small since junior high school."

"I'm hungry, too. My appetite has tripled since the baby."

Sean hesitated, then asked, "Would you like to have dinner together?"

"Of course I would."

Sean grinned, surprised by the relief that flooded through her at Jessica's answer. Sean liked being alone—normally—but after being surrounded by giggling women who made her feel a pang of loneliness that she had never acknowledged, she didn't want to be alone. Besides, Sean didn't know when, but at some point during their marathon session in the salon, she decided that she would like to be friends with Jessica, even if her husband was the scariest man whom Sean had ever seen stalk the halls of the Bureau.

"I don't mean to monopolize your entire day but . . . I can't exactly wear all this and dress like this," Sean said as she motioned to her face and then her worn jeans and wrinkled shirt. "I need new clothes and shoes . . . and probably new underwear."

"A shopping excursion." Jessica grinned wickedly, and Sean wondered if she should have kept her shopping trip to herself. From the gleam in Jessica's eyes, she could tell that Jessica would not follow Sean's idea of shopping, which included grabbing the first pair of pants she saw that were her size.

Jessica reached into the black purse she carried and pulled out a cellular telephone. Her fingers flew across the numbers as she said, "My best friend, Erin, would kill me if I went on a shopping excursion during the summer sale at the mall without telling her."

"I just want to grab a few pants and tops. . . . I don't know if I would call it an excursion. . . ." Sean's voice trailed off as she realized that Jessica wasn't listening to her as she spoke into the cellular telephone.

"Erin, it's Jess. We're getting to the summer sale after all." Jessica happily laughed as she gave her best friend their location. Sean's vision of a quiet, quick trip to the mall immediately disappeared. Jessica switched off the telephone, then turned to Sean. "Erin is on her way. She'll be downtown in twenty minutes."

"If you and Erin want to be alone—"

"Erin can't wait to meet you," Jessica said confused. "She likes to spend her money, my money, her husband's money—who also happens to be my brother—and I'm sure that she'd love to tell you how to spend your money."

"As long as you're certain that I won't be in the way—"

"You're stuck with me today, Sean," Jessica said, as she slung an arm around her shoulders. "Before we meet Erin we should grab a little snack, because Erin can spend all night in the mall, and it will be a long time before she'll stop for food."

Sean placed a hand over her grumbling stomach. "What do you consider a little snack?"

"Double cheeseburger, fries, and a soda," Jessica said simply.

Sean grinned at the answer. "You just became my new best friend." Sean didn't add that Jessica was probably her only female friend.

Logan heard the sound of a car cruise to a stop in the driveway of his brother's house in the hills of San Francisco. He tossed the television remote control onto the nearby leather chair, then ran to the front door, surprised that his heart began to pound against his chest. Logan threw open the door and his smile faltered when Jessica and Erin, her sister-in-law, walked toward the front door. Both women held a bundle of packages in their arms, which they transferred to Logan's arms as soon as they entered the house.

Logan glanced toward their two cars parked side by side in the driveway. There was no third car. There was no Sean. After his body's strange reaction to her that morning, he should have been relieved that she was not with Jessica and Erin. He had spent the whole day at work telling himself it was the basketball, the jogging, and the coffee that had caused the strange feelings. Then he had rushed to Cary's house after work, hoping that Sean would come home with Jessica so Logan could prove it to himself.

Logan ignored the disappointment that flowed through his body as he closed the door with one foot. He followed Jessica and Erin down the three steps into the sunken living room. The floor-to-ceiling windows framed the view of the twinkling city lights below the hills where Cary's house was located. Logan had spent more time staring out the window and imagining Sean in her robe than watching the television.

"What a day." Jessica sighed as she fell onto the sofa.

"I saw David's car parked in the street. Where is he?" Erin asked Logan, as she sat on the sofa next to Jessica.

"It's nice to see you ladies, too," Logan grumbled as he dropped their packages on the glass table near the sofa.

"Hi, Logan," Jessica and Erin chorused.

Logan tried not to, but their smiles were infectious, and he found himself grinning at them in return. "Your husbands went for pizza. They should be back soon."

"Pizza from Sergio's?" Jessica practically pleaded.

"As if Cary would dare to bring any other type of pizza into this house," Logan teased. He cleared his throat, then tried to sound innocent as he asked, "Where's Sean?"

"I invited her to come here for dinner, but she said that she had to prepare to leave for Santa Barbara tomorrow," Jessica said. Logan didn't miss her thoughtful expression as she studied him, then added, "I like her, Logan."

"She's definitely a strange one, but I like her, too," Erin chimed in.

"How did the salon appointment go? Did all of the employees escape with their limbs intact?" Logan asked.

Jessica laughed as she told him, "It was touch and go when the woman who gave her a facial began the extraction procedure—"

"What's an extraction procedure? It sounds painful," Logan muttered

"It feels exactly how it sounds," Erin answered with a shudder.

"Sean was great, Logan," Jessica said. "She's nothing like I imagined her from your description. You had me expecting a cross between Wonder Woman and Attila the Hun."

"And she's beautiful," Erin chimed in. "You're beautiful, she's beautiful . . . Jess told me that you and Sean are only neighbors. I don't believe that."

"Believe it, Erin," Logan said firmly. He hesitated, then said to Erin, "You said that she was beautiful. I've never heard anyone describe Sean that way. The salon must have worked."

Logan realized he was in trouble when Jessica turned to glare at him. He groaned, because once Jessica decided she liked a person, that person would be protected by her for all time. He should have known that better than anyone: he had known Jessica for less than a week when she had risked herself to save his life.

"Sean didn't need the salon, Logan. She thought that she did to feel better about herself, and that's because of the images this society sends to women that they're not beautiful unless—"

"I hear feminist rhetoric; that must mean my little sister is home," came David Larson's dry voice as he walked into the house followed by Cary. Both men carried large grease-stained boxes of pizza.

"Pizza." Jessica sighed in contentment as she jumped to her feet to cross the room. She grabbed the box from Cary's hands, then immediately ran to the wide kitchen that opened into the living room, where she ripped it open.

"I remember a time when my wife would greet me before she grabbed the food," Cary teased. Jessica looked over her shoulder at him and stuck out her tongue, which prompted Cary to laugh.

"Obviously Jess has been blinded by food, and that's why she allowed you to get away with that comment, David," Erin said as she crossed the room to press an intimate kiss against her husband's mouth.

The two argued more often than any other couple Logan had ever seen. Sometimes it irritated him, but most times it entertained him. Logan was not fooled by their numerous arguments. One had only to see the looks they gave each other when they thought no one else watched to realize that their two-year marriage was on solid ground.

Logan watched his brother walk into the kitchen and slide his arms around Jessica's waist. She leaned into his arms and lifted her head to press a kiss against his mouth. With the two couples temporarily entwined with each other,

Logan felt his usual sense of loneliness. He knew neither couple meant to make him feel left out, but it happened when two couples who loved each other spent time with a single man who couldn't date a woman long enough to broach the subject of introductions to his family.

"Logan, how many slices do you want?" Jessica asked as she playfully pushed Cary away to dole out the pizza.

"Two for now," he answered, then sat at one of the stools at the island in the middle of the kitchen. Jessica placed a plate of steaming, cheese-dripping pizza in front of him.

"What were you lecturing Logan on when we walked in?" David asked Jessica as he took the stool next to Logan.

"Sean," Jessica said as she glared at Logan. "Logan seems to think that Sean could be beautiful only after spending a day at the beauty salon."

"I agree," David said, then winked at Logan.

Logan laughed, then patted David's shoulder. Over the last four years, as Logan had grown close to Jessica, he had also grown close to her family. For better or worse, Logan counted Jessica, David, their mother, Karin, and Erin as his family.

"You're only agreeing to upset Jess," Erin said as she stood behind David to wrap her arms around his shoulders.

"Probably," David said with an apologetic shrug at Logan.

"How did Sean look?" Cary asked as he handed Logan a can of Pepsi, which Logan gratefully popped open.

"Gorgeous," Jessica answered. "She spent forty-five minutes with the makeup artist learning how to apply everything. I've never seen anyone concentrate on makeup so hard."

"She told me that her mother is a cop," Erin told David and Cary.

"One of the best sheriffs in northern California," Cary confirmed. "I heard about Sandra Weston through law enforcement circles before I moved to San Francisco."

"You can tell the truth, Logan. You're attracted to Sean, aren't you?" Erin pressed.

"Sean?" Logan sputtered. "Are you kidding?"

"What's wrong with Sean?" Jessica demanded as she slammed a plate of pizza on the counter in front of David.

"Nothing is wrong with Sean. She's just not my type," Logan answered.

"Why isn't she your type? Because you know that she wouldn't allow that grin of yours to get you out of trouble?" Jessica shot back.

David placed a hand on Logan's shoulder and shook his head in sympathy. "You've lost this argument. Jessica and Erin like Sean. Accept defeat and just start picking out china patterns for your future life with Sean."

David and Cary laughed while Jessica and Erin glared at the two men, their eyes promising silent retribution. Logan silently took another bite from his slice of pizza. He watched his brother place a kiss on Jessica's forehead while she continued to glare at him. Maybe one day he would have what Cary and Jessica had. Logan wanted that more than anything, but after five years of waiting, he was almost ready to admit defeat and become exactly who everyone thought he was.

Five

Logan glanced at his watch, then pressed the horn of his silver convertible BMW. Sean was late—as usual. They were supposed to have been on the highway to Santa Barbara an hour ago, but Sean had called him, still sounding half-asleep, and begged to put off their departure time by an hour. An hour had passed, and Logan sat in his car at precisely seven in the morning waiting for Sean. Now they would have to drive in Bay Area morning traffic, probably adding another hour to the five-hour drive to Santa Barbara.

He could admit that he wouldn't have been so impatient if he wasn't the least bit curious to see the new Sean. He had gotten home too late from Cary's house to knock on her door. If Sean didn't own a gun, he probably would have knocked, but he had forced himself to wait until morning.

He drummed his fingers on the steering wheel, then pressed one button after the other on the radio panel, searching for decent music. Logan suddenly realized that he didn't know how to take a vacation. Wasn't he supposed to be relaxed? Wasn't he supposed to be feeling a sense of freedom at the idea of no work for a few days? Instead he felt anxious about leaving San Francisco, and even more anxious that he was leaving San Francisco with Sean.

The entrance to their apartment building opened and Sean stumbled onto the porch, pulling one thigh-height suitcase behind her and tilting under the weight of another bag on her shoulder. Logan didn't withhold a silent curse as he noticed the large, dark sunglasses she wore to cover her eyes and the colorful silk scarf she wore around her head, which securely tucked around her neck. She wore her usual off-duty outfit of exercise pants and a tank top that boasted a quarter-size coffee stain above one breast.

Logan stared at that breast until his hand began to itch; then he got out of the car and immediately took her luggage from her to place into the trunk.

"Sorry, sorry," she mumbled as she sat in the passenger seat.

"No, you're not."

"You're right," she admitted with an easy shrug. He slammed the trunk closed and slid behind the steering wheel.

He turned the key in the ignition and the engine roared to life. Logan carefully pulled into the light traffic on their street. He knew that they wouldn't hit morning traffic until they merged onto the freeway. He moved to press the button to raise the roof, but Sean suddenly grabbed his shirtsleeve. He stared at her and automatically grinned at her smile, completely forgetting his irritation over her lateness.

"I love riding with the top down."

"What about your hair?" he asked uncertainly.

A blank expression covered her face as she asked, "What about it?"

"My dates . . . they complain about their hair if I leave the top down."

She appeared torn for a second; then she shrugged and said, "I have four days to be an irritating female. Right now I want the top down."

Logan darted occasional glances at her in between his scans of the road. The only skin visible on her face was her nose, lips, and chin. Logan stared at her lips. He couldn't explain it but he had become fascinated with them—their shape, their naturally pink color. He had spent half of the previous night wondering what they would feel like against every part of his body, and the other half of the night disgusted with himself for thinking about Sean like that.

"How was the salon?" he finally asked, so that he could pay attention to something else besides his dreams from the night before.

"Maybe all of the fumes went to my head, but I actually enjoyed parts of it."

"That was more than I thought you would admit."

"I like Jessica."

"I do, too," Logan murmured. "She's been very good to my brother, to my whole family."

Sean slightly reclined the seat and shifted and moaned until she found a comfortable position.

"Are you going to sleep?" Logan asked, surprised.

"Considering that I was up until five in the morning, trying to find the nerve to wear the clothes that Jessica and Erin convinced me to buy, I thought sleep was a good idea," she replied dryly.

"You bought new clothes, too? Neither Jess nor Erin told me that." Logan grinned as he asked, "What type of clothes did you buy that you're apprehensive about wearing?"

"You'll see when I change at the restaurant when we stop for lunch."

Logan couldn't imagine what Sean would walk out of the restaurant wearing. He didn't know whether to envision her in fatigues or all leather.

"We need to talk before you drift into dreamland," Logan said. "What exactly are you going to tell your family about me?"

"You're my friend."

"A friend does not take time off from work to escort you to a wedding," Logan retorted. He cleared his throat when he realized that he was a friend taking time off from work to escort her to a wedding.

"I will not tell anyone that you're my boyfriend," Sean said through clenched teeth.

"You don't have to sound so offended at the idea. Some women would consider me prime boyfriend material."

"Some women would," Sean agreed, but Logan heard the hidden insult in her voice. "I never told anyone that I was bringing a date or a boyfriend; Tina just assumed and spread it around the family. Whatever conclusion they come to about us will not be my fault."

"I'm a good boyfriend," Logan persisted. He forced a smile when he glanced at Sean and saw a smile playing around the corners of her mouth.

"I think the word 'boyfriend' automatically implies that the boy or man stays with one woman longer than a few weeks," Sean said, then added with a triumphant smile, "Therefore, I don't think it would apply to you."

"You're a regular comedienne, Weston," Logan muttered, even as he tried not to laugh.

She continued, "Besides, if I told my family that you were my boyfriend, they would expect . . . stuff."

"What stuff?" Logan asked.

"They would expect us to act the way a boyfriend and a girlfriend would act."

Logan noticed the sudden flush apparent in the walnut roundness of her cheeks. He laughed as he said, "Sean, I think that you're blushing. I didn't know that you could blush."

"A lot of black people turn red—"

"I don't mean black people; I mean you. Aren't you supposed to be invincible? Invincible women don't blush."

"Can I go to sleep now?"

"I have a few more questions," Logan casually answered, then turned the car onto the freeway. He groaned at the mass of cars in front of them on the multilane freeway and the mass of cars behind them. He concentrated on Sean as he inched the car forward along with the other commuters who left the city each morning to work in the South Peninsula. "I want to know about the Three Ts, besides the fact that they're beautiful and perfect and were put on this earth to irritate you. How old were you when your father married Tina?"

"Ten." Sean crossed her arms over her chest as if to ward off Logan's questions. Logan relented. She obviously didn't want to talk about her family, and he knew when to leave her alone. Surprising him, she continued in a quiet voice, "I spent one weekend a month and every summer with my father in Santa Barbara until I was seventeen. I was twelve the first time I heard Tracie and Terri call my father Dad. The summer I spent there after Dad married Tina, the four were still nervous around each other. Tracie and Terri were never openly resentful of my father, but I could tell that they judged his every action against their own father."

"What happened to their father?"

"The last that they heard he was in New York. I don't think they've heard from him in years. They don't talk about him. That first summer I thought that Tracie and Terri would never accept my father, but the next summer . . . The next summer I came back and they were one big, happy family. They called my father Dad. They had their perfect family unit, and I wasn't a part of it. I'll never be a part of it."

"Sean, you don't have to talk about this."

"It's not a big deal," she said dismissively, even as one trembling hand rose to readjust her sunglasses. "My father and my mother are complete opposites, and I'm like my mother. When I saw my father with the Three Ts, I knew what a perfect fit they were for him. Then I would come along and ruin the picture."

"Your father told you this?"

"Of course not, but I could tell. My dad wanted me to attend college in Santa Barbara to be close to him, but I chose to stay here. What was the point of living down there and constantly being reminded that I didn't belong with Weston family number two?"

Logan hesitated, then asked, "Are you and your father close now?"

"I like to think so, but I'll never be Tracie and Terri. He tells me that I'm special, but sometimes I wonder when he removes the blinders what he really thinks."

"Fathers never remove the blinders." Logan smiled at the memory of his own father. "My father thought that each of his kids could fly if we wanted to. My mother was the realistic one, but even she thought we could do anything if we worked hard enough."

"Do your parents still live in Arizona?"

"I thought I told you. . . . My parents are dead. A car accident." The same pain twisted his heart whenever he spoke the words aloud. The pain had lessened over time but a gnawing hole was still there, and Logan knew that it would never completely disappear. "It's been nine years."

"I didn't know. . . ." Sean's voice trailed off and she stared out the windshield. Logan raked a hand through his curls and focused on the car bumper in front of him.

"I still miss them," he quietly admitted. "Everyone says that I'm an exact replica of my father—looks, temperament, height. I'm even a cop, like him. As compliments go, that's the best one I've ever gotten in my life."

"You were young when it happened."

"Nineteen years old. I was in my sophomore year at University of Arizona. I went back home and joined the force to take care of Maggie."

"You must have been scared," Sean whispered.

Logan laughed at the understatement. "I was more than scared. Overnight I became the legal guardian of a sixteen-year-old. Maggie and my mother had been best friends, and there was nothing I could do to fill the void. I wanted Maggie to stop hurting, but I couldn't help her when I could barely keep myself moving."

Sean's hand drifted across the width of the seats to rest on his shoulder. The strength of her grip, the comfort of it, made him relax and notice the bright morning sun and the cloud-free crystal sky. A little more of the pain disappeared, allowing a memory of his mother's smile and his father's laugh to fill the darkness inside of him.

"I took night classes to finish college, and somehow Maggie made it through high school. I used to sit up at night praying that I didn't ruin her life too badly."

Sean squeezed his shoulder and smiled. "She's an officer in the navy. I think you did okay, Logan. You did better than okay."

Logan grinned at her, and, at her return smile, his heart almost leaped into his throat. He quickly averted his gaze to the traffic before he lost all common sense and leaned across the car to kiss her. Maybe he should have gone to the doctor's before driving to Santa Barbara, because there was no coffee in the car that he could blame his physical reaction on.

Logan tried to laugh as he said, "Wasn't I supposed to be grilling you about your family? How did we start talking about mine? I bet this is some Bureau tactic they teach you at the Academy."

Sean laughed, then replied, "I told you all of the high points from the Weston secrets closet." She removed her hand, then softly said, "I've never told anyone about how I felt growing up with the Three Ts. I never felt that I had the right. Tina treated me like one of her daughters, and Tracie and Terri treated me like another sister. I was lucky."

"You are lucky."

"You think I'm exaggerating about the beauty of the Three Ts," Sean guessed, a light tone replacing the sadness. Logan liked the lightness more.

"A little," he admitted.

"You'll see for yourself, Logan, and then I probably won't

see you for the rest of the week. Tracie may be getting married, but Terri is still single and just your type."

Logan's smile disappeared and he slammed on the brakes, causing the car behind him to angrily beep the horn. Logan ignored the blaring cars and turned to Sean. He took off her sunglasses to find her brown eyes wide and surprised.

"What are you doing—"

"No matter what you think you know about me, know this, Sean: I always leave with the woman I come with."

He held her gaze, daring her to contradict him, daring her to call him a flirt or a Casanova or any of the other names she usually hurled at him. She only stared at him, her mouth slightly open and her eyes wide with surprise and confusion. Logan nodded, satisfied, then carefully slid her sunglasses back in place and turned to the road again. They drove the next four hours in silence.

Logan impatiently tapped his fingers against the steering wheel, then got out of the car, slamming the door. Maybe he had overreacted four hours ago, but that was four hours ago. Sean hadn't spoken to him since then. She hadn't said more than three words to him over lunch. Logan was becoming irritated. He was becoming downright angry. After lunch she had spoken to him just to order him to wait outside the restaurant. While she worked her magic in the bathroom, he was supposed to enjoy the ocean breeze and the view of the Pacific Ocean only a few feet from the restaurant, which was situated in the sand.

Logan cursed at the thought. He didn't want to stare at the ocean. He would do plenty of that over the next week. He wanted to stare at Sean. He wanted to talk to her. He wanted to apologize for his reaction. He shouldn't have become so offended because she called a spade a spade. She thought that he was a flirt because he wanted her think that. He wanted everyone to think that because he was too insecure to tell anyone the truth about himself. He would rather be known as a heartless playboy than have anyone know the truth. He told himself that he shouldn't be angry because Sean thought that he was exactly the way he wanted her to think he was. He told himself that, but he still cursed.

Logan heard the sound of gravel crunching as someone approached him. He turned and all rational thought fled his mind as Sean walked toward him, moving like a dangerous animal tracking her prey in the jungle. Logan could no longer breathe because he faced the shocking realization that Special Agent Sean Weston of the Federal Bureau of Investigation was gorgeous.

He had never noticed how tall she was, how long her legs were, until he saw her in the dress. It was a red sleeveless dress that wrapped around her body and tied in the front with a very loose knot that all a man had to do was gently pull to reveal the lush curves of her body. The dress hugged and kissed Sean's curves as the neckline plunged past the point of being respectable, and the length stopped around midthigh. On any other woman Logan probably would have thought that the dress was nice, but on Sean . . . She made the dress a lethal weapon.

Logan's mouth went dry as his gaze continued down the length of the dress to the strappy red three-inch spiked heels that she wore. Like most men, he was a sucker for a woman in red high heels. Actually any color high heels. He once more looked over her entire body, and that was when he noticed the smooth sheen of her hair that partially curved over one eye, as if she constantly winked at him. And she wore makeup. Not just a dab of lipstick and mascara, but makeup that made her face seem like a beautiful portrait that belonged in a museum or, at the very least, on the cover of a fashion magazine.

For the last two years, Logan realized, he had been living next door to the most beautiful woman he had ever seen.

In midstride she suddenly stumbled, reminding him that,

red dress or not, she was still Sean. Like an ice-skater unable to balance, her arms flailed in the sky as she skidded on the gravel. Logan had been so shocked that he hadn't thought about helping her until he heard her scream his name. He raced around the car at the same time that Sean finally righted herself.

Logan froze when he saw the anger dancing in her eyes. She calmly—too calmly—smoothed down her dress, then smoothed one hand on her hair. Just like that, Logan went from drooling to biting his inner cheek to hold back his laughter.

She calmly assessed him, then said through her shiny red lips, "If you say one word, I will break both of your arms."

She waited for him to respond, but when Logan just stared at the ground, she got into the car. He walked to the driver's side and finally allowed himself to grin.

Six

The only way that Sean managed not to leap across the car and punch Logan in the face was because the dress was so tight that she could barely breathe, let alone raise an arm to smack him. She had walked out of the restaurant expecting to hear his compliments. She looked good. She knew it. It wasn't vanity; it was just a fact. Half of the men in the restaurant had watched her, looks of awe and disbelief on their faces. And what did Logan Riley do when he saw her? He laughed because she almost fell flat on her face. He would fall, too, if he had to wear high heels that should have been outlawed as cruel and unusual punishment.

Sean stared out the car window, not seeing the ocean scenery, the trees, or the sandy beaches as Logan drove through the hills toward her family's house. Sean continued to fume as the silence lengthened in the car. Logan was so irritating. He was so obnoxious. All she wanted was for him to say three simple words—"You look beautiful." She shook her head at the futility. She could have walked out the bathroom wearing nothing more than mascara and Logan would have gotten into the car and muttered about being late. She could just smack him.

"Are we almost there?" Logan asked, breaking into Sean's murderous thoughts.

"Are you in that much of a hurry to meet my family?" she snapped, taking the opportunity to glare at him.

"I'm in that much of a hurry to use the bathroom," Logan cheerfully responded. Sean continued to glare at him and he darted a quick glance at her before he turned to the road. He sighed, then asked, "What is it, Sean? You've been glaring at me since we left the restaurant. I'm not going to tell anyone that you almost fell in the middle of a parking lot."

"Don't you have anything to say about how I look?"

He glanced at her again, then said, "I like having full use of my arms."

"What are you talking about?"

"You told me that if I said one word, you'd break my arms." Sean rolled her eyes when she heard the laughter in his voice. He had been laughing at her the entire time.

"I wasn't talking . . . I meant that if you started laughing about my almost falling, I would break both of your arms, Einstein."

"And now you're fishing for compliments?" Logan uncertainly asked.

Sean groaned and clenched her hands together in her lap to prevent herself from running both hands through her hair, the way she always did. She couldn't do that with straight hair. She couldn't do anything with straight hair except hold her head very, very still.

"I'm not fishing for compliments," she said patiently. "I want your opinion. I look completely different, in case you haven't noticed."

"I've noticed," Logan murmured, his eyes trained on the road.

Sean waited for him to continue, and when he didn't she practically screamed, "And what do you think?"

"Do you really want to know what I think?" he asked in a strange voice that she didn't recognize.

Sean was shocked as she realized that she wanted to cry. Logan still thought that she looked the same. All of the makeup and the hair . . . She could have saved herself the trouble, as far as Logan was concerned. Then she reminded herself that she didn't care what Logan thought. This was all for her family, the Three Ts.

"Make a left here," she answered instead, while pointing toward a small road barely visible among the trees and brush of the hillside.

Logan followed her directions and less than five minutes later parked the car in front of the Weston house. Sean didn't wait for Logan to open her door but quickly scrambled from the car, which was difficult since she had to make certain to keep the hem of the dress at a respectable length and the bodice . . . Sean suddenly noticed the silence as Logan simply stared at the towering house behind her.

"This is amazing," he said in breathless wonder.

Sean followed his eyes and realized that to everyone else in the world, the house that she had been forced to call home one weekend a month and every summer as a child was actually a towering mansion. The red-tile, white-stucco mansion swept across half the hillside and boasted windows and glass walls on much of the bottom floor to take advantage of the perfect view of the Pacific Ocean in the distance below the hills.

Although Logan could not see it, there was an Olympic-size swimming pool in the back of the house along with a tennis court that Tina and her father used every day. The three-car garage boasted a Lexus, a Rolls-Royce, and her father's favorite new toy that he had bought three months ago—a 1965 Mustang. Sean could not picture her strait-laced, three-piece-suit-wearing father driving the car, but she also knew that Banning Weston would never purchase an item that he would not use.

Logan slowly got out of the car, still staring at the house in awe. "Why didn't you tell me that you were rich?"

"I'm not rich."

"Do not give me that poor-little-rich-girl routine." He tore his gaze from the house to look at her. "And to think of all those times you forced me to pay for pizza. You could buy the pizza restaurant."

"I'm not rich. My father and Tina are rich. Tina's maiden name is Harrison—"

"Of Harrison and Harrison?" Logan finished, his mouth forming a wide O. "They make everything—baby powder, diapers, lotion."

"My father was an executive at Harrison and Harrison in the San Francisco office when he and my mother were married. After the divorce, he accepted a transfer to the home office here in Santa Barbara. That's when he met Tina. After her father died ten years ago, my father became and still is the CEO and president of Harrison and Harrison." Sean grew uncomfortable under his intense gaze and walked to the back of the car to retrieve the luggage.

She quickly realized that she could not take her usual long, hard strides. With the towering heels, she had to take baby steps or she would fall flat on her face. With the cool breeze rising from the ocean to swirl around the top of the hill and her lightweight dress, Sean also realized that she was cold. Not to mention that her hair kept sticking to her mouth because of the lipstick. Being beautiful was uncomfortable.

"Why didn't you tell me?" Logan practically accused, meeting her at the trunk of the car.

"There's nothing to tell," Sean replied calmly.

"The fact that your family owns one of the richest companies in California is something that your boyfriend should know, Sean."

"You're not my boyfriend," she said through clenched teeth. "And they're not my family."

Logan's retort was interrupted by the sound of the front door opening. Sean cringed and turned, prepared for the assault from the Three Ts. Like a coordinated dance, the three women walked from the house and lined up in front of Sean.

Sean actually smiled at the identical looks of shock on their beautiful faces.

Tina, Tracie, and Terri all had flawless dark chocolate skin. They each had shoulder-length jet-black hair that fell in a perfect sheen past their shoulders, and they wore the casual clothes of the extremely wealthy that could never be completely casual. The three were petite—barely reaching five-foot-four—and dainty, or what Sean always pictured dainty to be. She always felt like the Jolly Green Giant around the Three Ts, especially now with the three-inch heels.

Sean sneaked a glance at Logan and was not surprised to see the gleam of male appreciation in his eyes as he assessed the three women. He snapped from his Three Ts–induced daze when he noticed Sean smirking at him.

"Sean, is that you?" Tina asked in a small voice as she stared at Sean from head to toe.

"Sean!" Sean grinned at her father's excited cry. Banning Weston ran from the house and swept past his wife and daughters to embrace her.

Sean loved her father. She would never understand him because he was as conservative and uptight as Sean and her mother were not, but Banning had always been Sean's best friend. She and her father resembled each other, with the same walnut brown skin and tall, athletic build, but whereas Sean cursed her long curls, Banning's close-shaven curls kept him looking young even if they were now streaked with gray.

"We were worried about you. You should have been here two hours ago," Banning chided as he hugged her again. "It's been too long, baby."

Banning glanced over his shoulder at his stunned, silent wife and stepdaughters. "What's wrong with you three?"

"Nothing, dear. Sean just looks . . . looks . . ." Tina's voice trailed off and she looked to her daughters for help.

"Don't you notice anything different about me, Dad?" Sean asked as she turned in a circle.

"No," Banning said blankly.

"There's nothing different, Daddy. Sean always looks fabulous, but today she looks more fabulous than usual," Tracie finally said, while winking at Sean. She crossed the distance and threw her arms around Sean, who stumbled slightly from the exuberance of the greeting. Tracie was twenty-two years old and four days from being a married woman, but she still greeted Sean as she had when she had been five. "I'm so glad that you could come to the wedding."

"We all are," Tina said, finally recovering from her shock as she hugged Sean and placed a soft kiss on her cheek. "You look beautiful, darling."

Sean was surprised that her vision blurred at the softly spoken words and the sincerity with which they were spoken. She had underestimated the Three Ts. What did she expect? That they would immediately run into the hills screaming when they saw her? She should have known that they would be happy just to see her, regardless of what she wore, because unlike her, Sean didn't think that the Three Ts had a jealous bone in their collective, perfect bodies.

"I'm glad that I finally have someone to help me deal with Tracie and her nerves," Terri said as she hugged Sean.

"What about me? Don't I help you with Tracie's nerves?" Tina asked, pretending offense as her gray eyes sparkled with amusement.

"Who do you think causes half of Tracie's nerves?" Terri teased her mother.

Sean noticed her father staring at Logan, who had watched the family reunion with a strange look in his eyes. Sean's heart pounded against her chest as she motioned toward Logan and mumbled, "This is my friend and neighbor, Logan Riley. He needed a vacation and thought that Santa Barbara would be a good place for one, so I invited him along."

Logan glanced at her before he shook hands with Banning, and with a surprised look on his face, accepted hugs from the Three Ts. Sean had never brought anyone to Santa Barbara with her. She had never mentioned men around the Three Ts or her father, mostly because there had been very few to mention. There had been one boyfriend in college who had told her after three months that she was "too much man" for him, and then a fellow agent at the Bureau, who had been transferred after four months. None had lasted long enough for her to consider introducing them to her father. Sean just prayed that none of the Three Ts would mention this fact to Logan, who would probably tease her about it for the rest of her life.

"I'm so glad that you drove down with Sean," Tina told Logan, and Sean sighed in relief as Tina acted as if Sean brought men with her on every visit. "We worry about her on the road alone."

"What do you do, Riley?" Banning demanded, as he stuck his hands in the pockets of his neatly pressed navy blue slacks.

"I'm a homicide inspector with the San Francisco Police Department."

"Homicide? Doesn't that mean murder?" Tracie asked, as she nervously began to finger the strand of pearls around her neck.

Logan smiled at her before he answered, "I investigate murders."

"And you like that kind of work?" Banning inquired, peering at Logan from behind silver-rimmed eyeglasses.

"I like solving puzzles," Logan answered. "And I like helping people. By the time I get a case, I can't help the victim, but there are usually people left behind who want answers. I try to give them that."

"Before the interrogation continues," Tina preempted Banning's next question, "we should get these two settled. We have a few guests coming over tonight for dinner, and I'm sure that you two will want to freshen up beforehand."

"Guests?" Sean tried not to sound panicked.

"Just a few," Tina promised. She noticed Logan reaching for their bags in the trunk and she quickly grabbed his arm. "Don't worry about that, dear. Max will see to your bags."

When Tina turned to lead him into the house, Logan looked at Sean and mouthed, "Max?"

Sean smiled in apology, then grabbed his arm and dragged him after Weston family number two, who moved en masse into the house. She struggled up the winding carpeted staircase after Tina, who moved with graceful ease in her high heels. Logan followed behind her, closely flanked by Banning, Tracie, and Terri, as if they were surrounding Logan to keep him from running. They reached the top of the staircase, which opened onto a hallway that branched in opposite directions.

"Sean, you'll stay in your old bedroom." Tina indicated down the long hallway, then motioned for Logan to follow her in the opposite direction. "Logan, your room is down here."

Sean hoped that her face didn't turn red as her father stared at her, as if waiting for a protest. She hid her smile when Logan winked at her before he followed Tina down the hallway.

"Once you get settled, come see me in the study," Banning told Sean. He hugged her once more, then pressed a kiss on her forehead. "I'm glad you're here."

He walked down the stairs, leaving Sean alone with Tracie and Terri. Sean forced a smile at them, then walked toward her bedroom. Unfortunately she heard the click of their heels on the wooden hallway floor as they followed her. Sean decided to ignore them and hope that the two got the message that she didn't want to talk. She silently opened her bedroom door. She froze as she realized that the room still stood as a testament to one summer when a fifteen-year-old Sean had allowed Tina to decorate the room however she liked if she drove Sean to target shooting once a week.

Within the room there were brown wicker, gauzy curtains,

a four-poster bed. . . . The room was everything that Sean's apartment in San Francisco was not. The room was everything that Sean was not, yet she found it strangely comforting. She fell onto the bed, then tugged off the heels, barely resisting the urge to throw them across the room in retaliation for the evil committed against her feet.

Sean gasped in surprise when her bedroom door slammed closed. She turned and warily watched Tracie and Tina fall across the queen-size bed next to her. Sean groaned as she recognized the looks on their faces: they wanted to have girl talk.

"Spill it," Tracie said with an excited giggle.

"Spill what?" Sean pretended ignorance, then walked into the private bathroom attached to the bedroom.

She smelled the lemon-scented cleanser in the air and knew that the room had been prepared for her arrival. There were fresh towels and washcloths on the rod, and the marble countertop gleamed in the sunlight. There was even a new toothbrush waiting on the sink. It was almost too perfect, but Sean was not so self-delusional that she didn't appreciate the care taken for her arrival.

Tracie and Terri followed Sean to the bathroom and stood shoulder-to-shoulder in the door frame. Sean didn't bother hiding her irritation as she glared at them.

"There's nothing to tell. Logan is my friend."

Tracie and Terri exchanged glances with each other, then looked at Sean. The two sisters were not twins, but they were separated by only two years, and Sean always felt that they shared the silent telepathy that some twins were purported to have.

"We aren't talking about Logan—although I want to hear that story—we're talking about the dress, the heels. . . ." Terri's voice trailed off as she nudged Tracie for help.

"The makeup, the hair . . . the cleavage," Tracie finished with wide eyes.

"When you were here for Mom and Dad's anniversary party, you definitely did not look like this," Terri added.

"This is the new me," Sean said, averting her eyes from their intense gaze.

The sisters seemed to wait for further explanation, and when Sean did not continue, they once more exchanged glances that Sean did not like.

"Well, I like it," Tracie said firmly.

"It's sort of a new look," Sean conceded, then brushed past them and into the bedroom.

"Tell us about Logan now," Tracie pleaded, once more falling onto the bed. "He's gorgeous."

"Tell me about Sheldon. I know that I met him at the anniversary party, but there were a lot of people and I . . ." Sean's voice trailed off as she tried not to admit that she couldn't remember meeting the love of Tracie's life.

"Please do not prompt her to talk about Sheldon. We'll be in here for hours and we'll miss the dinner party," Terri said with a dramatic sigh that made Sean actually laugh as Tracie glared at Terri. Anytime one of the Three Ts expressed anything besides cheerful femininity, Sean was pleasantly surprised.

"He's wonderful, Sean. I met him at Yale my junior year. We were in the same a cappella group—"

"A cappella?" Sean repeated, trying to keep the horror out of her voice. She remembered a cappella groups at her college. The men had all weighed about sixty pounds and stood no taller than her shoulders.

"Sheldon is a great singer," Tracie gushed. "He's already planning what to sing to me at the wedding reception."

"That should be great, Tracie," Sean forced herself to say. She was relieved to hear a knock on the bedroom door.

The door opened and a tall, muscle-bound brown-skinned man in all-black clothes walked into the room carrying her bags. Sean heard the soft intake of air behind her and noticed Terri move behind the wing-back chair in the corner of the room, as far from the man as possible. Sean reassessed the man at her stepsister's obvious reaction to him. His coal black eyes roamed the room until he stared at Sean, and although he tried to smile, Sean could tell that the smile did not reach his eyes. In the quick scan he gave her, Sean had the strange feeling that rather than cataloging her attributes, as most men would, he appeared to check her for weapons.

"Your bags." His deep voice carried through the room as he pointed out the obvious.

"You're not Max," Sean said bluntly.

"Max is helping Estelle in the kitchen. I'm Chancy Moore," he said. "Your mother wanted me to tell you all that guests will begin arriving in two hours." He glanced at Tracie and Sean, pointedly ignored Terri, then retreated from the room, softly closing the door behind him.

"Who was that?" Sean demanded, staring at Terri.

"He works at the corporation," Tracie said dismissively as she lay back on the bed, her hair fanning around her. "Sean, you haven't even said anything about your bridesmaid dress. Don't you think that it's the most beautiful thing you've ever seen—"

"Chancy lives here?" Sean asked suspiciously, while still staring at Terri. Terri silently held Sean's gaze, and Sean knew that Terri would tell her nothing.

"Daddy lured him from competition in New York. He needed a place to live while he gets settled," Tracie answered, as if the truth were obvious. "We have so much room here, especially since Terri moved to a condo in town last year and I'll be leaving soon, that Daddy told Chancy to stay for a while."

Sean was not satisfied with the explanation, but she knew Tracie wouldn't know the truth. Since Tracie was the youngest, Banning had always protected her. If either of her stepsisters knew the truth about Chancy's purpose in the house, it would be Terri. And Sean knew the truth had nothing to do with all the empty rooms available in the eight-bedroom mansion.

"Terri?" Sean crossed her arms, waiting for Terri to explain.

"What Tracie said," Terri said after a visible hesitation. She abruptly grabbed Tracie's arm and dragged her toward the door. "You probably want to freshen up before the dinner party. We'll see you in a few hours."

Sean waited two seconds after the two left, then tore out of the room and down the stairs to her father's study. She didn't knock but threw open the double doors. Banning looked up at her entrance from behind the massive maple desk. He saw Sean's expression, then slowly set down the pen in his hand and seemed to mentally prepare himself for her questions.

"Why aren't you surprised to see me?" Sean demanded, crossing the room to stand directly in front of her father's desk.

"I knew that you would want to talk once you met Chancy."

"Why did you hire the muscle, Dad?"

"He's just security for the wedding—"

"That's why you lied to Tracie about Chancy not having a place to live," Sean angrily retorted. "Whoever that man is, he is not the type to sit and watch caterers with sticky fingers. He's obviously an ex-cop or an ex-something. What is going on?"

"Nothing that you need to worry about, Sean—"

Sean raked her hands through her hair, momentarily forgetting about her perfect straight hair. "Trust me, Dad."

Banning seemed surprised as he said, "Of course I trust you, Sean."

"Why did you hire Chancy?" Sean practically pleaded.

Banning's expression didn't change as he tonelessly said, "I should have hired security a long time ago, Sean. We're a rich family and people recognize us."

"Has someone threatened you or one of the Three Ts?" Sean pressed as she sat in one of the leather chairs across from the desk.

Banning smiled through his somber gaze as he murmured, "I really wish you would stop calling them that."

"Dad—"

"There is nothing to worry about, Sean. I'm probably just becoming paranoid in my old age."

Sean glared at her father, wishing that she could read his thoughts. And like a guilty suspect, her father averted his gaze to the papers on his desk.

"I'd like to talk to Chancy," Sean finally said.

"I'll make certain that he makes time to talk to you."

Without another word, Sean walked toward the door with one thought on her mind: why wouldn't her father tell her the truth? She knew that he lied. There was a reason why Chancy lived in the mansion, and Sean knew it had nothing to do with a job at Harrison and Harrison. Banning was scared. Something had happened, and Banning would never tell her—and Sean knew exactly why: her father had never considered her a part of the family he had made with Tina, Tracie, and Terri. And the confirmation of her worst fears made her cry. She realized that she hated crying, which only made her cry harder.

Seven

She was driving him insane. Logan was surrounded by the beauty of the truly rich, by excellent food, by the "few" guests—which turned out to be about seventy-five people on the patio of the Weston home—and the only thought that ran through Logan's head was that Sean was purposely attempting to drive him crazy. He sat at one of the patio tables next to the pool, watching the throng of people talking, laughing, and sipping champagne. And Sean was one of them.

He hadn't seen her since she had disappeared into her separate bedroom when they had first arrived at the mansion. Logan had tried to find her, but in the confusion of the museum called a home, he had been lucky to find his way back to his room. He had gone to the beach, which had been a twenty-minute walk from the mansion, and when he had returned, he didn't have time to look for Sean because Tina had politely but firmly told him to shower and change for the party.

Logan had come down to the dinner party expecting to find Sean fuming in the corner of the patio because he had left her alone with her family for half of the day. Instead he walked onto the patio and realized that every man at the party watched one woman. He was not surprised when he followed their collective gazes to Sean, a Sean who flirted, giggled, and looked as if she belonged.

Under the twinkling stars and patio lights that cast a soft glow across the property, she shone like the moon. She wore a silver-blue strapless ankle-length dress made of the thinnest material that Logan had ever seen. The outlines of her underwear were apparent underneath the dress, and Logan wondered if she knew that. Then he heard her tittering, flirtatious laugh across the patio and realized that Sean knew exactly how thin and alluring the dress was.

She was all glowing brown skin and shining hair, and every man on the patio covertly—or not-so-covertly—watched her every move. And that involved a lot of movement. In the half-hour since Logan had been watching her, Sean had flirted and smiled at every man and woman on the patio except him. As the evening progressed, Logan decided that she made a concentrated effort to avoid him. And it was making him mad. She should be the one sulking in a corner alone, not him. He was normally the life of the party.

Logan slammed the glass of water he had held for almost an hour down on a nearby table. She could attempt to avoid him all she wanted, but he had not driven across California to be ignored by the only person he knew in the next three counties. He stalked across the patio, directing polite smiles at those women who openly stared at him, but his gaze was never gone for long from Sean. And judging from the way she turned her back to him, he could tell that she knew her time had run out. She couldn't ignore him any longer.

Logan stopped next to Sean, between her and the eighty-plus-year-old man in a three-piece suit whose vanilla-tinted face was flushed red as he openly gawked at her breasts. The man noticed Logan's hard glare and, with a curt nod at Sean, he quickly turned and darted into the crowd.

"You scared him, Logan," Sean said calmly, meeting his eyes.

"That's all you have to say to me?" Logan demanded harshly. He noticed the couple standing near them turn to stare at his raised voice. He grabbed her arm and led her farther toward the darkness of the hillside behind the house, away from the lights of the patio. He was surprised by his caveman tactics. He didn't grab women. But he was more surprised that Sean had allowed him to do that.

"What's wrong now, Riley?" she asked in a cool voice.

"You've been ignoring me."

"I have not been ignoring you."

"Yes, you have," Logan insisted. "I didn't come to Santa Barbara to be ignored—"

"No, you came to Santa Barbara for a vacation, remember? I forced you to come here, but I'm not going to force you to spend time with me. You're free until Saturday, the day of the wedding."

Logan glared at her, resenting the apathy that she showed and his own silent protest at the idea of not spending time with her until Saturday. Sean shot him a dry smile then tried to brush past him toward the patio, but she suddenly cried out in surprise. He saw her pitching forward in a flurry of wild arms with her left shoe heel caught in a small hole in the grass. He grabbed her waist and pulled her toward him to steady her.

"I still haven't learned how to walk in these," Sean muttered, glaring at the matching stiletto heels she wore. She appeared on the verge of saying more until she looked at him.

Logan didn't realize how close the two stood until he felt her warm gasp caress his lips. He noticed the smoothness of her bare shoulders. He noticed the sudden darkness of her eyes as she glanced at his mouth. His fingers on her hips flexed against the soft material of her dress that should have been her skin.

Logan forced himself to draw his hands from her waist slowly and carefully. He forced his gaze from her lips even as the truth hit him like an iron glove in the stomach: he wanted her.

"Thanks for saving me from another embarrassing moment," she softly whispered, her arms still on his arms where she had grabbed for balance.

"You look beautiful, Sean," Logan's voice matched the level of hers.

"Do you really think so?"

"Me and every other man here."

"You don't look so bad either," she reluctantly said, as one hand moved to straighten the collar of his powder blue shirt underneath the charcoal gray suit that he wore.

"Even Prince Charming tries to look nice for the ball." She stared at him, unspeaking, and Logan saw the desire in her eyes. An ache throbbed in his groin.

The sudden charged silence between them was broken by light applause from the patio. Logan turned to watch the band move into position and begin to play a soft waltz. The crowd began to pair into couples and create a dance floor near the pool.

"Do you want to dance?" he impulsively asked.

Sean darted a quick glance at him before she once more turned to the dancing couples. "I'm a horrible dancer."

"Dancing is a lot like sex. It takes the right partner." He hadn't meant for his voice to sound so husky, so seductive, but there was something about the darkness and inhaling the familiar scent of Sean's raspberry-sweet aroma that made his voice automatically drop a few octaves. Logan realized with half embarrassment and half wonder that his body liked Sean's aroma more than he thought. In a split second, he had become almost painfully aroused.

Logan's thoughts drifted from his anatomy problems when he suddenly noticed the speculative gleam in her eyes. He tried to hide his smile. He should have known that Sean would not allow that comment to pass.

"You do know that your flirting doesn't work with me, don't you?" she said matter-of-factly.

Logan felt a wolfish grin cross his face—which, of

course, made Sean look more suspicious. "That sounds like a challenge to me."

"Call it whatever you want, Riley, but before you waste your time, you should know that you're not my type."

"Oh, really?" Logan asked lightly. He thought that maybe he should feel offended, but he wasn't. He always loved a challenge, and whether Sean knew it or not, she had issued one.

"Really," Sean firmly answered. "You're too . . . smooth."

"Some might consider that a compliment."

"It's not meant to be one," Sean bluntly replied.

"Then it's an insult?"

"It's not meant to be an insult. It's the truth. I've never paid much attention to men like you. You smile at a woman and expect her to fall into your arms. It all comes too easily for you. Commitment is a four-letter word. That's not what I'm looking for in a man, if I were looking for one, which I'm not."

Her words shouldn't have mattered to him. He knew she was wrong, and maybe one day she would realize it, too. He shouldn't have cared. She was just Sean, not a woman who he thought could be the one who could break the five-week curse, but for some reason he wanted her to see him as he really was, not the image that he presented to everyone.

"Is that how you see me?"

"I've lived next door to you for two years. I've seen your parade of women, a different woman every weekend."

"It sounds like you have me all figured out." Logan closed the distance between them. Whether she realized it or not, she tried to take several steps back, but the fence surrounding the tennis court blocked her. Logan grinned when he saw the understanding that she was trapped dawn in her eyes. He had Sean on retreat. He hadn't thought that it could be done.

Logan raised his hand to brush strands of hair from her

eyes. He smiled when she flinched. As if she'd suddenly realized her response, Sean's chin rose a fraction of an inch as if steeling herself for a fight. He brushed the hair from her face, his fingers lingering on skin that surprised him by its softness. He had never thought of Sean as soft. He had touched women, but for some reason he couldn't remember any feeling as soft as she did. She lost the fighting look in her eyes, and Logan actually thought that he heard Sean sigh. That was ridiculous. Sean Weston did not sigh.

"I accept your challenge, Weston," he finally said.

"What are you talking about?"

"You're threatening my image as a playboy."

Sean quickly corrected him, "That's not what I meant. I was just saying that even though you're handsome and charming, you're not—"

"I'm giving you ample warning," Logan cut her off in a soft voice, as he trailed his fingers down her face to her lips which glistened in the moonlight. He touched them, half expecting Sean to suddenly bite him, but only her sudden heavy breath touched his fingers. He tried to read the strange look in her eyes, but whatever she thought, she kept locked behind her dark expression.

Logan reluctantly removed his fingers from her, then casually said, "Sheldon invited me to his bachelor party."

Confusion danced in Sean's eyes at his abrupt change of subject. She finally asked, "Are you going?"

"I thought I would." He watched her closely as he added, "Earlier, your father invited me to play golf tomorrow morning."

"Why?"

"Because he wants to get to know his daughter's boyfriend." Logan grinned in triumph when irritation flickered across her expression.

"I never told him that you were my boyfriend. I knew that he would jump to that conclusion, which is exactly why

I wanted you to talk to other women while I talked to other men tonight."

"No women here interest me like you do, Sean."

"You're flirting with me again," she accused.

Logan grinned, then grabbed her hand. "Dance with me, Weston."

She attempted to pull away, but Logan held firm. "I told you that I don't dance."

"Guess what? You have the right partner tonight." Logan ignored her protests as he dragged her toward the patio.

He ignored the curious glances in their direction as he shouldered to the center of the dancing area. Sean darted nervous glances at the couples moving around her, and Logan could tell that she was on the verge of bolting at any second. He knew that she hated any situation that she was not in control of. She hated those situations because they made her nervous—they made her human, and Sean Weston hated to be reminded that she was human. Logan almost felt sympathy for her, but she had insulted his skills and . . . and, more important, Logan wanted to dance with her. More than anything he could remember wanting in the last five years.

Logan watched Sean nervously tuck hair behind her right ear, completely ruining her sophisticated, beauty-salon hairstyle. And if Logan hadn't believed she was beautiful before, he definitely did at that moment.

"Don't move," he ordered in a soft voice. He quickly ran to the band and signaled to the bandleader.

Sean watched Logan across the patio talk to the bandleader. She didn't know why she remained in the spot where he had left her. She stood alone in a mass of dancing bodies, and because Logan had told her not to move, she wasn't going to move. Sean didn't think that she could move even if she wanted to. Her knees were too weak. Logan Riley was flirting with her. And for one brief second in the darkness she had thought that he would kiss her.

Sean shook her head at her thoughts. She would not buy in to whatever game Logan was playing. Even though she was attracted to him, she would not kiss him or do anything else with him, just because he suddenly found her attractive. She knew why he suddenly cared about flirting with her and whether she challenged him . . . the clothes, the hair, the makeup, and the shoes. She looked like one of the women he would date.

She had seen his expression when he had first seen her at the party. He had looked surprised, then amazed, and if Sean didn't know better she'd have thought he looked like he wanted her. Now she knew the truth. He didn't want her. He wanted the image she portrayed. But she was still herself, and as soon as Logan remembered that, the sooner they could return to their regular exchange of insults.

Sean sighed as Logan walked back toward her, a sexy smile on his face that set off small trembles of desire through her body. She had lied to him. Maybe men like him didn't have a chance with her, but he did. If she didn't live next door to him and if she didn't know his turnover rate with women, Sean wouldn't have been able to resist him.

Logan reached her just as the band abruptly stopped the waltz music and a lively tango melody filled the air. Sean watched as numerous couples stalked from the dance area while darting angry glances at the band. Amid the soft lights and clinking champagne glasses, the tango music seemed out of place.

"This is not the tango crowd, Riley," Sean warned him as he wrapped an arm around her waist.

"I know." He winked at her just as he slammed her against his body.

Sean cried out in surprise, then laughed at his answering grin. Her smile disappeared when she saw Terri and Banning standing with the other guests who watched Sean and Logan, as if expecting a show. Banning encouragingly waved at Sean, and Sean forced herself to smile before she looked at Logan.

"Are you going to embarrass me?" she demanded, attempting to keep her expression pleasant for her father.

"I will have you know that I am the best tango dancer in the precinct. I don't usually dance with amateurs, but I'm making an exception for you."

"Should I break your leg now or wait until all the guests leave?"

"Relax, Weston; you may even find yourself having fun."

He grinned, then, with a quick snap of his hands, spun Sean away from his body and into the few couples who danced around them. The couples darted out of the path of her spin. Sean tried to apologize, but Logan grabbed her arm and snapped her around until she whirled back against his body. The room continued to spin as, to the beat of the music, Logan bent her backward until Sean thought that she would spilt in two; then he whipped her upward. Her hair slapped her in the face, but when she saw the excitement in Logan's eyes, she could only laugh.

Slowly the crowd created a circle as people turned to watch the two dance in a series of simple moves that Sean would have tripped over if Logan didn't have a firm hold on her waist. Sean began laughing, despite her vow not to give Logan the satisfaction. He laughed with her, then twirled her around the floor until she felt as if she glided across the room. Her hair flew; her dress flew and probably bared her underwear to the crowd, but she was dancing. Sean couldn't stop smiling as she felt like the star of her own personal musical.

The song abruptly came to an end with a resounding last note, and Logan spun her around one last time, then draped her over his body. Sean hadn't realized that every eye at the party was on them until the applause began. Logan carefully released his hold on her, and Sean felt the loss of his warm hands, leading her and guiding her. Logan bowed to the crowd, then motioned to Sean, who dramatically curtsied—or at least her version of a curtsy.

Sean glanced at the various smiling faces and bowed again. She turned to bow to the people behind her when she saw an older man standing next to Sheldon and Tracie. He smiled and clapped like the others, but Sean's blood ran cold. She peered through the crowd at the man's familiar face. He noticed her stare and abruptly turned and walked toward the house.

Ignoring the continuing applause, Sean began to push her way through the crowd, her eyes trained on the man's broad back as he disappeared into the house. She ignored the compliments directed at her from the various people whom she shoved past. She broke free of the crowd and ran as fast as the three-inch heels would carry her into the house. She cursed as the man's shadow disappeared out the front door. Sean hopped on one foot to pull off one shoe, then the other, and sprinted toward the door.

She flung open the door just as a black limousine with tinted windows disappeared down the road. Even if she could reach Logan's car, she would never be able to maneuver it through the gaggle of other cars that lined the driveway and the road to follow the man.

"Sean," Logan said as he ran to a stop at her side. He glared at her as he muttered, "You left me standing alone in front of everyone. The dance wasn't that bad, was it—"

"I think I just saw Carl Madison," she whispered in disbelief.

"What would the biggest weapons dealer in the United States be doing in Santa Barbara?"

"I don't know, but I plan to find out." She walked into the house, with Logan close on her heels.

Eight

Sean dragged her hands through her hair as she sat in the massive chair behind her father's desk. The house was still and silent, a sharp contrast to the voices and music only hours earlier. Sean had waited until close to four in the morning, when she thought that everyone was asleep, to creep into her father's office to turn on the computer and log in to her e-mail account to wait for a message from a fellow agent in the New York office.

Sean stretched her arms over head then curled her legs underneath her body in the wide, comfortable chair. She wore sweatpants and a much-loved and much-washed T-shirt. Her toes and the arches of her feet still hurt from the pinch and the towering height of the shoes that she had forced herself to wear, but she still felt the most comfortable she had since she'd walked out of the restaurant that afternoon. She decided that it was time to rethink her plan. She could not permanently damage her feet just to prove to herself that she could be part of Weston family number two.

Sean heard the study door opening and whirled around in the chair, prepared to lie to her father about her presence in his office at such a strange hour. Logan slipped through the door and softly closed it. She groaned as he walked across the darkness lit only by the blue light from the computer. She tried not to notice the long brown legs and their thick dusting of dark hair from the calves to the muscular thighs that disappeared underneath the snug blue shorts he wore. Fortunately or unfortunately for her, he also wore a T-shirt. She knew that he generally slept shirtless. The image had assaulted her almost nightly since she'd discovered the disturbing news a few months ago after she knocked on his door for a late-night snack.

"Has your friend e-mailed the file yet?" Logan asked eagerly, then glanced at the computer.

"What are you doing awake?"

"I want to see the FBI file on Carl Madison. If a dangerous individual like Carl Madison is hanging around your family—and coincidentally me—then I want to know about it."

"Your concern is touching," she dryly responded. Logan grinned in response and she once more felt that strange rolling movement of her heart that happened only when he was around. It had become almost debilitating. She groaned deeply, in what she hoped that he thought was irritation but was mostly for her to calm the flutters in her stomach, then said, "When I told you that I was going to ask my friend to e-mail me the file on Madison, I didn't mean that you had to wake up at this ridiculous hour to wait with me."

"I couldn't sleep," Logan said with a shrug.

Sean wondered if he was haunted by images of her in his dreams, as she had been haunted by images of him. She shook her head at the thought. Logan had probably had too much champagne at the party and that was why he danced with her and flirted with her. Judging from the fact that he hadn't looked at her once since he entered the study, he probably had forgotten about his flirting earlier that evening. She told herself it was for the best, but she still stared out the windows at the now-dark patio, remembering the charged moment when she thought that he would kiss her.

"I still don't understand why you didn't tell your father," Logan said, breaking into her fantasies.

"What would I tell my father? That I suspect a fugitive

from the law is a guest at his daughter's wedding? He would just think that I'm trying to get attention."

"Your father wouldn't think that, Sean."

"Did you notice Chancy?" Sean asked, ignoring his softly spoken comment.

"He's an ex-cop, probably now a bodyguard." Sean was surprised that Logan had noticed Chancy's obvious law enforcement training. Logan grinned at her as he said, "I may just be a local cop, but I know a law enforcement officer when I see one."

"Did you talk to him?"

"No, but I watched him tonight. He's good. Has your father told you about any trouble around here that would prompt him to hire Chancy?"

"No," Sean spat, then stared at the computer screen. "He didn't even tell me why he hired Chancy, except that the family is rich, and apparently all rich people need security. I can't believe that he never told me he was going to hire a full-time security specialist."

"Maybe he doesn't want you to worry."

"Maybe," Sean murmured.

There was a silent pause before Logan asked, "Who exactly is this friend in the Bureau who's going to work at six in the morning just to e-mail you a file?"

Sean heard the too-casual tone and for a second she wondered if Logan was jealous. "Just a friend."

"Is this friend a boy or a girl?"

"What is this? The third grade?" Sean asked while laughing in disbelief. "Why do you care?"

His expression was too serious when he softly responded, "I care, Sean."

"Stop it, Logan," Sean demanded. "Stop the flirting, the caring, and . . . and the looks."

"What looks?"

"You know what I'm talking about," Sean snapped. "You look at me like I'm the only woman in the room."

"That's what Prince Charming does," Logan said with another casual shrug that made her want to scream.

"Will you get over the Cinderella thing, Logan?" Sean cried in frustration. "I want us to go back to how things were before I put on a short dress and makeup."

"You have to admit that the dancing tonight was a nice touch," Logan said, ignoring her outburst. "All of the women at the party were sighing at the romance of it all."

"Is that why you danced with me? So that other women would sigh?" Sean heard the disappointment in her tone and she quickly turned to the computer to avoid his searching gaze. She sounded like one of those indecisive women who irritated her. First she told Logan to stop treating her as though she were special; then she wanted to pummel his face in because he danced with her only to increase the members of his fan club.

Logan turned the chair she sat in, forcing her to look at him. He placed his hands on the armrest, effectively trapping her within the chair. Sean refused to give him the satisfaction of showing her discomfort and arousal at his nearness. She forced herself to hold his gaze even when his familiar soapy-clean scent wrapped around her and made her heart race.

"I danced with you because I wanted to," Logan said firmly. Electricity crackled in the air as the two stared at each other for an eternity; then Logan moved back, breaking the moment. Sean deeply inhaled the fresh air, trying to rid her mind of his scent. He added with a careless shrug, "The fact that we looked so good together on the dance floor was a bonus."

"You're so proud of yourself."

"Maybe I should start charging you for my services."

"Or you could return to San Francisco.

"Not for all the money in the world," Logan said, shaking his head. "If Carl Madison is really a guest at your sister's wedding, I want to be here when he's caught. He's been eluding the law for almost two years, while pumping countless illegal weapons across state lines every week. Anyone involved in his capture and the elimination of his operation will have an instant boost to his—or her—career."

"Of course," Sean murmured, chiding herself for hoping that his reason for remaining in Santa Barbara involved anything other than business.

"Besides, I have to stick around and see your next outfit," he added with a sexy grin that made her stomach turn into a liquid roller coaster. "So far each dress has shown more flesh than the previous one. I'm betting you'll be naked by the wedding."

Sean silently gasped at the image of Logan, with a dark, hungry gaze, staring at her standing completely nude before him. She forced a dry laugh as she muttered, "In your dreams, Riley."

"In my dreams you've been naked for a while." Sean's mouth dropped open at his quick response. Apparently whatever challenge she had unwittingly issued was still in effect. He laughed at her obvious shock, then mused, "I think I just rendered you speechless."

"What are—"

Logan cut her off as he indicated the computer screen and smugly said, "You just got a new message from a Sally Barker. Sally. That sounds like a female to me."

Sean forced herself to turn to the computer screen. With one trembling hand she directed the mouse to open the e-mail sent by Sally Barker. The file opened and a large color picture of the man Sean had seen on the patio filled the screen.

"Is that the man you saw earlier?" Logan asked, leaning over her shoulder to read the words on the computer screen. His scent once more enveloped her in a warm cocoon and ruined her ability to think clearly. She shook her head and told herself to stop allowing Logan to get to her. If he wanted a fight then he had met his match with her. She refused to surrender to his sensual maneuvers. She repeated that to herself over and over.

"If I didn't see Madison then he has an identical twin in Santa Barbara."

She scrolled down the screen to read the document that outlined the illegal activities of Carl Madison and his gun-smuggling empire that supplied guns to gangs and criminal networks in all fifty states through a complicated smuggling scheme that neither the FBI nor local police had been able to infiltrate. The file ended on the fact that Madison was not considered dangerous, labeling him as the brains behind the vast operation, but danger followed him. He had disappeared from surveillance eight months ago after an attempt on his life by a rival gang, the Donalds, that wanted to gain control over his territory.

"You should call the Bureau," Logan said as Sean turned off the computer.

"I don't want FBI crawling all over the house the week of Tracie's wedding."

"You would rather place your family in danger?" he asked incredulously.

"He's not listed as dangerous. If anything, he's an accountant who's fooling a lot of people. Besides, I don't even know if that was really him I saw tonight. I only caught a quick glimpse of his face."

"Madison may not be dangerous, but the Donalds are. The base of their illegal operations is in Chicago, but even I've heard about them in San Francisco. They're ruthless and vicious. If they want Madison dead, it's only a matter of time before he is dead."

"I know who the Donalds are."

"Sean—"

"If I call my supervisor and a team is sent out and I'm wrong . . . I'll be the laughingstock of the Bureau. After the Jell-O incident, I don't need any more red marks next to my name." She realized her mistake in mentioning the "Case of the Exploding Jell-O Bowl," as it was known throughout the Bureau in San Francisco, when Logan arched one eyebrow.

"What Jell-O incident?"

"The point is that I have to be certain that the man I saw is Carl Madison," Sean said dismissively. She stood and stretched her arms over her head, feeling too tired to deal with Logan's seductive pull any longer. She had made enough of a fool of herself around Logan for one day. She needed to escape before her defenses lowered even more and she begged him for his kiss.

"You're not the only one on the line here," Logan insisted. "If my captain finds out that I had an inside lead on Madison, but didn't notify anyone, then I'll be at a desk for the rest of my career."

"You don't have jurisdiction in Santa Barbara."

"Carl Madison has committed crimes in San Francisco. I'm certain that the local cops will work with us more willingly than with you and the Feds."

Sean refused to admit that Logan was probably right. Local police tended to stick together and to automatically distrust federal agents. She stared at him, trying to read his blank expression. She finally gave up, then said, "What do you want to do?"

"We'll wait and see if Carl Madison or his identical twin comes to any more wedding events. In the meantime, you print the picture of Madison and we'll show it to your family and the local police. If he is in town we can notify our respective agencies and they can be here within the hour."

"Deal," Sean said, nodding.

"Shake," Logan ordered, while holding out his hand.

Sean knew that she was being childish, but she didn't want to touch him. His large brown hand looked too inviting, too warm. Against her will, she remembered the feel of his hands on her waist, the way his fingers had dug into her skin, almost as if he didn't want to release her.

"I'm not going to bite you, Sean." He grinned as he added, "At least, not yet."

She refused to react to his flirtatious remark and reluctantly placed her hand in his grip. His fingers fluttered over the pulse in her wrist, and her blood pounded all over her body at the feather-soft touch.

She snatched her hand from his grip as if he were a poisonous snake. Logan just smiled at her and continued to lounge on top of the desk like a hired male model. Sean tried to think of something to knock the smug smile off his face, but the only response she could think of was to whirl around and rush toward the door. She glanced back at him over her shoulder to find him still watching her.

Sean yelped as her left knee bumped into the edge of the coffee table in the center of the room. Because she had been practically running to escape Logan's stare, the sudden obstacle caused her to become airborne and she sailed through the air to land on the plush rug near the door. She quickly scrambled to her feet, hoping that the faster she stood, the less chance Logan would have to notice that she fell. She glanced at him once more and found him watching her with a strange smile. He didn't laugh or tease her or even ask if she was all right. He just watched her.

Sean practically ran from the room, making certain to keep a careful watch for any other pieces of furniture that appeared from nowhere.

As Sean sailed into the air in the middle of the study, Logan realized that he might be falling in love with her. Sean Weston, with her uncontrollable hair, her wide mouth and equally as wide smile, and her rumpled clothes. He felt as though he sat in a roller coaster that was about to plunge downhill and leave his stomach at the top. He could not be in love with Sean Weston.

When he thought about finally opening himself to the

pain of loving someone again and eventually being hurt by that person, Logan had never pictured the woman, but it couldn't be Sean. He knew that he had created the challenge with her. He wanted to have an excuse to touch Sean because he wanted to flirt with her, to touch her, to hear the soft sigh that she probably didn't know escaped her lips when he leaned close to her. He was acting as though he were attracted to her, and Logan couldn't think of any other reason except that he was.

Logan walked from the study as if in a trance and began to think about every moment he had spent with Sean over the last two years. He placed a hand on his rolling stomach as he realized that he possibly could have been attracted to her from the first moment he saw her, when she wore a pair of baggy, food-stained sweats and an oversize sweatshirt. Logan refused to believe himself. There was no way he could be sexually attracted to a woman like Sean.

Logan liked women who wore skirts and dresses, women who didn't think a good weekend involved cleaning guns or sitting with a six-pack in front of the television to watch a football game. He liked women who pretended interest in his work but who wanted only to tell their friends that he was a cop and not hear about the specifics of being one. He liked women who expected him to have all of the answers and . . . Logan shook his head as he realized that he didn't like those women. Maggie was more like Sean than like the women he dated. Jessica would have hit him for even comparing her to those women. All of the important women in his life were nothing like the women he searched among for his soul mate.

Logan had wasted his whole life on women whom he couldn't hold a conversation with. He could talk with Sean. He could do a lot of things with Sean, and Logan realized with unsettling certainty that he wanted the majority of those things to include a bed and a naked Sean.

Logan cringed at the direction of his thoughts. He had

been celibate for five years—five long years that only his brother and sister knew about. After too many failed relationships to count, which had all lasted five weeks or less, Logan had vowed never to give his heart, his soul, or himself to a woman unless they had passed the five-week mark. When he had made the deal with himself, he had never thought that he would find himself five years later still waiting. He had been tempted over the last five years—almost to the point of insanity, but he had never felt physical pain at keeping his promise until Sean Weston.

The moment in the darkness at the party once more invaded his thoughts, along with the almost painful ache in his groin. Her skin had smelled like a forbidden ambrosia. He remembered the powerful pull he felt toward her, the need to take her in his arms and shoot anyone who came near. He remembered her wild laughter when they danced, and how every move he made she matched with equal passion.

Logan suddenly groaned. He was losing his mind. He was a flirt, and he was flirting with Sean because there was no other woman around he could flirt with. That was it. No further discussion.

As he headed toward the stairs, Logan caught a glimpse of white from the swimming pool. He opened the glass patio doors, wondering if his tired eyes deceived him. Then he saw Terri wrapped in a white silk robe sitting on a patio chair staring at the night sky. She abruptly buried her face in her hands, and her shoulders shook from the force of silent sobs.

Logan hesitated. It was none of his business, but he still found himself walking outside the house. After raising a little sister, Logan could not bury his instinct to stop female tears. He loudly cleared his throat, and generally made enough noise to wake the dead as he closed the patio doors. By the time he turned to Terri, she had managed to wipe away any evidence of her tears except for the slightly swollen eyes.

"Logan," Terri greeted with a weak smile.

"I didn't notice anyone else out here," Logan said, hoping that he sounded surprised to see her in the darkness.

"With all the excitement around here, I can't sleep. We didn't hire a wedding coordinator because Mom, Tracie, and I wanted to do everything. Sometimes I wish that we had hired one. You wouldn't believe how much work goes into one day. I bet this is how Broadway directors feel the night before a show opening. In between work and the wedding, I haven't been able to sleep in the last five months." She abruptly stopped talking to take several deep breaths, since Logan hadn't heard her pause for air since she had opened her mouth.

Logan didn't comment on the forced cheerfulness in her voice but instead sat in the patio chair next to hers. He noticed that Terri tried to move farther into the shadows to hide her tearstained face from him, but it was too late.

"I'm really glad that you came with Sean," Terri continued in her too-bright voice.

She smiled, then glanced at her bare wrist. She sighed in surprise. "Look at the time. . . . I have to get up in two hours for work, so it's been nice talking to you, Logan, but . . ." Her voice trailed off when Logan gently wrapped his hand around her wrist. With wide, frightened eyes, she stared at him, and Logan almost wished that he could have accepted her acting skills as easily as she had accepted his.

"You aren't wearing a watch, Terri," he gently said. He released her wrist and she instantly crossed her arms over her chest.

"I'm just stressed," she answered his unspoken question about her tears. When Logan continued to stare at her, she repeated in a more insistent tone, "I'm just stressed."

"You sound like you have a lot on your mind," Logan finally said, giving her an easy escape.

Terri smiled, her relief obvious on her shadowed face. She smiled as she excitedly bobbed her head. "You're right."

"I'll see you tomorrow," Logan said.

"Thanks . . . I mean, I'll see you." She jumped to her feet to leave, then paused for a second as she uncertainly glanced at him and said, "Logan . . . Don't tell anyone about this. I don't want to worry anyone."

Logan silently nodded; then Terri turned and quickly ran back into the house. He sighed, then placed his feet on the chair she had just vacated. Now he remembered why he never took vacations. Somehow he always worked harder on vacation than he did at work.

Nine

Too early in the morning to be legal, Logan squinted at the cruelly bright sun as he walked out the front door of the mansion de Weston. He immediately pulled his sunglasses from his shirt pocket and rammed them over his eyes. Logan was once more reminded that he was getting old. He could no longer stay up until five in the morning, then wake up at seven for an early tee time with Banning. Actually Logan couldn't remember ever being able to do anything like that but, like most adults, he liked to think that life had been so much better and easier when he was younger.

Smiling as if it were not a crime to be awake that early, Banning waved at Logan from the driver's door of his forest green Lexus. Because it was Sean's father, Logan forced a smile and gave a small wave in return.

"There's coffee in the car," Banning called to Logan.

Logan moved toward the promise of coffee and slid into the leather passenger seat of the luxury car. Banning grinned, then sat behind the steering wheel. The engine came to life with a surprisingly silent hum. Logan noticed only long enough to grab the thermos of coffee from the cup holder.

"It's another beautiful Santa Barbara day," Banning commented as he slowly and carefully steered the car down the narrow road toward the main street. "The weather channel said that it will be a perfect eighty degrees from now until August."

Logan grunted in response as he gulped down the coffee. He wished that he could have been better company, but the little sleep he had managed to snag throughout the night had been constantly interrupted by images of Sean. Sean in the red dress. Sean in her robe. Sean in a white shirt with ketchup stains. Sean in a tub of Jell-O. Sean wearing nothing and holding her lush breasts in her hands, offering them to him.

". . . what do you think, Logan?" Banning concluded whatever he was saying while Logan daydreamed about his daughter.

"I think . . . I think that sounds good," Logan stammered. He caught sight of the beach in the distance as Banning directed the car through the hills.

"Have you had a chance to go to our famous beaches?"

"Yesterday afternoon," Logan answered.

"Beautiful women, beautiful beaches."

Logan smiled his wholehearted agreement, then asked, "Do you like it here?"

"I have a good life."

Logan had the strange feeling that Banning wanted to say "but." Banning remained silent and Logan shrugged away his notion. He stared out the window, noticing that the road Banning drove wound higher and higher into the hills above Santa Barbara.

"Do you like golf, Logan?" Banning suddenly asked.

"To be honest, I've been only once. Some cop buddies and I went. We got kicked out after one of my friends . . ." Logan's voice trailed off as he realized he shouldn't tell Sean's father that particular story. He nervously cleared his throat, then lamely finished, "I like golf."

"Don't tell anyone, Logan, but I hate golf," Banning said matter-of-factly. "I can't stand the sport. I know there's supposed to be an almost religious aspect to the game, but each and every time I step onto the green, I have to restrain the urge to run over my golf clubs with the cart."

Logan stared surprised at the older man, who paradoxically appeared the epitome of the typical wealthy golfer. Banning parked the car on a dirt lot next to a battered pickup truck. Logan got out of the car and looked across its hood. Three large, colorful, kite-looking objects—three times the size of a man—littered the cliff, which ended abruptly in a steep drop to the ocean. If Logan didn't know better, he would suspect that the kites were really meant for hang gliding, where a man strapped himself to the objects and pretended to be a bird. Logan laughed at his thoughts because he knew better. Sean's father was the president of a multimillion-dollar corporation. Men like him did not hang glide.

Two men with long hair got out of the truck next to Banning's car and waved at Banning as if they knew him.

Logan glanced at the ocean below them, way below them, then turned to Banning. Banning looked almost giddy as he pulled a black helmet from the backseat of the car. He replaced his eyeglasses with a pair of Oakley prescription sunglasses.

"This doesn't look like a golf course, Banning," Logan said, attempting to keep the panic out of his voice.

"What does it look like, Logan?" Banning asked casually.

"It looks like a death trap," Logan practically screamed just as one of the tall, blond men approached Banning to shake hands in a complicated series of moves that Logan hadn't even seen on the streets of San Francisco.

"Ban the man," the surfer dude greeted with a wide grin. "You brought a friend?"

"This is Logan Riley. He's my oldest daughter's boyfriend."

Logan knew that Sean would kill him for not correcting her father on his role in Sean's life, but he was on the verge of death. He couldn't be expected to keep all of the facts straight.

"The daughter in San Francisco?"

"That's my Sean," Banning said with a confirming nod. He motioned to Logan, then said with a long-suffering roll of the eyes, "He's a virgin."

"Not since I was fifteen," Logan protested, his voice slightly cracking.

"Calm down, Logan. I meant that you're a virgin to gliding," Banning patiently explained, then looked at the surfer—or paraglider—dude and shared a condescending laugh.

"Maybe I should give you a chance to calm your friend down," surfer-paraglider dude said to Banning. "Chaz and I have already gone up today. It was amazing, Ban."

Banning practically jumped up and down, then turned to Logan as the surfer-paraglider dude walked away to join Chaz and to make fun of Logan. Logan walked around the car to stand directly in front of Banning. He clenched his hands into fists to restrain the urge to hit the older man. Logan would never admit having a fear of heights, but he did believe that any rational man would keep his feet on solid ground if given a choice, and he considered himself a rational man.

"What happened to golf? Weren't we supposed to play golf? Unless I've missed some major development in the sport of golf, golf does not include cliffs and hang gliding . . . and the land being so far away. In fact, golf takes place on the land, the solid land, underneath your feet."

"I told you that I hate golf," Banning said, his mouth twisting into a smile underneath the mustache.

"Fine! We don't have to golf," Logan exploded. "Are golfing and plunging to our deaths the only things to do in Santa Barbara? What about a nice walk on the beach? That sounds fun, doesn't it?"

Banning's smile disappeared and he slowly took off the sunglasses. Logan watched him, not feeling the least sympathy for the poor-little-me routine he knew Banning was trying to pull. That routine didn't work for grown men who owned multimillion-dollar homes and operated a corporation that was regularly listed in *Forbes*.

"For the last eight months, something has been missing in my life," Banning abruptly said.

"Like what?" Logan asked in disbelief.

"I don't know, Logan, but I do know that I've spent my whole life being exactly what everyone told me to be, and now I don't know where I stop and where everyone's image of me begins," he explained in a quiet voice that reminded Logan a little of Sean when she was sad. "For over thirty years I wake up in the morning, put on a suit, put on a tie, put on the right shoes—no rubber soles. I eat a bowl of oatmeal, drink a glass of orange juice; then I get into a sensible car and I go to work, where I spend ten to twelve hours ensuring that I can do the same thing the next day.

"I'm fifty-seven years old and I don't know who I am. All I know about myself is that I have one ex-wife, three daughters, and a second wife. Everything I am is defined by other people. That's not how a man should define himself."

"How does hang gliding fit in to any of this?"

"It's marginally safer than bungee jumping," Banning replied with a smirk that made Logan laugh. "I know it seems insane to jump off a cliff with basically a kite attached to your back, but the feeling that comes from hang gliding is amazing. There's nothing on earth like it."

Logan sobered, then hesitantly asked, "Does your family know what you're doing?"

He saw the momentary panic on Banning's face before he quickly shook his head and said, "Of course not. They would worry or think that I'm crazy."

Logan kept his own opinions about Banning's state of mind to himself, then peered over the cliff once more. The only reason that Logan hadn't flipped open his cellular telephone to call Sean or the men in the white coats was because he understood Banning. Even the wealthiest men in the world had to feel truly free for a little while.

"What else have you done besides hang gliding?" Logan asked, almost afraid of the answer.

"Bungee jumped—the momentary thrill is not worth the fear. Parachuted out of a plane, one of the most amazing ways to almost die. Joined a drag race one Saturday night; they laughed at my 1965 Mustang, but those high school punks didn't know what I had under the hood—"

"You're making my stomach hurt," Logan muttered, glancing at the older man who no one would ever guess was a daredevil. Logan glanced over the cliff once more, then asked, "Are you certain that this is safe?"

"Chaz and Arnold may not look like it, but they run a tight operation. You can't get much safer than those two."

"How does it feel being that far off the ground?" Logan asked curiously.

"There's no explanation, Logan," Banning said with a contagious smile that made Logan forget that he was dealing with an old man in the middle of a midlife crisis. "I don't have to explain it, Logan; you can feel it for yourself. Just have a few hours of training and a practice run; then you can feel how amazing it is."

"I'd rather live vicariously through you," Logan quickly responded.

"You aren't going to stop me?" Banning asked, surprised.

"I'm not going to stop you . . . on one condition."

Logan didn't think his thoughts were that visible until Banning groaned and muttered, "You want me to tell Tina and the girls what I'm doing."

"I have a feeling that they'll be more understanding than you give them credit for, especially Sean."

"You've just met me, Logan. I'm the man everyone depends on to know what time the plane leaves or how much money to leave for tip in a restaurant or the safest stock to buy. If I told my wife and daughters that I was jumping out of planes and paragliding over the beach, they would . . . they would lock me up."

"Or they would join you," Logan suggested.

Banning's mouth dropped opened in disbelief, and even Logan could not keep a straight face at the thought of the Three Ts jumping from a plane. In unison, both men laughed.

"I can't see the Three Ts . . . I mean—"

"I know what Sean calls them," Banning said dismissively.

Logan cleared his throat, then continued, "I can't see Tina, Tracie, or Terri jumping out of that plane with you, but Sean . . . Sean would do almost anything for you."

"For anyone whom she loves," Banning said in a quiet voice that made Logan's palms sweat.

Logan wiped his hands on his khaki pants, then glanced at Arnold and Chaz. He couldn't believe that he was going to say it, but he heard himself ask Banning, "Only a couple of hours of training?"

Banning grinned as he excitedly asked, "Do you want to fly today, Logan?"

"Hell, no, but let's do it."

Banning whooped, sounding strangely like Maggie and her navy friends, then galloped across the cliff toward the death traps also known as gliders. Logan took a deep breath, then followed him.

Sean walked down the stairs, sighing in relief at the heavy silence that told her no one was in the huge Weston household. Tracie and Terri finally had given up on trying to get Sean to go to shopping with them at the crack of dawn, but only because Sean had promised to meet them for lunch. After luxuriating in bed until ten o'clock, she had showered and taken too much time applying makeup and doing her hair, and now she had only thirty minutes before she had to meet two of the Three Ts in downtown Santa Barbara for lunch.

Sean walked into the kitchen and headed directly for the refrigerator. It had been difficult to eat at the party, with the dress cutting into her stomach and Logan staring at her with heated eyes that made her want to leap across the patio onto him. And since she had missed breakfast that morning, she was ravenous. Sean was more glad that Logan was not in the house than that her family wasn't. She could deal with her family. She had twenty-seven years of practice. However, she could not deal with Logan. He was playing some type of game that Sean knew if she even asked for the rules she would be lost.

She had wanted to hate Logan when he first moved next door to her. He was too gorgeous and entirely too charming. He was everything that a tough-talking, gun-toting woman like her was suspicious of. But Logan made her laugh. He understood her weird obsession with guns. He hadn't even commented when she installed a punching bag in the middle of her living room. How much more perfect could one man be? But he didn't want her.

Logan didn't want any woman for long. He was the typical commitment-shy male, and proud of the fact. Besides, even if he were looking to marry someone, Sean knew—compared to the typical women he dated—that she would not be the woman he turned to. She had spent the entire night telling herself that Logan's flirting, heated glances, and accidental touches were just to relieve himself of his boredom.

Sean had just grabbed a can of soda from the refrigerator when Tina walked into the room. Sean quickly stuck the can inside the refrigerator, then pasted a huge smile on her face. The Three Ts would never drink anything as fattening as a soda. The Three Ts probably weren't even human enough to want to drink diet soda. No wonder she felt stifled in this house.

"Good afternoon, Sean," Tina sang. In her hands she held a flower basket that overflowed with blooming fragrant red roses. "I thought you went shopping with Tracie and Terri."

"I'm meeting them for lunch."

"You still hate waking up early," Tina guessed as she set the basket on the kitchen counter.

"I should get ready to go meet them. See ya."

"Sean, wait. I want to talk to you."

Sean silently groaned, then smiled through clenched teeth at Tina. She should have known that Tina would not let her escape that easily. Tina settled onto a wooden stool at the counter, as if preparing for a long heart-to-heart talk.

"It's been so long since your father or I have seen you. How are you doing?" Tina asked.

"Great."

"How's work?"

"Good."

"I like your new look."

"It's a temporary change," Sean firmly said.

"Why is it temporary?"

"I can't go to work in heels like this and a dress that barely covers my . . . It wouldn't be appropriate."

"Of course not for work, but for the weekends and dinner dates," Tina tried with a cheerful laugh.

Sean snorted in response, but didn't tell Tina that the last "dinner date" she had gone on had been a blind date that ended abruptly when she pinned her date's arm behind his back and slammed him onto the floor of the restaurant after he "accidentally" squeezed her breasts. The coward hadn't even apologized before he bolted, leaving her with the bill.

"I like Logan," Tina said with a warm smile.

"I think it's impossible for a woman not to like Logan."

"That dance last night . . . You two seem like more than friends."

She stared at every item in the kitchen besides Tina, then finally said, "We're just friends, Tina."

"You like him, don't you?" Tina said speculatively as she peered at Sean. "You've always been good at hiding your feelings, but I can tell. You may even love him."

"Tracie's wedding sounds like it's going to be the event of the season," Sean said cheerfully, desperately attempting to switch the subject.

"Sean, how are you?" Tina whispered, her voice full of emotion. Sean darted a nervous glance at the door. She could admit it now; Tina scared her. Tina was so emotional and caring and kind. Sean always felt as if she were the big, bad wolf around fragile Tina, who never screamed or yelled or became impatient.

"I honestly am fine, Tina."

"How about money? Your father said that you still haven't touched the account that we set up for you."

Sean sighed, accepting the fact that she would not be able to escape this conversation. She sat in one of the chairs at the round kitchen table.

"I appreciate the thought, but I don't need the money."

"We want you to have it. Maybe you could move out of that little apartment and find a nicer place—"

"I'm doing fine, Tina. Honest. I love my job; I love San Francisco. I have a good life."

"But no one to share it with," Tina pointed out.

"Not having a man is not the end of the world," Sean snapped. She noticed the brief flash of hurt cross Tina's face and Sean sighed in frustration. "I'm sorry."

"I just want you to be happy," Tina said.

"I am." Sean stared at her hands for a moment, then politely asked, "How are you?"

"Your father is doing wonderful things at the company. He just hired another thirty employees and the profits are soaring this quarter. Although I am worried because the doctor said that his blood pressure is a little high—"

"I asked how you are, Tina, not how Dad is."

Tina appeared flustered and she instantly shot from the stool. She pulled a glass vase from one of the cabinets and partially filled it with water from the faucet. She busily began to arrange the flowers inside the vase.

Sean wondered if Tina had forgotten about her question until Tina blurted out, "I'm bored, Sean."

"Excuse me?"

Tina walked across the kitchen and dropped into the chair next to Sean. Sean noticed the desperate look in Tina's eyes as she grabbed Sean's hands.

"Do you know what you do every Wednesday at three o'clock?" Tina demanded.

"Wednesday at three o'clock? I have no idea," Sean said confused.

"I do," Tina practically shouted. "For the past ten years, every Wednesday at three o'clock I go to Rachel's Nail Salon. I get a manicure and a pedicure and my nails are painted Malta Maroon. And every other Tuesday at noon for the last five years, I play a game of tennis with Kate Pherson. And every Sunday for the last three years, your father and I go to the country club for dinner, where I order a Caesar salad. I am so sick of Caesar salad!"

Maybe the tight dress and tight shoes had cut off all circulation to her brain, but Sean found herself clutching Tina's hands in sympathy. "I hate Caesar salad too," Sean confided. "I hate most green foods."

Tina stared confused at Sean for a full second before she began to laugh—a loud, obnoxious laugh that sounded as though it should have come from Sean. Sean found herself laughing, too, even though she wasn't certain whether they laughed at Sean or Tina.

"I've missed you, Sean," Tina said softly, the amusement still dancing in her eyes.

"I've missed . . . I've missed being here, too," Sean admitted, surprised by how much she meant it. She noticed tears shining in Tina's eyes, and Sean quickly steered the conversation to a safer subject. "You have to find something that makes you happy. For me it's guns."

"Guns?"

"I love the smell of gunpowder and the weight of the gun in my hands. I could spend hours looking at the Beretta catalog . . ." Sean's voice trailed off as she pictured her tiny stepmother with a gun in her hands. She quickly added, "You should find an activity that's suited to you."

"Like what?"

"What do you like to do?"

"Cook—"

"That's something that you do for other people. This has to be something just for you." Sean suddenly snapped her fingers together as she said, "When I was younger, I remember that you loved to watch ballet. Maybe you could take a few classes."

"Ballet?" Tina laughed and placed her hands on her cheeks. "I'm fifty-four years old; I can't take a ballet class or . . . I'd look like a fool."

"Do you still care how you look to other people?" When Tina appeared speechless, Sean shrugged, then asked, "Have you told Dad how you feel?"

"Of course not. You know your father. He likes routine, I wouldn't want to upset him."

"He likes you a lot more than he likes routine. You should talk to him. Dad may surprise you."

Tina didn't answer but threw her arms around Sean, who tried not to show her surprise. She couldn't bring herself to return the embrace but she did pat Tina on the back.

The emotions were getting too high, so Sean reached inside her bra for the paper that she had folded and placed beside her breast. Tina's expression turned incredulous; then she started when Sean pulled out a folded piece of paper.

"Could you look at a picture for me?" Sean showed her

the computer image of Carl Madison. "Do you know this man?"

"No," Tina said, then hesitantly asked, "Don't you have a purse, Sean?"

"Have you ever seen this man around the house or any of the other wedding activities?"

"No. Who is he?"

"No one." Sean forced a casual smile, then refolded the paper and stuck it back into her bra.

"Would you like to borrow one of my purses?" Tina asked.

Sean was on the verge of answering when she heard the front door close. She could hear her father and Logan's loud male voices as they walked toward the kitchen. When the two entered the room, Sean could instantly tell that they had been doing something they shouldn't have. Her father practically glowed with happiness, while Logan looked . . . he looked gorgeous, as he always did.

Banning dropped a kiss on Sean's forehead, then pressed a hard kiss on Tina's lips, who shot a surprised glance at Sean. Sean stared at Logan, who grinned at her with a smile so pure and contagious that she could only smile in return. Only Logan could make her smile for no apparent reason.

"Logan, do you want a beer?" Banning asked as he stared into the refrigerator and grabbed a bottle.

Logan broke from his smiling contest with Sean and answered, "No, thanks."

"Banning, those beers belong to Chancy," Tina admonished.

"He won't mind," Banning said dismissively.

"Where have you two been?" Sean asked, glancing from her father to Logan.

"Golf. It was a great day for golf," Logan said with a wicked smile that Sean knew meant he was lying and had had a lot of fun with whatever made him lie.

"How did you do, Banning?" Tina asked.

Banning momentarily averted his gaze from his wife, then murmured, "The same as always."

He noisily began to search the drawers for a bottle opener. Sean stood and smoothed down the white tank dress that she wore.

"Are you going somewhere?" Logan asked her.

Sean momentarily lost her breath as she met his gaze. He partially leaned against the kitchen wall, and he watched her with such promise and possession that she felt a strange kinship with animals hunted in a jungle. He looked . . . sexy and dangerous. Like a pirate. Except law-abiding Boy Scout Logan Riley could never be a pirate. Instead Sean pictured him as a really dangerous Canadian Mountie. Whatever dangerous man he looked like, it made the heat rush through her body and focus in the center of her body, which radiated for him.

"I'm meeting Tracie and Terri for lunch," she said in a voice that sounded slightly shaky. "I should leave now."

"Can I talk to you for a moment?" Logan asked, not moving except for his eyes, which touched every curve and valley of her body. Sean wordlessly nodded her consent, even though her brain screamed in warning.

"Sean, take the Lexus," Banning called after her.

Sean gave her father a wave of acknowledgment, then followed Logan. He walked down the hallway that led toward the back of the house. She thought that he would walk to the den, but instead he whirled around in the middle of the darkened hallway. She flinched at his sudden movement and somehow found herself backed against the wall.

Logan grinned the sexy, dangerous smile that always made her want to dip her tongue into his dimple. He moved toward her until her breasts skimmed the front of his shirt. Even through their clothes, Sean felt the contact to her toes.

Her entire body reacted. Her breasts grew heavy, her ears burned, and her legs trembled. She realized that she hadn't been tripping over her heels for the past twenty-four hours; she had been tripping over Logan.

"Where are you going to hide your gun in this dress?" he asked in a husky whisper as both of his hands skimmed over her hips and came to rest around her waist.

"Gun," she blankly repeated, desperately trying to remember what the word meant. Logan's amused smile made her realize that she sounded like a fool. She forced herself to think and said the first thing that popped into her head: "I showed Tina the picture of Madison. She's never seen him."

"I showed your father, too. He's never seen him either." Even though Logan talked about a simple subject, his voice promised long nights and sweaty bodies. His eyes dropped to her breasts, emphasized and displayed in the dress. Even though she wore clothes, under his hot gaze she felt naked and vulnerable.

"What exactly did you and Dad do this morning? You two don't act like men who played golf."

His large, warm, callused hands skimmed over her bare arms to rest on her shoulders, sending sparks of lightning through Sean's body. She tried not to squirm.

"How do we act, Sean?" he asked, his eyes resting on her mouth.

"Like two men who traveled to hell and back and had a really good time doing it."

"I'm glad I came back," Logan whispered, then smiled again. Sean would berate herself later, but at that moment, with Logan close and her body aching for him, she decided for the first time in her life to lose.

She didn't know if he pulled her to him or if she pulled him to her, but her hands suddenly held bunches of his shirt material and his hands clutched her shoulders. Their lips slammed into each other in a blinding force of desire and lust. Sean couldn't see anything else or hear anything else except Logan. Every sense in her body was focused on his lips, on his soft, slick lips that tasted like salty ocean air and undeniable Logan.

He dug into her shoulders, and Sean took the moment to taste his bottom lip more fully. She ran her tongue across it, tasting him, and she almost fell again at the moan he made in the base of his throat. He groaned louder, and his hands moved from her shoulders and trailed down the side of her body to rest on her waist. Sean wanted him to touch her breasts, which were smashed against his hard, unyielding chest. She wanted him to touch her any- and everywhere that he wanted, but Boy Scout Logan kept his hands on her waist.

They stood thigh-to-thigh, their bodies pressed almost as close as two bodies could be. Sean squirmed against him, trying to move his hands on her by force of mental will. He still didn't get the hint. She tried to speak to tell him what to do with his hands on her body, but Logan took her open mouth as an invitation to slip in his tongue. If Sean had been a fainting woman, she would have collapsed at the burst of emotions that exploded through her at the touch of his impossibly cool tongue inside of her mouth.

His tongue felt foreign until he began to bathe hers in his sweetness, and then she felt as if it would be impossible for her to live without his tongue inside her. Her hands clung to his shoulders for a port in the storm as powerful lust began to wash over her body, flinging her into the sky. His tongue bathed her lips, then swirled around her mouth, exploring every crevice as if she were his to explore.

She could have kissed him forever. His kisses, his total sweet devastation and possession of her mouth, were almost enough to make her shout his name. She tried to pull him even closer, but as she pulled on his shoulders, Logan began to move from her arms. She finally recognized his attempt to move out of her bruising embrace, and Sean abruptly dropped her hands from his shoulders.

She didn't want to look at him. She didn't want him to

see the desire that she knew was apparent in her eyes. She wished she weren't breathing as if she had just run a fifty-yard dash. She wished that she could be calm and sophisticated and laugh off the kiss, and not lick her dry, swollen lips in hesitation and shock. She had just kissed her next-door neighbor, and she would have given her favorite pair of handcuffs to continue for the next one hundred years.

Sean stared at Logan's running shoes and prayed that he would just walk away and give her time to compose herself. Of course, Logan didn't move. Several seconds of silence passed between them, until Sean finally forced herself to look at him. She was surprised to realize that Logan looked as stunned as she felt.

She had to fill the silence. She brushed hair from her eyes with what she hoped was a sophisticated, casual move; then she stammered, "Well, that was . . . That was . . . What was that? It was—"

Logan leaned toward her and placed a sweet kiss on her lips, instantly shutting her up. What was a brief, almost chaste kiss became spine-tingling as his lips caressed her bottom lip for a long, torturous second. He reluctantly pulled away from her, and Sean hadn't realized that she had closed her eyes until she noticed that his lips were no longer on hers. She opened first one eye, then the other to find him watching her with a bemused smile.

"You're going to be late for lunch with your sisters," he rumbled.

Sean tried to speak, to joke, to tease, to do anything that would lighten the moment. When she only stood there like a mute, Logan turned and walked down the hallway back toward the kitchen. She took one step toward the stairs and instantly teetered on the too-high heel and caught herself on a nearby table before she tumbled straight to the floor.

Ten

Sean winced as she got out of the car. Her knees still stung in sharp pain from her fall. She had never been the most agile woman on the block, but after a Logan Riley kiss, she couldn't even hold her balance anymore. The thought sickened her. She was a strong, independent woman who forgot all of those qualities as soon as she got close to one man.

Sean slammed the car door, then spotted Tracie and her fiancé, Sheldon, clinging to each other in front of the restaurant where the sisters were to have lunch. Sean didn't want to be smug, but the chaste kisses Tracie and Sheldon shared were nothing like the heart-stopping clash of mouths she had just experienced with Logan. Maybe she did mean to be smug, but Sean could not imagine Sheldon Cameron, with his matching suspenders and belt underneath a black suit, ever kissing Tracie the way that Logan had kissed Sean. Although, judging from Tracie's adoring gaze, Sheldon didn't have to do anything but breathe for Tracie to be turned on.

"Hi, kids," Sean greeted them.

Tracie and Sheldon turned to her with identical goofy smiles. Sheldon was the same height as Sean, and while that made him tall enough for Tracie, Sean couldn't help but compare him to Logan's towering height. Logan would dwarf him at the bachelor party. Sheldon had the soft, groomed features of a well-educated man who had never done manual labor a day in his life. He was attractive, in a preppy way, but Sean could never find a man attractive who didn't have a dimple or gold eyes that penetrated her soul.

"Sean, we need to talk so I can figure out if what Tracie has told me about you is true," Sheldon greeted her.

"No matter what anyone says, I did not tell her to cut her hair herself when she was eight," Sean stubbornly insisted.

Tracie giggled while Sheldon glanced from Tracie to Sean with a confused expression on his face.

"Where's Terri?" Sean asked, switching the subject.

"She went to the bathroom inside the restaurant." Tracie stared at Sheldon, who placed a soft kiss on her lips. "I was just saying good-bye to Sheldon and making him promise to have fun tonight."

"It won't be fun without you, sweetie," Sheldon promised in a sickeningly sweet voice.

"Thanks for inviting Logan to your bachelor party, Sheldon," Sean said.

"I hope that he won't be disappointed. My friends and I . . . we're not exactly the cop type," Sheldon said, then darted a nervous glance at Tracie.

Sean wanted to respond that Logan wasn't the trust-fund-baby type, as Sheldon and his friends probably were, but instead she pulled the folded picture of Madison from the small purse that she had picked up after Tina made her feel self-conscious about her old carrying place.

"Before I leave you two to finish saying good-bye, do either of you know this man?"

Sean was not prepared for the identical looks of shock and foreboding on their faces. Tracie frowned, then glanced at Sheldon, who had gone as pale as his mocha-colored skin would allow. Sheldon nervously cleared his throat and said, "We've never seen him before. Why do you ask?"

Sean studied the couple for a moment. Over the last four

years as a federal agent, she had grown apt at telling when a person lied. Sheldon lied. Tracie had always been a horrible liar, and she could barely look Sean in the eyes.

"His name is Carl Madison. He is a wanted fugitive, and he has very dangerous people looking for him. If you know him, Sheldon, you have to tell me," Sean urged with as much gentleness as she was capable.

"I don't know him," Sheldon weakly insisted.

"Then why do you look like you just saw a ghost?"

"I have no idea what you're talking about."

"Sheldon—"

"He said that he doesn't know him, Sean. Leave him alone," Tracie said, coming to her fiancé's defense. Sean was surprised by Tracie's sharp tone: Tracie never screamed at her. The Three Ts had been full of surprises since her home-coming yesterday, and Sean didn't know if she liked all of them.

"This is not a game," Sean tried again, staring at Tracie, then Sheldon. "If he's here in Santa Barbara, I need to know."

"We don't know him, Sean," Tracie repeated in a louder voice that made several people on the sidewalk stare at the trio.

Sean slowly folded the paper, then stuffed it into her purse. She ignored Tracie as she said to Sheldon, "If you change your mind about talking to me, you know where to find me."

She walked into the coolness of the restaurant and sighed in relief to escape the tense moment. Sheldon and Tracie were hiding something. Sean spotted the public telephones in a hallway to the right that also led to the rest rooms. She quickly ran to the phones before Tracie followed her into the restaurant. She punched in the familiar number to Special Agent Eddie Morton, the closest thing to what she could call a friend at her office. Although Sean wondered if she frightened Eddie sometimes. Whenever she walked near him, he would flinch as if prepared for a blow, or he would drop something. She wondered if her disastrous blind date, who had been Eddie's friend, had spread vicious rumors about her.

"Special Agent Morton," Eddie answered.

"Eddie, it's Sean." She heard him mutter a curse before he yelped. "Eddie, are you all right?"

"I just spilled soup on myself. . . . I'm fine, Sean." His voice sounded several octaves higher than when he had first answered the phone. "I thought that you were on vacation."

"I am, but I need you to do a background check for me."

"Why don't you call—"

"I need it to be quiet. I don't want anyone to know that I've asked."

"I don't know, Sean," Eddie said reluctantly. "I think the Jell-O incident is still too fresh in the minds of a lot of people. You're still radioactive goods around here. Being seen with you is hazardous to my career health."

"Will you people ever let me live that one down? So what, I spilled a bowl of green Jell-O on the face of the director of the FBI. He took a shower, washed his hair, got a new suit. . . . It turned out fine," Sean impatiently snapped.

"Is that why since the incident happened you've been assigned to deliver arrest warrants in some of the most dangerous parts of the city?"

"The man obviously does not have a sense of humor," Sean muttered, then pleaded, "Eddie, I'm asking for your help. It may turn out to be huge in a few days and I'll make certain that you get some of the credit, but right now I want it to be quiet. Please."

"Just this once, Sean," he reluctantly agreed.

"I need you to check out Sheldon Cameron. I don't have any pertinent information for you except that he attended Yale University three years ago and he now lives in Santa Barbara and works at Harrison and Harrison."

"No Social Security number or driver's license number?"

"No."

"And you're not going to tell me what this is about?"

"No."

"How can I reach you?" Eddie muttered, sounding like a prisoner being led to the gallows. Sean quickly gave him her father's number, then glanced over her shoulder toward the entrance. Tracie had still not entered the restaurant.

"Thanks, Eddie; I owe you one."

"Do you really mean that, Sean?"

Sean didn't like the eager tone in his voice. "Maybe," she finally answered.

"I just . . . with the potential for lawsuits . . . But then I told myself that we rarely talk, so I couldn't make this a hostile workplace environment—"

"What are you talking about?" Sean snapped impatiently.

"When you get back to the city, maybe we could go for a beer."

"Why?" Sean asked, confused. When he didn't respond, she briefly slammed her eyes closed as the realization hit her: Eddie Morton had a crush on her. For a woman who had never dealt with a crush before, Sean didn't know what to say.

Eddie seemed to understand her silence and he quickly said, "It was a stupid idea. We work together; we should not become involved . . . but other agents have done it."

"I'm kind of in love with someone else." Sean's palms suddenly grew damp as she realized it was the truth. She had never proclaimed her love for Logan, and saying it out loud made it seem more real and feel more painful.

"Kind of?" Eddie asked, sounding more amused than upset.

"He doesn't know, and it's this big unrequited thing that's been going on for two years but . . . I love him, and sometimes I don't think that I'll ever be able to stop."

"Maybe you should tell him. He doesn't know what he's missing."

Sean giggled like a schoolgirl, then quickly cleared her throat to sound more adult and not as though she were laughing at Eddie's expense. "You flatter me, Eddie."

"After my last girlfriend dumped me, I figured that a woman like you would be no-frills and simple."

"I think I'm insulted," Sean muttered.

"It's not an insult, Sean. You're the kind of woman who, in about five years, all of us guys will be wondering how we missed you. We'll be done with the tight dresses and big hair, and we'll just want a woman who'll drink a beer and not complain if we want to invite the guys over for Superbowl Sunday," Eddie said. He sighed at the apparent loss of one day having no-frills, simple Sean, then promised, "I'll call you as soon as I find out anything."

Sean listened to the dial tone for a second, then replaced the receiver. How had that gone from a man declaring his interest in her to insulting her? She shook her head in disbelief, then walked into the nearby women's bathroom. The problem with wearing makeup was that it always had to be refreshed—another lesson learned from Collette, the makeup artist.

Sean froze in the doorframe when she saw Terri in an overstuffed chair in the small lounge area of the bathroom. She lay in the chair with her head resting against the back of it and her legs outstretched before her. The pink high heels that matched the pink sundress she wore were neatly lined up on the floor. Her mouth was pinched into a line of pain, and Sean could tell from the tight expression on her face that the pain continued.

Sean told herself to leave. Terri hadn't seen her. She could walk out of the bathroom and find Tracie and tell her to take care of her sister. Sean could even find the table they'd reserved and not become involved at all. But Sean could do none of that. For some reason the Three Ts were breaking down, and Sean was the only one who could pick up the pieces—whether she wanted to or not.

Sean closed the door with a louder-than-necessary thud. Terri's eyes flew open and she instantly jumped from the chair as if it had bitten her.

"Sean, hi. This is a lovely bathroom, isn't it?" Terri chattered desperately. Her hands frantically ran through her tousled hair as she stepped into her heels.

"Sit down, Terri."

"Why? You're here and we can eat. I just needed a little rest after a whole morning of shopping with Tracie. Since it usually takes her and Sheldon half an hour to say good-bye to each other, I knew that I had time to recuperate."

"Tell me what's wrong," Sean said, not having to pretend concern when she saw the panic in Terri's eyes.

"Nothing's wrong."

"When we were little you told me everything, whether I wanted to hear it or not. You trusted me. Has that changed?"

Terri appeared on the verge of denying everything; then she abruptly fell back into the chair. She buried her face in her hands, then finally looked at Sean.

"I'm pregnant."

Sean had to sit in the chair next to Terri at the news. She hadn't known what she expected when she saw Terri's obvious unhappiness. Maybe Sean thought it was something simple, like a broken fingernail or finding that her favorite dress was no longer in season. Not pregnancy. Terri?

"I didn't even know that you were seeing someone."

"I'm not," Terri responded with a determined expression on her face.

Sean's mouth hung open at the declaration. She had never considered herself to be conservative, but she also could not imagine her straitlaced sister sleeping with a man outside of a relationship. Terri still slept with a stuffed teddy bear. How could she be pregnant?

"Dad and Tina must have been surprised when you told

them," Sean said carefully, already knowing the answer, judging from Terri's defensive posture.

"I haven't told them. You're the first person I have told, besides the doctor, but I guess the doctor knew before I did, so he doesn't count."

"You haven't even told the father?"

"Especially not the father," Terri snapped angrily, as she jumped to her feet. She began to pace the length of the lounge in long, angry strides.

"He has a right to know, Terri."

"He has no rights," Terri exploded.

"For a man you're not seeing, you feel very strongly about him."

Terri glared at Sean as she once more sat in the chair, the anger continuing to dance in her eyes. "Stop your cop tactics on me."

"What cop tactics?"

"I'm not going to tell you who the father is."

"It's your decision, Terri," Sean relented. Terri nodded in righteous indignation, then averted her gaze from Sean's. "But you're going to have to tell Dad, Tina, and Tracie soon. You can't hide something like that unless . . . unless you don't plan to keep it."

As if by reflex, Terri's hand covered her stomach as she glared at Sean. "I'm keeping my baby."

"How far along are you?"

"Nine weeks."

Sean suddenly grinned as she thought of Terri in a perfect five-hundred-dollar dress holding a baby girl wearing an equally expensive infant version.

"Congratulations, Terri."

Terri appeared in shock as she stared at Sean. "Congratulations? That's all you have to say?"

Sean pretended to think for a few more seconds; then she teased, "And I guess this means that I'm not the designated driver tonight for the bachelorette party."

Terri laughed, but her smile quickly faded as her hand rubbed over her stomach. "What am I going to do, Sean? I love him," Terri whispered as her eyes filled with tears.

Sean was never one to touch, but if touching was ever required it was at this moment. She kneeled in front of Terri and grasped her hands. Terri's hands were too cold, and Sean anxiously began to rub them between hers to generate warmth.

"You don't have to think about this now. Let's get through the next three days and then we'll sit down with Dad and Tina and tell them everything."

"You'll face them with me?" Terri asked hopefully.

"Of course I will." Terri threw her arms around her, and Sean found herself smiling. "Now you need to eat. I need to eat."

"I came in here because I was so nauseous, but now I'm starving," Terri agreed.

She and Sean stood and both automatically went to the mirror behind them. Sean laughed at the humor in the situation as in unison they both reached into their purses for the requisite weapons.

"I thought for certain that Logan would have told you about last night," Terri confessed, as she quickly combed through her hair.

"What happened last night?"

"He caught me crying on the patio. I made him promise not to tell anyone, but the way you two are together, I thought that he wouldn't be able to keep it from you."

"Logan can be very closemouthed when he wants."

"He seems like a nice guy."

"He is." When Sean saw the smile cross Terri's face, she quickly added, "He's just a friend, Terri."

"What kind of friend takes off from work to go to a family wedding?" Terri asked, a sharp glint in her bright eyes.

"He's on vacation."

"There are a million places in California alone that Logan

could have gone if he just wanted a vacation, besides Santa Barbara. I think that he wanted to be with you."

"Terri . . . You're still a romantic."

"No, I'm not," Terri said seriously. "I'm a realist now, and Logan cares for you. I don't think that . . . the father of my baby ever really cared for me. He cared about my money, but not me."

"Don't cry, Terri. You'll ruin your makeup," Sean whispered, turning to her stepsister as her eyes began to fill with tears. Sean quickly wiped at the tears that fell down Terri's face, ignoring her own. She suddenly grew angry as she saw sadness and longing cross Terri's face. "I can hurt him, Terri, the sperm donor for your baby. I can break an arm, shoot off a kneecap . . . whatever you want."

Terri laughed as she said, "You're still the same, Sean."

"Still bloodthirsty?"

"No, still protective of those you care about," Terri corrected, while squeezing Sean's hands.

Sean didn't know how to respond to that one. Either Terri was completely wrong about her—and Terri was rarely wrong—or Sean did care about the Three Ts. Since Sean didn't trust herself to respond, she turned to the mirror to comb her hair.

Logan stepped from the shower feeling refreshed and . . . and alive. Although he had screamed like a woman in a horror movie, Logan had gone hang gliding. And he had loved it. The sensation of being that high above the ground with only a pair of wings snapped to his back by Chaz and Arnold, instead of making him think about death made him think about life. He told himself that was the reason he had kissed Sean as if his life depended on it. He told himself that after a near-death experience, a man needed to reaffirm his life. How did a man do that? With sex, and Sean just happened to be there.

He had walked into the house and seen Sean looking surprisingly happy to see him. When she forgot that she found him a minor annoyance, she gave him the sweetest, most innocent smile. Logan had never noticed that his heart skipped a beat every time she smiled until after his near-death experience. He had seen that special smile and all he could think about was flying over the water.

And kissing her had been better than flying, better than the wind whipping over his face. Logan had not expected that. He didn't know what he expected when he touched her, but an overpowering, earth-shaking kiss had not been on his mind.

Logan heard the shrill ring of his cellular telephone, which he had left on the bed. He quickly wrapped a towel around his waist, then ran from the steam-filled bathroom. He grabbed the phone on the fifth ring.

"I thought I would have to leave another message," came his little sister's annoyed voice from the other end of the telephone. *Little* wasn't exactly the word he should have used to describe a United States Navy officer. Twenty-five-year-old Maggie Riley was not little in any sense of the word.

She stood close to five-ten, and with her confident swagger and rigid posture that suggested years of military training, Logan sometimes wondered who was more frightening, Cary or Maggie. He had decided last year after Maggie broke a man's nose in the mall for grabbing her behind that Maggie was the scariest, because at least Cary knew how to control his anger.

Judging from her harsh tone, Logan was glad that she was across the country in Washington, D.C., so he would not have to be face-to-face with the infamous Maggie Riley temper. He had forgotten to call her and tell her that he would be in Santa Barbara for the weekend. As gruff as she pretended to be, she worried about her brothers like a mother hen; her ranting only covered her worry. Sometimes Logan wondered if he had raised Maggie or if she had raised him.

Maggie continued in a gruff voice, "I left four messages on your machine over the last two days. If Cary hadn't known where you were, I was going to book a flight out there and hunt you down."

"I should have told you that I was going out of town, Maggie. I'm sorry."

"I'll forgive you this time, only because I want to know what the hell is going on." Logan laughed at Maggie's curious, demanding tone. "Cary told me that you went to Santa Barbara with Sean, the woman you told me could drive a monk insane."

"Sean isn't that bad," Logan defended.

"I've never talked with her. The one time I saw her she was dressed in combat gear and going on a raid. I'm just going by what you told me about her. What gives, Logan?"

"She wanted support at her stepsister's wedding."

"From you?" Maggie asked, surprised.

"We're friends."

"Since when?"

"Why am I getting the third degree? A friend needed help and I got a place to stay while on vacation."

"And that's all?" Maggie pressed.

Logan told himself that he wasn't going to tell Maggie anything about the kiss that had scrambled his brain or about the strange feelings that raced through his body whenever Sean smiled at him.

Naturally he heard himself say, "I kissed her."

He heard Maggie's sharp intake of air on the other end of the receiver. Logan didn't blame her. Maggie had helped him through every heartbreak he had experienced since he was ten years old and his thirty-year-old math teacher had told him he was too young for her but to look her up in another ten years.

"I thought that you were going to forget the five-weekers

and concentrate on finding a woman for the long term," Maggie said, bringing his thoughts back to the present.

"Do you think I start out hoping that my relationships will only last five weeks?" Logan asked annoyed.

"I don't know, Logan. Explain why all of your relationships have ended by the fifth week—"

"I didn't end any of those relationships," Logan pointed out.

"That's right. You allowed yourself to be dumped on by women who didn't even deserve you." Maggie's frustration was apparent even over the telephone as she said, "I told you that I was going to find a woman for you. You're too nice. You can't be trusted around women."

"You make me sound like an idiot."

"You said it, not me. But given your track record I think we both can agree that I need to screen any future five-weekers for my own protection."

"Your protection? Why?" Logan asked while laughing in disbelief.

"Because the next woman who rips out your heart, I'll have to rip out hers—literally."

Logan laughed, then wondered if he should have been encouraging Maggie's violent streak. He laughed again when he realized that Maggie reminded him of another woman whom he had been thinking about too much.

"I have a feeling that you and Sean would get along really well."

"What's so great about her?" Maggie demanded. "This isn't just about sex, is it, Logan? It's been so long since you got any that it's probably going to your head."

Logan forced himself not to press the disconnect button, because he knew that Maggie thought she was helping, but he felt slightly nauseated at the idea of anything relating to sex and his little sister. He firmly believed that the two subjects should never mix.

"We haven't slept together, Maggie," Logan said through

clenched teeth, then added, "Not that it's any of your business."

"That's not a surprise, since you haven't slept with anyone in the last five years."

"Do you make it a point to bring that up every conversation or does it just slip out every time?"

Logan rubbed his eyes, feeling as though he needed another shower to wash off the grime that inevitably covered him when he thought of his numerous failed relationships. He also cursed himself for the day he had told his sister that he hadn't slept with a woman for five years. He wanted to make love, not mate like wild rabbits, which practically made him a leper in this day and age. Actually, Logan thought that lepers had some rights. A heterosexual twenty-eight-year-old man who willingly abstained from sex had no rights in the modern dating world.

"Logan, you're a nice, sweet, kind man . . . which is exactly why I don't trust your judgment when it comes to women. Women can be conniving and cruel and backstabbing—"

"You sound like the guys in the locker room at the station," Logan interrupted, while shaking his head in amusement.

Maggie audibly sighed, then reluctantly asked, "Do you really care about her?"

"We're friends . . . of course I care about her."

"Maybe it's time, Logan. You've been alone for five years. At least your relationship with Sean has lasted longer than five weeks."

"I wouldn't call what we have a relationship. We kissed, but that doesn't mean anything. A lot of friends kiss, right?"

Maggie ignored his rambling and muttered, "I guess I'll have to trust you, although I don't like it."

Logan smiled at her reluctant agreement to allow him to live his own life; then he asked, "How are you doing, Mags? Was there a reason that you were trying to reach me?"

"I just wanted to hear your voice."

"You aren't having any more problems with the jerks in your unit, are you?" Logan's anger returned with renewed intensity every time he thought of anyone treating his sister with disrespect.

"I can handle these idiots. I have pretty thick skin; I grew up with you and Cary."

"You've been grilling me about my sex . . . love life this entire call. What about you? Are you still seeing that Rob guy?"

"Rob? Rob . . . Oh, that was over weeks ago. I'm now seeing this marine, Kenny; although he is a marine, so I don't know how long it will last."

"Maggie, be careful," Logan said, not attempting to keep the worry out of his voice.

"Don't worry about me. Unlike you, brother, I don't plan to ever give anyone the power to hurt me." He heard a mix of voices in the background, and Maggie mumbled something to someone before she said to him, "I have to go."

"I'll call you when I get back to San Francisco."

"Promise me that you won't allow this woman to hurt you, Logan."

"I promise," he said with a laugh. Although he had a feeling that he would break that promise unless he managed to keep the entire Weston family and half of the guest list between himself and Sean.

Eleven

After getting dressed, Logan searched the mansion for his new playmate, Banning Weston. Banning had promised to take Logan hang gliding at least once more before Logan and Sean left. Logan couldn't wait. He never thought he would willingly hurtle himself into space, but there was something about the sport. If he had told Maggie, she probably would attribute his hang-gliding obsessions to his lack of sexual activity. She would say that Logan needed something to fill the void—and he realized that she would probably be right.

With Banning nowhere to be found, Logan walked into the kitchen. He and Banning had eaten hamburgers, like real men, after their death-defying flight, but Logan realized that he needed a snack before going to Sheldon's bachelor party that night.

Logan briefly wondered what the women in Tracie's bridal party would do that night. He quickly shut those thoughts from his mind as he thought of Sean. Regardless of his conversation with Maggie, Sean was his friend and nothing more. Logan cringed at Sean's reaction if he told her that she would be his next five-week victim. She would laugh in his face. He valued her friendship too much to ruin it all for her inclusion on the list of five-weekers.

Logan was in the middle of preparing a turkey breast

sandwich when Chancy walked into the room. Chancy's stony features attempted to crack into a smile when he saw Logan.

"I didn't know that anyone was in here," Chancy said.

"The kitchen is big enough for both of us."

Chancy shrugged in response, then moved to the pantry, where he pulled out a bag of chocolate-chip cookies.

"Where did you find those?" Logan asked, surprised. "The most fattening thing I could find in this kitchen was the mustard."

"At Banning's last physical the doctor told him to watch his cholesterol, so Tina threw out anything that Banning would consider good. I keep a private stash that Tina doesn't know about." Chancy peered into the bag before he said, "And I think that Banning found it."

"Poor Banning."

"That's what a wife will do," Chancy muttered. Logan noticed the faraway look in Chancy's dark eyes before he suddenly glanced at Logan and offered the open bag. Logan smiled in excitement as he reached into the bag and ignored Chancy's laughter at him.

Chancy sat at the counter and watched Logan finish his preparations for his sandwich. "Sean was not anything like I expected her to be."

"What do you mean?" Logan set the finished sandwich in front of Chancy, who nodded in appreciation. Logan began to arrange the condiments for a second sandwich.

"The way this family talks about her . . . I just expected her to be more . . . hard."

"Don't let the clothes fool you, man; Sean is as hard-ass as they come."

"Is she really an FBI agent?"

Logan eyed Chancy, who stared at the uneaten sandwich in front of him. "Why do you ask?"

"If she is an FBI agent, then she has the power to hurt someone who hurts her family?"

Logan set down the knife but kept it close. He pulled the folded paper from his back pocket, then showed the picture of Madison to Chancy.

"Do you know this man, Chancy?" Logan demanded.

Chancy's expression grew blank. "No."

"I know you're security. Why is Banning lying to his family about your position?"

Chancy tiredly sighed, then muttered, "I'm an employee like everyone else, Logan."

"I'm going to ask you one last time; do you know this man?"

Chancy seemed to notice Logan's harsh tone for the first time. His eyes grew wide as he met Logan's gaze. "What is this about?"

"I only have to make one phone call to find out who you really are," Logan warned. The day was too beautiful for Logan to play bad cop, and his lips still tingled from the memory of kissing Sean. Logan didn't have the will to continue arguing with Chancy. He bit into his finished sandwich, sighing in satisfaction at the quality of it. Who said that he couldn't cook? He glanced at Chancy, then said neutrally, "I'm not going to tell anyone, except Sean. What's going on around here?"

"I am a security consultant," Chancy confessed. "Without telling their daughters, Banning and Tina hired me three months ago."

"Pepsi?" Logan asked, turning to the refrigerator.

"I'll have one of my Pepsis." Chancy placed emphasis on the word *my*, but Logan ignored him and grabbed two bottles from the refrigerator.

"What happened three months ago?" Logan asked, continuing Chancy's story.

"Tracie and Sheldon went to Los Angeles for the weekend. On the way home, on the highway around four o'clock in the morning, someone shot at their car. No one was hurt."

"A warning?"

"This family is wealthy and well known throughout the country. It could be a disgruntled ex-employee, a current employee, a nut job who thought he could kidnap Tracie and hold her for ransom. The possibilities are endless. Banning called me."

"Why did he call you?"

Chancy appeared offended by the question. "I may not be Sandra Weston, but the right people know who I am."

"I take it that Tracie and Sheldon did not file a police report."

"It would have generated too much publicity," Chancy confirmed, while shaking his head. "Tracie dismissed the entire incident as her having been in the wrong place at the wrong time. She didn't want anything to mar her wedding, which is why Banning kept my true reason for being in the house from her and Sheldon."

"Have there been any incidents since the shooting?"

"Not even a car trying to cut Tracie off on the freeway. I'm beginning to think that maybe it was kids playing a prank. I have to admit that I am glad that Sean is here. Since she's spending time with Tracie, Banning has given me a little time off. A man can take only so much of watching a woman shop before he goes insane."

"What about the ex-boyfriend or ex-girlfriend angle? Maybe Sheldon and Tracie's marriage is hurting someone who wants to hurt them in return," Logan offered.

"Have you met Sheldon and Tracie?" Chancy asked with an almost incredulous expression. "I don't think they would know how to make anyone angry at them, unless just because they're so perfect, someone would want to hurt them."

"I see your point," Logan murmured. "What about Terri? Have there been any attempts on her life?"

Logan noticed Chancy's momentary hesitation before he gulped soda from the bottle. He slammed the bottle on the counter harder than necessary. "Terri is fine."

Logan decided not to comment on the abrupt change in

Chancy's mood. Instead he tapped the piece of paper that still lay on the counter. "What about him? Have you seen him hanging around the house, around the family?"

Chancy scrutinized the picture for a moment, then reluctantly shook his head. "I haven't seen him. Who is he?"

Logan folded the paper and stuck it in his pocket as he explained. "His name is Carl Madison. He sells illegal weapons to the highest bidder, which usually means gangs, the Mafia, anyone and anything that can destroy our streets. A rival gang is hunting him. They want him dead far more than we want to arrest him."

"Why do you think someone like that would be around this family? If I didn't live here every day, even I wouldn't believe how perfect these people are."

"Sean thought that she saw him last night at the party."

Worry was visible on Chancy's face as he murmured, "I'll keep a lookout for him."

Logan's entire body hummed when he suddenly heard Sean's voice. She and her sisters walked into the house, their heels clicking on the hardwood floor, and their laughter brightening the room. Logan barely restrained the urge to immediately run to the front door. He noticed that although Chancy remained seated, his clenched hands betrayed tension in his body.

Then Sean entered the room and Logan felt . . . He felt sick. He wanted to vomit. He didn't want to stand next to her or be in the same room with her. After five years of abstinence, Logan didn't think that he could stand one more second without feeling Sean beneath him. If he didn't leave the kitchen that second, he would drag her onto the table, ignoring her stepsisters and Chancy, and take whatever she would give him.

Sean walked into the kitchen, and she instantly noticed the strange look on Logan's face. For a split second as he stared at her, she wondered if she should be frightened of him. She couldn't read his expression, but he didn't have the usual angelic Boy Scout glow around his face. At that moment he looked dangerous. Sean shrugged away her strange thoughts, then moved toward the refrigerator. She was starving. Lunch at the restaurant her stepsisters had picked had consisted of three pieces of lettuce and a piece of chicken that was half the size of her palm.

"How was lunch?" Chancy asked, his eyes on Terri. Sean noticed that Terri promptly turned on her heel and walked out the room.

"Very little," Sean muttered in response as she yanked open the refrigerator door. She noticed the remnants of sandwiches in front of Logan and Chancy. She moved next to Logan and grabbed the half-eaten sandwich from in front of Chancy. She took a large bite out of the sandwich and briefly closed her eyes at the richness of mayonnaise. Fat-filled, glorious mayonnaise. "There was a card-carrying member of the Bread Police at the restaurant, who made it his goal in life to make certain that no one in the restaurant got more than one roll. At thirty-five bucks a plate, I think I deserved more than one roll."

"You just like to give people a hard time, Sean," Tracie said with a laugh.

Sean noticed that Logan stood absolutely still as he stared at Tracie. She took another bite of sandwich, then cursed when she noticed a glob of mustard land on her dress. Logan glanced at her, then quickly looked back at Tracie. Sean nudged his side with one arm.

"You're quiet, Logan. What kind of trouble did you get into while I was gone?"

"Nothing much." Logan glanced at his watch, but the move was so quick that Sean knew he hadn't seen the time. The food suddenly seemed like lead in her stomach as she noticed that he purposely avoided her eyes. The kiss. His behavior was because of the kiss. "I have to call . . . call Cary. He's waiting for my call."

Logan didn't look at anyone but practically ran from the kitchen. Sean turned to Chancy and demanded, "What's wrong with Logan?"

Chancy shrugged, while Tracie dramatically insisted, "I thought that I was supposed to be the nervous one. How can I be nervous when all of you are?"

"What makes you think that Logan is nervous? Logan doesn't get nervous. He's too arrogant," Sean said, then finished the sandwich with a disappointed sigh. She focused on Tracie, who dramatically dropped onto a stool.

"He was nervous about something," Chancy agreed. A sudden smug smile crossed his face as he looked at Sean. "Come to think of it . . . Logan didn't start acting strange until you walked in. I think there's a connection. Did you two have a fight?"

"Logan was the same as he's always been," Sean lied unconvincingly, which made Chancy laugh in response.

"And then there's Dad." Tracie moaned, continuing her railing against all the people in her life who ruined her chance to garner sympathy. "He's been running around the last few months acting all secretive and weird. He bought that thirty-five-year-old Mustang out of the blue, and I'm beginning to wonder if he even likes Sheldon."

"Dad has been acting secretive and weird?" Sean asked surprised.

"Who wouldn't like Sheldon?" Chancy muttered between clenched teeth. "He's perfect for a Harrison woman. Wealthy, intelligent, Ivy-league education. Not like an ex-marine who doesn't even own a decent suit."

"And don't get me started on Mom," Tracie continued, becoming angrier. "She's been moping around talking about being young and old. I'm going to stick her in a retirement home right now if she doesn't stop it."

"Your mother is not moping—"

"And Terri is the worst," Tracie exploded, cutting off Sean's attempt to defend Tina. "When she's not working or spending all of her time with the caterer or the florist, she's running to the bathroom."

"Bathroom?" Chancy questioned. Sean saw the moment when Chancy stopped enjoying Tracie's diatribe and became . . . panicked. "Why is Terri running to the bathroom?"

"No one cares about me," Tracie wailed. "I'm taking one of the biggest steps in a woman's life, and no one in my family seems to care."

"They care, Tracie. We all care," Sean muttered automatically, as she wondered whether she had done something to make Logan angry.

"Then someone had better show it soon or . . . or I'll elope." Tracie turned on her heel and ran out of the kitchen.

Sean tried not to laugh, but when she saw Chancy's own attempts to hide his smile, she did laugh.

"At least they're human," Chancy murmured, then shook his head.

Twelve

Sean slammed the door to her bedroom and tried not to obsess over Logan's reaction to her in the kitchen. If he wanted to act as though the kiss meant nothing, then she could, too. She would force herself to forget how her heart pounded, how her body throbbed, and how her mouth tingled—all from being that close to him. She groaned because she knew that she would not be able to forget that.

If she couldn't make herself forget, she could at least force herself to think about something else. Like pain. Sean yanked off her dress and pulled on a pair of leggings and a matching exercise top. She vowed to work out in the gym in the basement of the house until she completely forgot about Logan Riley and his stupid dimple.

Sean stormed through the house toward the gym, anticipating the torture she would inflict on herself. The gym was large and filled with enough state-of-the-art equipment to rival any commercial health club, and she planned to use every instrument. She stopped in the entrance of the room and cursed when she saw Logan and his dimple lying on a workout bench, lifting a bar of weights. Her self-lecture flew out the room when she saw the smooth muscles gliding underneath the sleeveless shirt he wore and the cinnamon brown legs that stretched from his snug gray sweat shorts.

Watching his body strain under the weights was like watching a world-class symphony come to life.

She should have run out the room. She should have avoided all contact with the insufferable jerk who acted as if kissing her senseless meant nothing to him. But, as with everything else in her life, Sean preferred direct confrontation.

She walked across the room and stood at the end of the bench and loudly cleared her throat. With a loud clang that echoed through the cavernous room, Logan set the bar on the stand; then he sat up on the bench and glared at her.

"What are you doing here?" he demanded, sounding more irritated than she felt.

"Don't worry, Logan; I'm not going to attack you like you attacked me in the hallway this afternoon."

Logan's eyes widened as he sputtered in disbelief, "I attacked you? That's interesting, because I thought we were kissing. I didn't know that I was attacking you. Is that how they teach you in the Bureau to fight off attackers?"

"Be careful, Riley, before I show you exactly how I fight off an attacker."

A strange smile suddenly crossed his face. He slowly stood and closed the distance between them. He stopped until he stood close enough to her for another kiss, and Sean was forced to look up at him. She knew that he did it to intimidate her, but he didn't fool her. Logan would never hurt her. No woman's heart would be safe with him, but he would protect her and care for her as long as she didn't place too many demands on him.

"Have you ever punched anything that could punch back?" Logan asked, a challenging gleam in his eyes.

Sean smiled in response, then pretended to take a step toward the punching bag in one corner of the room. Instead of taking another step in that direction, she whirled around, kicking her foot toward his face. Logan ducked in time, and her foot sailed through empty air. He laughed, then moved to the large blue floor mat in the middle of the room. She cautiously followed him, while trying not to return his smile.

"We should both be resting up for the parties tonight," Sean said, even as she assumed a fighter's stance.

"If you're too chicken to fight me . . ." His voice suggestively trailed off.

Sean screamed in attack and swung her fist at Logan. He ducked; then he counterattacked with a swing at her. Sean jumped back from his fist, then barely evaded the quick kick he sent in her direction. She had known that he was good from the few times she had watched him beat the crap out of the punching bag during the times they worked out together, but she truly hadn't truly known what a good fighter he was until she saw the speed and precision of his fists and feet. Sean could tell that he moved more slowly than he was capable of to avoid hitting her, and it made her angry.

To regroup, Sean did a series of backflips across the mat, out of the range of his lightning-fast hands and feet.

Logan laughed; then he taunted, "Stand and fight, Dominique Dawes."

"You're just jealous."

"Jealous of a few flips?" Logan snorted in indignation.

"You're jealous that I have more grace and skill in my pinkie finger than you have in your whole body," Sean replied; then, in a very unfighterlike move, she stuck out her tongue at him.

Logan laughed, then turned his back to her. Sean suspiciously watched him; then her mouth dropped open in utter shock as he began to flip in a whir of hands and feet across the mat. He stopped directly in front of her; then he winked at her. In a quick move he suddenly leaped toward her.

Sean avoided his tackle by moving to her left, which placed him behind her, so she never saw the foot that he landed squarely in her back. Sean grunted more from surprise than from pain as she fell to the ground from the force of his kick. A person's back was broad, and strong enough to withstand most hits. And Sean knew that was the precise reason why Logan had hit her in the back. She jumped to her feet and glared at him.

"Are you going easy on me?" Sean demanded.

"I wouldn't dare insult you like that," Logan said innocently, then raced across the mat toward her.

She stood her ground and they began to exchange punches and kicks, quicker than anything that Sean had ever experienced in all of her years of sparring and Academy training. With all the flying fists and feet, Logan never hit her. He allowed her to block his every move, never bothering to take advantage of his obvious speed. The feminist in her was angry with him for treating her like . . . like a woman, but the small part of herself that she refused to accept as romantic realized that was one of the reasons why she had always loved him. Because even though no one else saw her as a woman, Logan Riley did.

In a move that had Sean blinking in surprise, Logan wrapped his arms around her waist and tackled her to the ground. Sean hit the mat with a grunt and Logan quickly moved on top of her. He grabbed her fists, which had been pounding his arms, and pulled them over her head, pinning her hands to the mat. Sean pretended to grow tired from her struggles, and she saw the triumphant smile cross Logan's face as he stared down at her.

Sean smiled back at him; then, in one quick move that had Logan blinking in surprise, she swung her legs to hook around his shoulders and slammed him into the mat with a momentum that caused her to swing to a sitting position. She scrambled to straddle his body as Logan laughed, surprise evident in his tone. She mocked his movements and held his hands above his head. Unlike she could have done in the reverse position, they both knew Logan could have broken her grip at any moment. He didn't. He suddenly became so still that Sean could feel his heart pounding against his chest.

She was on the verge of teasing him about surrendering to her when his smile disappeared and his eyes grew dark with desire. Sean almost jumped off him when she felt the hard length of him grow against the inside of her thigh. The smart thing for her to do would be to move off him. A small part of Sean wanted to. The conquering warrior in her refused to move.

Sean thanked the warrior; then, without warning to herself or Logan, she leaned down to cover his mouth with hers. At the touch of her lips to his, her hands released his and immediately traveled to caress his face. As their tongues battled as fiercely as their bodies had, Logan's hands moved to her waist, then slid down to cup her bottom, pressing her closer to his hardness. Silk flowed throughout her body, making her grind against him.

Sean sighed inside his mouth, and Logan dug his fingers into her full bottom, feeling the warmth through the thin material that clung to her like a second skin. Logan had thought that he would be able to resist her, but now he knew the truth; he wouldn't be able to keep his promise to his sister. He wouldn't be able to keep his promise to himself to make love only to a woman who passed the five-week mark. Logan had to have Sean. She was like a drug in his blood. Every time he touched her, tasted her, smelled her, he needed more. No other woman had ever driven him this crazy, and Logan wondered if he would ever be satisfied.

Her tongue swept through his mouth, leaving sparks of passion. She nipped his lips, then ran her tongue over the slight tingling pain. Her hands moved into his hair as her mouth seemed to devour him, one long, searching kiss after another. Logan tried to breathe. He tried to remember to breathe, but he could only inhale Sean.

"Excuse me." Logan heard Banning's insistent voice, and judging from his tone, it was not the first time that he had spoken. Sean sprang off Logan and was across the room before Logan could blink. Logan rose to his feet, feeling slightly unsteady. He yanked down his shirt, hoping that Banning would not look below Logan's waist. No such luck. Banning met Logan's eyes again, then arched one eyebrow.

Logan glanced at Sean, who frantically smoothed down her pants even though they were wrinkle-free. Since Sean was obviously not going to be any help, Logan forced a smile in Banning's direction.

"Good afternoon, Banning," Logan said, attempting to sound as though his hard-on were not the result of Banning's daughter.

"What exactly was going on in here?" Banning asked in a tight voice.

"We . . . we were exercising," Logan answered lamely.

"What type of exercising?" Banning responded.

"Dad, is there something that you wanted?" Sean finally broke out of her self-induced trance.

"Maybe I want to exercise. This is an exercise room."

"You're wearing slacks and a tie," Logan said in disbelief. He nervously cleared his throat when both Sean and Banning shot him a silencing look.

"I was looking for you," Banning finally said to Sean. "We need to talk."

"About what?" Sean asked.

"About Chancy."

Logan cleared his throat to remind the Westons that he was still in the room. "I'm going to—"

"Stay, Logan," Banning ordered. "You already know everything I'm going to tell Sean."

Logan felt her accusing eyes on him before she turned to her father and said, "Chancy is not just here because he's a Harrison and Harrison executive who needs a place to stay, is he?"

"Two months ago someone shot at Sheldon and Tracie while they were driving on the highway. Chancy is a bodyguard; I hired him immediately after the incident to protect Tracie. We still don't know why it happened, whether it was intentional or not, but I didn't want to take any chances with the family's safety." Banning visibly tensed as he waited for Sean's reaction.

Logan glanced at her and, instead of seeing the anger he expected, he saw hurt—a hurt so deep that he had to resist the need to wrap his arms around her. As if she remembered that she was Sean, anger flashed into her eyes.

"Why didn't you tell me, Dad?"

"Sean—"

The explosion both men had been expecting finally came. "Did it ever occur to you that I could have helped? Did it once cross your mind that your daughter, who works for the Federal Bureau of Investigation, could have done something to catch whoever did this? Did you think that maybe I could have given you names of bodyguards or contacts within the Bureau down here? Once, Dad, even once, did you think about me?" Sean seemed too overwhelmed to continue speaking, and she turned her back to Logan and Banning.

Banning glanced to Logan for help, and Logan silently shrugged in response.

"I'm sorry, Sean," Banning finally said. "It just happened so fast . . . and I knew that you would be here soon for Tracie's wedding. I know that you're an agent, Sean, a good agent, but you're my daughter first, and when I think of protecting my family, I think about protecting you, too." Banning lowered his eyes as he said softly, "You never ask us for anything, Sean, but I know that sometimes you struggle. You have to pay bills, deal with criminals, deal with your mother . . . I didn't want to add to your list of worries, too."

Sean spun around, and Logan's heart tore as he saw the tears in her eyes. "Maybe I wanted to worry, Dad. That's what families do, but I was never a part of this family, was

I?" Her voice trailed off in a sob and she ran out the room. Banning cursed, then glanced at Logan.

"Should I go after her?" Banning asked Logan uncertainly.

"When Sean gets like this . . . it's better to leave her alone."

"What can I do to fix this?"

"Show her that she's a part of this family.

"She's always been a part of this family . . . but she's not like the other girls. She takes on so much that I just wanted to spare her," Banning responded desperately. "When I first married Tina, Sean tried her hardest to keep Tina and the girls at a distance. I didn't know how to bridge the gap. Sean is loyal to her mother. I think she always thought I betrayed her mother by marrying Tina, but . . . I just don't know what to do, Logan."

"You should have told her the truth about the car shooting, Banning. Why do you constantly underestimate her?"

Banning glared at him as he said through clenched teeth, "She's my daughter."

"She's also a grown woman who just happens to be one of the best young agents in the FBI. She's your greatest ally, Banning. She can handle it. You don't know how lucky you are to have her love."

"I guess that makes two of us," Banning said with a knowing smile. He abruptly sobered as he said, "Tell me what to do, Logan. You know her better than I do."

"Make it right between you two."

"I don't know how."

"Yes, you do," Logan said as he placed a hand on Banning's shoulder. "Trust her."

Banning stared at Logan a second longer, then walked from the room, a dejected slump to his shoulders. Logan groaned and raked both hands over his face. He knew that he should have gone to the beach and found a bikini-clad beach bunny to make him forget about Sean Weston and the pain she was in.

Logan knocked on the door to Sean's bedroom. After a few seconds with no response, he pressed his ear against the door, hearing only silence from the other side. That didn't mean anything. She probably sat on her bed, glaring at the door, hating the world. Logan figured that after his twenty-minute shower and change into clothes for the bachelor party that Sean would have calmed down enough to talk to him. As he banged on the door, he realized that apparently she hadn't.

Logan grew impatient and tried the doorknob. It was locked. He pounded on the door again. He was just eyeing the door to test its strength for a good kick when Sean swung it open. Instead of looking on the verge of tears, as Logan had half feared, she looked mad as hell. Without a word she spun around and returned to the open suitcase that he could see in the middle of the large bed.

Logan walked into the room and silently closed the door behind him. He watched Sean move in a frenzied storm as she stalked into the bathroom, then threw an armful of stuff into the suitcase. Next, she yanked clothes from the hangers in the closet and dumped the whole heap into the suitcase.

"You can't just leave," he finally said.

She ignored him as she made a trip to the wicker chest of drawers in a corner of the room. She unloaded the clothes on the suitcase, then said neutrally, "There's a flight to San Francisco in an hour. There's so much room here that I doubt anyone will even notice if you stay here for the rest of your vacation—"

Logan rolled his eyes in frustration, then blocked her path to the suitcase as he stood in front of the bed and grabbed her arms. He ignored the warning in her eyes as she stared at his hands on her.

"Did you hear me? You can't just leave, Sean."

"Let go of me, Logan," she whispered through clenched teeth.

"Maybe your father didn't handle things as you would have, or even as I would have, but he told you the truth. Are you going to run away while someone may be trying to kill your sister or are you going to help your family?"

"Get your hands off me. Now."

Logan continued, "You can act like you don't care, but I know the truth. You're angry because you're hurt, but Banning didn't want to hurt you, Sean. In his own twisted way, he was trying to protect you from having to worry about them because he knows something that you try to hide from everyone else, something that I figured out a long time ago; you became an FBI agent not because of the guns, but because you want to help people. You want to take their pain away, no matter what the cost is to you. You can hate Banning for a lot of reasons, but you can't hate him for wanting to take that burden off you."

A lump formed in his throat when he saw tears swimming in Sean's eyes. With any other woman, Logan would have wrapped his arms around her and told her that everything would be all right. With Sean, he didn't know what to do, except not mention her tears. He felt completely helpless. When she tried to move from him, he released his hold on her arms. She wiped the tears from her face and wrapped her arms around herself.

"They've never accepted me, Logan," she suddenly whispered in a tiny voice that made his soul hurt for her. "I didn't think it mattered to me. I told myself that if they didn't want me then I didn't want them either, but it hurts. It hurts a lot more than I thought it would."

He framed her face with his hands and forced a smile when she finally met his eyes. "You say the word and we're out of here. I'll throw our suitcases in the car and we'll be on the highway before your father even knows that we're gone."

"I hear a 'but' coming on," she whispered with a groan that made Logan grin.

"But before we leave, you should know what I see. I see a group of people with whom you have nothing in common except that they're your family. And when I see the love in their eyes when they look at you, being family is the only thing that matters. Do you really want to leave them at a time like this?"

There was a long pause when Logan thought she would hand him her suitcase, but she finally said, "I guess since we're already here, we may as well stay."

He smoothed hair from her face, then forced himself to remove his hands from her soft skin. His gaze drifted to her glistening lips and he immediately felt like a pervert. She had been on the verge of tears less than a minute ago, and all he could think about was kissing her.

"I should leave for the bachelor party," Logan murmured to himself, but for some reason he could not force himself to move as Sean continued to stare at him.

"Logan . . . I . . ." She seemed unable to continue as she stared at the ground.

He could have made her ask. He probably should have, just to remind her that she was human, but for some reason he didn't. Without a word Logan wrapped his arms around her. When she clung to his back and rested her head on his chest, he knew he had done the right thing. She didn't need to be reminded of her vulnerabilities; she just needed someone to hold her, and Logan wouldn't have allowed anyone else to take the job.

She abruptly moved from his arms, and Logan caught the uncertainty in her eyes. Her brow furrowed, and Logan knew that she was probably trying to think of something to make him forget the fact that he had seen her cry.

He threw his hands up in surrender and said, "I know, I

know—if I tell anyone that you lost the fight, you'll break both of my arms."

Her mouth dropped open in disbelief before she corrected him. "I didn't lose the fight. When Dad walked into the gym, you were on the bottom and I was on the top, remember?"

Logan grinned as he said, "I have a secret for you, Weston: I like being on the bottom."

She rolled her eyes at his flirtatious smile; then she laughed. Logan winked at her, then walked out of the room, closing the door behind him. He raked both hands over his face, attempting to forget the fact that for one moment on the other side of the door, he had caught a glimpse of what caring for a woman for longer than five weeks could bring.

Thirteen

After hang gliding in the morning, fighting a duel to the death—sort of—in the afternoon, and finding out that one woman's tears meant more to him than most women's smiles, Logan was bored out of his mind as he sat with Sheldon and his friends in a private room of the Santa Barbara Country Club. The room was outfitted in dark colors and heavy oak paneling that exuded the wealthy's idea of masculinity. The men's brandy snifters were never empty, and the smell of illegal Cuban cigars filled the room. While Logan liked smoking cigars as much as the next man, judging from the looks on the faces of the six other men in the room, and the fact that they had been in the room drinking brandy and smoking cigars for the last three hours, it was more than sad that this was the bachelor party.

Logan normally wouldn't have said anything, except that Sheldon looked almost as bored as Logan felt. His five friends, who had all been introduced to Logan as "Kappa" this or "Omega" that, smoked their cigars as if this was their version of paradise. Logan decided that within the next few minutes he would excuse himself to the bathroom, then run for his car and drive back to the Weston mansion. Maybe Banning would want to go drag racing.

"How exactly do you know Sheldon, Riley?"

Logan looked at the man who sat next to him. He vaguely

remembered that his name was Walter Simmons, of the Boston Simmonses. Since Logan didn't know anyone in Boston or care about Walter Simmons or the rest of the Simmonses, Walter Simmons's pedigree meant nothing to him.

"Tracie is my friend's stepsister." Logan forced himself to sound remotely interested in Walter, even as he mentally began to count down the next five minutes until his escape.

"Tracie's stepsister?" Walter's face momentarily frowned with concentration; then he abruptly smiled and snapped his fingers together. "The stepsister in San Francisco? Sam, Sheila . . ."

"Her name is Sean. Sean and I are neighbors in San Francisco."

"San Francisco . . . Do you know Barry Flowers?"

Logan tried not to cringe at the name game Walter started. Logan wanted to tell Walter Simmons of the Boston Simmonses that he was certain that he didn't know anyone that Walter knew.

"No, I don't know Barry Flowers."

"Stanley Hatcliff?"

"No."

"Everyone knows Stan," Walter mused. He appeared to more closely scrutinize Logan as he said, "What is it that you do again?"

"I'm a cop." Logan noticed the sudden silence in the room as all six pairs of eyes focused on him. He heard the collective gasps of horror and disbelief. He glanced at Sheldon, who suddenly became interested in his cigar. Logan explained further, "I'm a homicide inspector with the San Francisco Police Department."

"Explain something to me, Logan," one of the men said, leaning forward in his chair toward Logan. Logan remembered the man as Elton Multon of the Chicago Multons. "As a seemingly intelligent black man, how can you be a police officer?"

"Elton—"

Elton interrupted Sheldon's admonishment as Walter and a few other men in the room nodded in agreement with Elton. "No matter how hard you try, you'll never be one of them. You'll always be one of their lackeys, one of their houseboys that they use to beat and persecute your own people."

Logan decided to simply ignore the comment. He had spent half of his life dealing with comments from black men and women who called him a sellout and every other name in the book for being a police officer. Once upon a time those comments had hurt him, but after receiving the heartfelt gratitude and smiles of too many people of every color during his years on the job, he had stopped explaining himself to people a long time ago.

"Elton didn't mean that, Logan," Sheldon said quickly. "We all know what a hard job you have. I know none of us would do it."

"Maybe you're right, Sheldon," Elton reluctantly agreed, then grinned as he said, "Besides, if I had to be a cop just to catch a piece like Sean, sign me up for the Academy right now." A loud round of laughter sounded through the room, except from Sheldon, who looked frightened as he stared at a motionless Logan.

Logan's anger roared through his body like a tidal wave about to bury an unsuspecting shoreline. He had never felt such pure anger. He rarely allowed his emotions to control him, but seeing Elton's leer as he mentioned Sean's name and hearing the laughter about her—his woman, and Logan accepted that she was his woman—made his entire body clench with the need to hit something or someone.

Before Logan had even made the decision to move, he was across the room and had kicked over Elton's chair. The chair rocked backward and, with a loud crash, Elton and the chair sprawled onto the floor. Logan stood over Elton, praying for him to move. If Elton made an attempt to stand, or even breathe, Logan decided he would break his arm. But

Elton was more intelligent than he looked, because he remained completely still and stared wide-eyed at Logan.

In a corner of his mind, Logan noted the sudden silence in the room as the other men held their breath, waiting for whatever would happen next.

Logan's voice sounded surprisingly calm to his own ears as he said to Elton, "You can talk about me, Elton. You can even talk about cops. But if I ever hear you talk about Sean with such disrespect again, you won't be able to move your mouth for the next month. Do you understand me?"

Elton dumbly nodded, then darted glances at his friends, who remained in their chairs behind Logan. Logan forced a smile onto his face and, judging from the frightened look that crossed Elton's face, realized that his smile probably resembled the dangerous smile that Logan had seen sometimes on Cary's face.

"Consider yourself lucky that I'm in a good mood. Otherwise I would tell Sean what you said, and then, along with your mouth, you wouldn't be able to move your arms," Logan said.

Sheldon hesitantly crossed the room to stand behind Logan, and Logan felt his tentative hand on Logan's shoulder.

"Elton opens his mouth without thinking, Logan. He didn't mean anything by it," Sheldon quickly said.

Logan held out his hand to assist Elton to his feet. It was a move to show no hard feelings and to give Elton's hand an extra squeeze that would maybe grind a few bones, but Elton quickly scrambled to his feet of his own volition. He took several steps from Logan to stand behind Walter, who intently stared into his glass of brandy.

"I'm sorry this happened, Sheldon," Logan said, not sorry at all, but he wanted his apology on record in case Sean discovered the incident and blamed him for ruining Sheldon's bachelor party. "I'll leave now so you can get on with the party."

"Wait," a meek voice said. Logan turned to the man sitting next to Walter. Logan didn't remember his name, but he remembered the sweaty palm that had shaken his hand. "Don't leave."

"Shut up, Howard," Elton snapped, his bravado returning now that he stood across the room from Logan.

"We need help, Elton. The five of us couldn't think of anything to do but sit here and drink brandy like our fathers. Sheldon was about to fall asleep from boredom until Logan almost kicked your teeth in," Howard told Elton.

"I'm not bored," Sheldon said, not sounding convincing.

"We want to have fun, Logan," Howard said, turning to Logan and ignoring Elton. "Where can we go to have fun? It's Sheldon's last night of freedom."

"I don't know Santa Barbara," Logan said helplessly. "If we were in San Francisco I could help, but here I'm a visitor like you all."

"You have an idea of what we can do?" Sheldon said hopefully.

"Most bachelor parties go to a . . ." Logan's voice trailed off as he suddenly grinned and thought of Sean's reaction when she saw him. "This city's club scene isn't that big, only a few clubs on State Street. How much do you want to bet that's where the women are?"

"We can't crash the girls' party," one of the other men said with a flabbergasted laugh.

"Yes, we can," Sheldon said firmly as he jumped to his feet. "And we are."

"What about freedom?" Walter protested. "Other women?"

"I've had twenty-plus years of freedom. I want to be with Tracie now," Sheldon simply responded.

"I'll drive," Logan volunteered, which caused a round of applause and approval. In a deep mass of excited laughter, the men left the room, except for Logan, Sheldon, and Elton. Elton avoided Logan's eyes as he turned to Sheldon.

"Do you still want me to hang out tonight?" Elton asked stiffly.

"We've known each other since we were ten years old. Of course I want you to hang out."

Elton didn't look at Logan as he stormed from the room. Sheldon muttered after Elton's departure, "And you've been an ass since you were ten years old."

"I'm sorry that happened," Logan muttered, hating the fact that he apologized. He knew that if Elton had made his comment around Sean, he would be limping to the hospital right now, but Logan was a little more restrained than Sean, and he liked Tracie. Logan didn't want to be responsible for ruining her fiancé's bachelor party.

"I'm not," Sheldon said firmly. "Elton deserved a lot more for what he said tonight than being dumped on his ass."

Logan smiled in gratitude, then grinned as he imagined the potential outfits that Sean could have worn for the bachelorette party. He hoped that it was something short and tight and illegal in a few Midwestern states.

"The women are going to be surprised to see us," Logan said.

"I hope so." Sheldon grinned as he rubbed together his hands like a villain in a black-and-white movie.

Logan followed Sheldon and his friends into the club. Their objective had become clear after they left the first two clubs as soon as they walked inside and saw no bachelorette party. Sheldon was obviously going through Tracie withdrawal, and Logan could admit that he wouldn't mind seeing Sean. He told himself it was to make certain that she had recovered from that afternoon in her room, but there was a deeper truth: he just needed to see her. It was that strange urge that caused him to drive a group of loud, obnoxious rich men from one bar to the next.

Logan peered through the darkness of the room at the numerous people who filled the warehouse-size club. Bright lights, momentarily illuminating how many women wore too little clothing, flashed through the club almost in beat to the music—loud music with a driving beat that pounded in Logan's chest and reverberated through the building. People of all shapes and colors moved on the dance floor in a large mass of arms and bare flesh. Men in a uniform of black clothes stood at the bar attempting to look cool while blatantly eyeing any woman—or women, since they all traveled in packs of three—who dared to walk past them.

"Wait here, Sheldon. We'll bring you a drink," Howard screamed over the loud music. He nudged Logan and yelled, "Do you want water, designated driver?"

Logan shook his head in answer, not bothering to attempt to talk over the music and general noise of the club. He suddenly remembered why he hadn't gone to a club in months. The members of the bachelor party abandoned Sheldon and Logan to make a push toward the bar.

Two women in clothes that Logan felt belonged in the bedroom and not in public—although he definitely was not complaining—bumped into him. He moved out of their path, but they brushed against him again, then giggled at each other and continued to walk. Logan stared after them. When one turned over her shoulder to wink at him, he grinned in response. The women's path was suddenly blocked, and they separated to walk around the obstacle. The obstacle was a woman who looked the picture of original sin in second-skin black leather pants, black stiletto heels, and a blinding red halter top.

Logan's gaze finally made the path to the woman's face, and his grin instantly disappeared. Sean crossed her arms over her chest as she glared at him. For several seconds the two stared at each other; then she abruptly turned and disappeared into the crowd.

"Busted," Sheldon announced, while jabbing Logan in

the side, apparently having witnessed the silent exchange with Sean.

"Maybe I do need a drink," Logan muttered.

"At least we know that they're here," Sheldon said cheerfully, then ordered, "Go talk to Sean."

"Did you see that look she gave me?" Logan shook his head as he involuntarily shuddered at the promise of pain in Sean's eyes that had been apparent even across the dark room. "I'm not going anywhere near her."

"I don't see Tracie or the rest of the bachelorette party anywhere. Ask Sean where my woman is," Sheldon said as he pushed Logan in the direction Sean had disappeared.

"Are you aware that you're sending me to my death?" Logan muttered, allowing himself to be pushed.

"I think the French call it the *little death*." Sheldon laughed at his sexual innuendo, then patted Logan on the back. "Give her hell, buddy."

Logan watched Sheldon push his way through the mass toward his friends at the bar. Logan turned in the opposite direction and shouldered through the crowd of people toward Sean. When he finally saw her standing against a wall in the back of the club, giving any man who came within ten feet of her a death look, Logan could only grin. Maybe Sean would break his heart after only five weeks, but Logan had a feeling it would be the best five weeks of his life.

Logan gave the man standing next to Sean a hard glare, and the man quickly moved from the wall. Logan leaned against the wall next to her, but Sean ignored him and continued to watch the dancers.

"Where's Tracie? Sheldon's looking for her." Logan felt like an idiot, screaming over the loud music, especially when Sean finally looked at him and pointed to her ears as if she couldn't hear him.

Logan smiled at her response, then wrapped one arm around her waist and pulled her flush against his body. Her eyes widened as she slammed into him. Every inch of her wonderful, sinful body was pressed against every inch of his, and Logan didn't bother to hide what feeling her did to him. Her eyes widened as she felt his erection press against her thigh, and she placed both hands against his chest and tried to push him away. Logan refused to budge.

He had spent all night itching to see Sean, and he finally decided that the reward for his trials and tribulations *was* Sean. Whether she wanted to be or not. Logan maneuvered her a few feet into a dark corner of the room and pushed her back against the wall. He was encouraged that she didn't protest, but only pulled his shirt to keep his body pressed against hers. Logan leaned close to her right ear and pulled the fleshy earlobe between his teeth. She instantly stilled against his chest, and Logan felt her tug his shirt material in her hands.

"I asked you where Tracie is. Sheldon is looking for her," Logan whispered, then ran his tongue over the part of her ear that he had bitten, soothing the brown skin.

Logan ran his tongue along the length of her neck, tasting the saltiness of her warm, soft skin. He felt her shiver, and he grinned before he placed an openmouthed kiss on her neck. Logan hadn't purposely given a woman a hickey since his early days in high school, but now it was his new mission. He wanted to claim her as his own. He wanted all the men who covertly watched her in the club to know that she belonged to him. Of course, Logan would never tell Sean that. She would probably hit him.

Sean's hands traveled from his shirt to link around his neck and drag him closer to her. Logan was no longer satisfied with her neck but moved to loom above her mouth.

"Do you really think that you can flirt with other women and then kiss me?" she said in a silky whisper.

"What other women?" Logan blankly asked, hoping that she'd fall for his act of innocence.

Sean only smiled, then leaned toward him. Logan groaned when he felt a sudden hand on his shoulder. Keeping his hands on Sean's waist, Logan reluctantly turned and narrowed his eyes when he saw a grinning Tracie and Sheldon. He barely restrained a curse when Sean's hands fell from his shoulders and she pushed him in the chest. Logan took a reluctant few steps from her, but kept one hand on the small of her back. He could feel a small strip of bare, soft skin in between the waistband of her pants and the hem of her top that he rubbed a thumb across. Sean shot him a dirty look, but Logan also noticed that she didn't move.

"I told Sheldon it was you two back here in the corner," Tracie said, looking from Sean to Logan.

Sheldon not-so-discreetly winked at Logan, then said to Sean, "I'm glad that Logan found you."

"I can't even hear myself think in this place," Tracie screamed over the noise. "Sheldon and I are going to the coffee shop down the block."

"You can't leave your bachelor and bachelorette parties to have coffee," Logan said, amazed at their plan.

Sheldon and Tracie blankly looked at each other, then back at Sean and Logan before Sheldon said, "Why not?"

"Because . . . because it's . . . You just can't," Logan stammered. He looked to Sean for help but she only smiled at her sister. Logan turned to Sheldon and Tracie and tried again. "You're supposed to be having fun. You're supposed to be enjoying one of your last nights as single people."

"It's after midnight. I've had about as much fun as I think I'm going to have tonight," Tracie whined.

"And I wouldn't have asked Tracie to marry me if I thought being single was so much more enjoyable than marrying her."

Sean squeezed Logan's arm to silence him; then she said to Tracie, "Where's Terri and the rest of your bachelorette party?"

"Terri wasn't feeling well, so she went home ten minutes ago," Tracie explained. She then shrugged and said, "I think that my bachelorette party is officially over. Debbie ran into an ex-boyfriend whom she's now kissing in another corner of the club, Heather is dancing on the bar and allowing men to stick money in her pants, and the rest of the girls are wandering around the club paying men to take off their shirts because they're still bitter that I didn't want to see male strippers tonight."

"See why I need to get her away from here?" Sheldon said, obviously appalled by Tracie's friends' behavior. He placed a protective arm around her shoulders.

Tracie glanced at Logan before she said, "Sean, do you need a ride home?"

"I'll drive her home," Logan preempted Sean's answer. Sean glared at him, but he continued to look at Tracie and Sheldon.

Tracie grinned as she brushed a kiss against Sean's cheek. "Have fun." Sheldon winked at Logan once more, then grabbed Tracie's hand and led her toward the exit.

Logan felt Sean's glare on him and he slowly turned to her. He had a feeling that he wouldn't get anywhere near her for that hickey he desperately needed to see on her long, graceful neck.

"Take me to the house now," she said simply, then brushed past him and stalked toward the exit.

Logan enjoyed watching her move before he noticed that he wasn't the only man doing so. He hurried after her, making certain to glare at each and every man who stared after her.

Fourteen

Sean told herself that she wouldn't talk to Logan. She had seen the look of pure sex that he shot those two women in the club. If he hadn't seen her, Sean had no doubt that he would be doing something hazardous to his health with one or both of the women at that moment. Of course, as soon as he touched her in the club, she couldn't remember why she was angry anymore. She could only think about how sweet he had been in her room earlier that evening. And there was no other word for it but sweet. She had known that Logan could be charming, flirtatious, even chivalrous, but she had never thought of him as sweet until he held her in his arms and allowed her to—for once—stop holding the world on her shoulders.

Sweet or not, he had still given those women a look of promise that made her want to scream. She didn't know who she was more angry with now: Logan because he was Logan, or herself because she turned into a spineless woman whenever he was near. And since when did she care whether Logan flirted with other women? She could admit that she had always cared, but now she definitely had a legitimate reason. He had kissed her. He had touched her as though she were more precious than his gun. And Sean became angrier when she realized why: Logan was a superficial, simple male who looked at the exterior, and that was all that mattered.

She had been so busy thinking of all the reasons why she should be angry with him that she didn't notice until the car stopped that they were not at the mansion. She glanced at the unfamiliar surroundings. The car stood on a cliff, with the expanse of ocean and sand glowing through the darkness beneath them. A dark, deserted road lay behind them, and Sean saw the lights from other houses in the distance. She refused to be swayed by the sound of the ocean through the open car window and the lingering salt breeze.

Sean glared at Logan, who stared out the windshield at the darkness. She said through clenched teeth, "This is not the house. Where are we?"

His grin, visible in the light of the moon glowing through the windows, made her momentarily forget her anger. "Your dad told me this morning when we drove by this place on our way to hang . . . to the golf course that high school kids come here to make out. Now I know what you didn't do when you spent your summers here."

She refused to be embarrassed and snapped, "You're not cute, Riley."

"Yes, I am."

"Why did you bring me here? Is this part of the challenge?"

"I want to talk."

"I want to talk, too," Sean said emphatically. "I want to talk about why you think that you can kiss me anytime you feel like it."

"I want to know if you're all right about this afternoon," Logan quietly said, then looked at her, his brown eyes caressing her across the car. When Sean didn't respond, Logan continued, "If you need to talk, you can talk to me. You know that, right?"

Maybe it was his gentle tone and warm eyes, or the fact that he didn't try to flirt with her or seduce her with soft words. Sean didn't really care why, but sitting in the car with him, she had to taste him again. She had to feel his hands on her, all over her, making her feel like no other man had made her feel before.

Without warning she unclasped the seat belt, then moved across the car to straddle his lap. Her behind dug into the steering wheel, one knee slammed into the gearshift, and her head jammed against the roof, but feeling the hardness of him underneath her made the pain disappear. And seeing his wide grin and surprised eyes made the pain enjoyable. His hands instantly dug into her waist to steady her and to hold her against him.

"Tell me the real reason why you brought me here," she whispered as she leaned her face to within a breath of his luscious mouth. "We could have talked in the coffee shop with Sheldon and Tracie."

"Talk?" Logan repeated, as if he had no idea what the word meant.

Sean smiled in response, then said, "Maybe we can . . . relax in the backseat until you figure it out."

She expected him to laugh at her. She didn't expect him to move her to the backseat of the car so fast that her head spun. She lay on the leather seat and Logan moved over her. Their long bodies were cramped in the confines of the car, and Sean had a feeling that she would also have a cramp in her neck if she remained in the same position, but as soon as Logan's lips met hers, she couldn't move to save the world.

They met in a fury of arms and tongues and lips. Sean laughed at Logan's frenzied attack as his hands raced across her body from one end to the other, his mouth never ceasing the sweet, brutal attack on hers. She grabbed at the shirt he wore, not surprised when she heard buttons tear and spring across the car to the floor. She pushed the shirt from his shoulders and sighed into his mouth when she felt the bare warmth of his skin. He was so warm and hard. The contradiction almost drove her over the edge. His tongue raced through her mouth while his large hands squeezed her thighs, imprinting his heat through the leather pants.

Logan trailed hard, demanding kisses down her neck to the cleavage visible in her top, as she ran her hands over his back. All around her, the air seemed filled with Logan, and she never wanted it to end. She sighed his name when he worked one breast free from the top and the strapless bra she wore. He squeezed the flesh that she always dismissed as unimportant, except when he was around; then his mouth covered the peak and Sean's hips involuntary reared off the seat as she realized how extremely important breasts could be to a woman.

He lapped one nipple as he worked the other breast free from her top. He traveled to the other breast, giving it the same undivided attention. Sean wrapped her arms around his head, pulling him closer, wanting him closer. His hands traveled down her partially bare stomach to press into her center through the leather, and Sean gasped his name again as her entire body shuddered at the powerful emotions Logan caused in her. It partially scared her, but she was too driven by desire to fully comprehend her fear.

"It's been so long," he murmured as his tongue brushed across a hard nipple that made her buck off the seat in ecstasy at the liquid warmth he released in her body.

She heard the snap of her pants; then Logan tried to pull the leather down her legs, but it stuck to her skin. She groaned in protest when he raised his head from her breasts to look at the pants. He tugged at the pants harder and Sean almost slid off the seat from the force of his pull.

"You taste so good, so soft, and . . . and how do I get these damn things off?" Logan muttered, his voice hoarse with desire and frustration.

Sean panted as overwhelming emotions raced through her body. He expected her to think? When she saw the impatience in his eyes, she forced her brain to work through the

haze of pleasure that was driving her closer to her meta-
phorical cliff before he tore off her two-hundred-dollar
leather pants with his bare hands. She spotted the bar over
her head and said in between gasps for air, "I'll hold on and
you pull."

Logan nodded in understanding as Sean grabbed the bar.
After several pulls that had Sean stretched across the backseat like a taut string, Logan pulled the pants, which took
her underwear, over her bare feet—Sean didn't know when
had she lost her shoes. He threw the pants in the front seat,
then smiled at her. Sean grinned in response and held out
her arms for him.

Then she saw it flicker across his eyes—the hesitation.
She was nude except for the halter top that was a thin band
underneath her breasts, while he still wore his pants, hover-
ing above her. It was over.

Sean cursed him for making her feel undesirable, and she
cursed herself for giving him the power to do so. She felt
the tears sting her eyes and she instantly reached for her
halter top to pull it over her breasts. One of his hands stilled
hers and the other covered her right cheek in a strangely
gentle manner, when nothing had been gentle between them
since they had sat in the car.

"You are so beautiful, Sean," he whispered, sounding almost awed.

She couldn't help dryly responding, "You don't have to
sound so surprised."

Logan briefly smiled, then whispered, "What surprises
me is that I'm not as surprised as you think I am."

Sean had no snappy comeback or retort for that one. And
she knew in that short space of time that she and Logan
would not make love that night. As if all the air suddenly
left his body, Logan tiredly sighed and carefully began to
move off her. Cool air caused by his movements wrapped
around her legs, making her feel more exposed than her bare
body already was.

As if she had no pride or dignity, Sean grabbed his shoulders and said, "Don't stop, Logan."

He smiled—a strange smile that didn't quite reach his eyes—and fell onto the floor of the car. "I can't see your underwear, but here are your pants."

"Just like that, we stop. . . ." Sean's voice trailed off, more from confusion and surprise than from anger. She sat up on the backseat, causing Logan to bump his head against the seat as he recoiled from her as if she were a poisonous snake.

He quickly averted his eyes, then grabbed his shirt, which hung over the front seat, and through a series of contortionist movements pulled it on. Sean barely noticed his elbow that accidentally jabbed into her knee, because she was too shocked. They had been two seconds from bliss—and she knew that it would have been bliss—but out of the blue he had stopped.

Sean stared at Logan, who made every attempt possible not to look at her in the small confines of the car. She raked a hand through her hair and felt the familiar unruly curls. She knew that her makeup had probably come off in their gymnastic movements and that without the clothes and hair, she looked like . . . she looked like herself. She didn't need to ask Logan why he had stopped. She knew why.

As if sensing the gathering storm of her mood, Logan abruptly climbed into the front seat to open the driver's door. "I'll wait outside until you're dressed."

He slammed the car door just as Sean, in a burst of anger, threw her shoe at his back. It sailed through the open window and harmlessly bounced to the ground. Logan didn't pause as he stalked toward the shelter of the trees.

Logan parked the car in front of the mansion. Without waiting for him to turn off the engine, Sean jumped from the car and ran toward the front door. She hadn't bothered to find her other shoe, and since she had only one she must have left it in the car to hopefully poke Logan's next date whom he almost slept with in his car.

She had to escape Logan before she exploded and hurt him or, more likely, hurt herself, because she wanted to scream and yell and she knew that Logan would calmly explain that he simply did not want to sleep with her. He had come to his senses and stopped before he did something that he regretted. She should have respected that, but it only made her angrier. Once more, she felt hurt and unwanted, like the clumsy little girl she was. And the hurt quickly transformed into rage.

Logan hadn't said one word to her during the fifteen-minute drive back to the mansion. She wouldn't have thought he noticed that she was in the car except for the occasional nervous glances that he darted in her direction, as if he thought she would suddenly jump out of the car. Sean wanted to reassure him that she wasn't jumping from any vehicle. Whether she could restrain herself enough not to throw him from the car was another story.

Sean fumbled with the keys in the lock even as she heard Logan's slow, steady footsteps behind her. Risking life and limb, Logan calmly placed his hand over hers. He took the keys from her hand and unlocked the front door while Sean just glared at him, her trigger finger itching. Logan still wouldn't meet her eyes but instead stared at her shoulder. She finally rolled her eyes and tried to storm into the house and to hopefully slam the door in his nose.

Except there was one very large problem: Logan wouldn't move from in front of the door.

"Move." Sean spat out the one word with as much loathing as she could manage.

"I'm sorry—"

"I am walking a fine line. If you don't want to push me over the edge, you will not insult me by saying that word."

"What word?" Logan asked confused.

"Sorry," Sean said through clenched teeth. "You're not

sorry; I'm not sorry. We're two adults who allowed alcohol to rule our feelings—"

"I haven't had a drink all day," Logan quietly said, momentarily halting her angry tirade.

"Is that supposed to make me feel better?" Sean finally blurted out. "You were perfectly sober when you attacked me in the car and perfectly sober when you rejected me in the car?"

"I did not reject you, Sean."

"What do you call it?"

"I . . . I . . ." For some reason he was unable to continue. He dragged both hands down his face, then plopped onto the top porch step, looking the picture of dejection as he stretched out his legs in front of him.

Sean was the one who should have been angry. She was the one who had been wronged in this whole situation, thrown aside like an empty clip of ammunition. Instead she felt a strange feeling akin to tenderness as she stared at Logan's lowered head. She released a sigh of disbelief at her own actions but she still sat next to him on the porch, cringing as the leather waistband bit into her skin.

Since Logan continued to be as still as a statue, Sean groaned and ran her hands through her hair. Suddenly the words he had spoken in the car suddenly played in her brain like a distorted recording: *It's been so long.* She stared at Logan, who continued to look at his hands. She shook her head at the notion. Logan was a sexy man who went on dates four nights a week, who had sex with women four nights a week. She tortured herself nightly thinking of him with other women.

For the first time since Sean had known him, she asked herself how many times Logan had come home the night of a date. Every time. How many times had women slept over at his apartment? Often. But the women left his apartment early in the morning and they always looked . . . Sean could only call it frustrated or disappointed or even annoyed. Was

Logan even more of a Boy Scout than she thought? Is that what he meant when he said that it had been too long? That was a ridiculous thought. She must have misunderstood.

"Logan, in the car you said . . ." She took a deep breath, then tried again, "What did you mean when you said that it had been too long?"

"Exactly what you thought I meant," Logan said, finally meeting her eyes.

Sean was momentarily speechless, then managed to ask, "How long has it been, Logan?"

She didn't think he would answer her as several seconds ticked by, but then he softly said, "Probably longer than it has been for you."

"I doubt that. The only offer I've had in the last three years has been the occasional marriage proposal from a suspect trying to get out of trouble."

Logan halfheartedly smiled, then dryly proclaimed, "I win."

"What are you talking about?"

"I haven't had sex in five years."

Sean's mouth dropped open as all of her anger immediately drained from her body. Everything that she had ever thought about Logan was . . . wrong. She thought of him as the love-'em-and-leave-'em type. She thought of him as parading from one bed to the next, leaving behind a trail of bitter, brokenhearted women.

"You're lying," she whispered, noticing underneath the soft porch light the flush that covered his face.

"I haven't had the best luck with women. In fact, I've had horrible luck with women," Logan admitted with a bitter laugh. "I meet a woman, everything goes great; then in the fifth week of our relationship she dumps me. It's like clockwork. Every woman—and there have been a lot of women—since I started dating at fifteen has dumped me either before the fifth week or by the fifth week. I'm starting to think I'm cursed. My sister calls my ex-girlfriends five-weeker number one, five-weeker number two . . . I couldn't take it any-more. Even I can take a hint. I'm obviously not meant for a long-term relationship, so I decided to take a hiatus from relationships.

"At first I thought that I should just concentrate on one-night stands and leave the commitments to other men, but that didn't work for me either. The whole situation always made me feel . . . don't laugh, but it made me feel dirty. So I decided that I wouldn't sleep with a woman, that I wouldn't commit my heart to a woman, until we passed the five-week mark. In five years that hasn't happened and here I am. I hadn't even come close until tonight."

"Until tonight?" Sean repeated in a strained voice.

"It started with Janice. I thought that I loved her. I pictured us married and in love like my parents had been." A faraway look entered his eyes as he leaned inside the door frame. "I met her when I returned home after my parents' death to take care of Maggie. She was the cheerleading coach at Maggie's high school.

"Around week four of that relationship, I unexpectedly went to her apartment early one evening and caught her in bed with my partner. She told me that I didn't spend enough time with her. Then there was Belinda. She was a nurse in Arizona. That five-week relationship ended with a 'Dear John' e-mail. She wrote that I was too nice for her and she was moving to Las Vegas with her ex-boyfriend. Next came Olivia. She told me after a few weeks that I wasn't ready for a commitment because I canceled a date to testify in court. Then Carrie—"

"I get the picture, Logan," Sean snapped, irritated at the thought of each and every woman from his past.

"It's been a series of bad relationships, one after the other. We get along fine for a few weeks; then something clicks and . . . a week later I get a bottle of wine attached to a note sent to my house or a sing-o-gram announcing our breakup."

"A sing-o-gram?" Sean repeated, trying really hard not to laugh at the forlorn expression on his face.

Logan continued, oblivious to her silent laughter, "I can't take the breakups, the heartaches . . . I can't take any of it anymore, Sean. My parents had the perfect marriage, the perfect relationship. They were high school sweethearts who had kissed only each other. If they had that, why can't I find a woman who can stand to be around me for more than five weeks?"

"I don't understand it. You're almost perfect. What's wrong with you that I can't see?"

Logan grinned in the middle of his pouting and said, "You think that I'm perfect?"

"Almost perfect," Sean mildly corrected him. "But then again, I've never dated you. Obviously something has to be wrong with you or all those women wouldn't have dumped you."

"Thanks for putting it so bluntly," Logan dryly responded. Sean shrugged in apology but waited for his answer. Logan threw up his hands in frustration as he said, "I don't know what's wrong with me. Five-weeker number nine told me that I was too nice. So I tried being mean, and five-weeker number ten told me that I was too mean. I just cannot win."

Sean told herself not to ask, but through clenched teeth she muttered, "How many five-weekers have there been?"

Logan hung his head in shame. "You don't want to know."

Sean suddenly snapped her fingers, then shook his arm, causing him to look at her. "You're like a swan, Logan."

"A swan?"

"I read about this in a magazine. Swans mate for life. They take one look at another swan and they know if that's the swan for them. If it's not, then they immediately move on—no dinner, no coffee, no movie. If it is, then they spend the rest of their lives with that one swan—"

"This had better have a point soon."

"The point is . . . the five-weekers weren't right for you because you're waiting for your matching swan. Your heart knew the truth as soon as you met all of them, and subconsciously you sabotaged the relationships so you could continue the search for your one true swan. There's nothing wrong with you except that you're a romantic, the last of a dying breed. You want true love and nothing else will do."

"Maybe," Logan said with a look that told her he didn't believe one word.

"That has to be the explanation."

"I know the explanation: I'm forever destined to be alone."

"Now you're being dramatic," Sean scolded. She stared at beautiful Logan, then murmured in disbelief, "I just can't believe it. All of this time . . . I thought that you . . . Five years? Are you sure?"

"We're both tired. We should get some rest," he said, attempting to change the subject as he stood.

Sean forced a smile and nodded in agreement. She slowly stood and felt another shot of tenderness as she saw the guilt and regret that swam in Logan's eyes. She had been wrong about him. Completely wrong. He wasn't a playboy; he was the most perfect man in the world. He couldn't fool himself into settling for a relationship like other people. He needed true love.

For that reason, Sean thought that she and Logan would have been perfect for each other—except for one big problem: Logan didn't see her as his mate-swan either. She had been there during a weak moment, and as a result he had almost broken a promise to himself. For a man like Logan, who prided himself on old-fashioned concepts like honor and integrity, she knew he probably thought that his behavior in the car had been unacceptable. And even though her lips still tingled and her body still ached for his touch, Sean wanted Logan to feel better.

"Now I understand about everything that's happened between us, and I don't want you to blame yourself. You're only human. A healthy guy like you . . . you had to falter at some point," Sean stammered. She didn't have much practice with forgiving and forgetting, but she wanted to do it right for Logan. "It's been five years. You were desperate and I was available, and I'm glad that you stopped before something happened that we both would have regretted. If I were a guy who had waited five years for the perfect woman . . . I would have stopped, too."

"I'm not waiting for the perfect woman. According to you, I'm waiting for a swan," Logan muttered, shooting her a censuring look.

Sean ignored his jibe and continued, "I also am wearing red tonight. I read in an issue of *Cosmopolitan* that no man can resist a woman in red."

Logan's somber expression melted into a dimpled smile as he laughed. He shook his head; then he said, "I'm glad that we're friends, Sean."

She tried not to choke on the word *friends,* the most offensive f-word in the English language, and instead responded, "Me, too."

"And I'm glad that you aren't making a big deal out of the kisses and . . . and the car. I don't know what's gotten into me. Maybe it's the Santa Barbara air, but since we've talked I feel much better. And I can guarantee that nothing like that will happen again."

"I'm glad," Sean lied.

"By the way, if you tell anyone about this conversation, I'll torture you with another appointment at the beauty salon." Sean failed miserably in withholding her laughter, but she nodded in understanding. A strange longing suddenly entered his eyes as he softly added, "You're almost as sweet as you taste."

Sean bit her bottom lip over her smile, refusing to show

her pleasure at being described as "sweet"; then she ran into the house and up the stairs toward her room.

Sean opened her bedroom door and stepped into the darkness. She glanced around the room to distinguish potentially knee-bruising furniture, but the closed curtains blocked out any light and her eyes had not adjusted to the darkness. Since she didn't need any more bruises on her knees, Sean turned to flip on the light switch. Seeming to emerge from the shadows of the room, a masked man who stood tall and broad-shouldered in all black crashed into her. The force of his tackle knocked the air from her body as they both slammed into the door, with the right side of her body meeting the unyielding force of the door first.

Sean didn't have time to scream as his arm moved from around her neck to cruelly squeeze over her mouth. His other arm wrapped around her waist and partially lifted her off the floor as she frantically kicked her legs in an attempt to connect the heel of her foot with his shin, as her hands scratched at the glove-covered hand over her mouth. A small part, the rational part of Sean, wanted to scream off her pretty little head and pray for Logan to take care of the big, bad wolf. The other part of her, the slightly insane FBI agent part, became angry that someone would dare to attack her in the place where her family lived.

The man slammed her against the door again, causing a searing pain to race through her shoulders, which took the brunt of the impact. Using her sudden stillness as she tried to clear her head from the pain, the man whirled her around to face the door, and before she could brace herself he moved his hand from her mouth to slam her head into the door. Pain centered like a laser beam in her forehead as tiny dots of white light danced in front of her eyes. Her knees grew weak as she fought the urge to welcome the darkness and close her eyes.

The man lifted her off the ground by her neck, as if she weighed no more than a sack of potatoes, and Sean came to life again, twisting and struggling like a live electrical wire in his bruising grip. She couldn't breathe, and the combination of panic and anger made her move faster and harder. His other hand moved around her waist to control her, but her wild movements threw him off balance and, as one, the two crashed into the door again, causing him to loosen his hold around her neck.

The man grunted as this time he took the full force of their combined fall against the door. Sean instantly drove one elbow into his stomach. The man yelped in intense pain and his arms instantly fell off her as he doubled over. With a loud scream of anger, Sean grabbed a handful of the face mask—and hair, she hoped—then used her lower body as leverage and his forward momentum to flip him onto the floor.

The man sailed over her shoulder and landed on the floor with a loud crash, slamming into the nightstand near the bed, causing the entire structure to topple to the floor. The lamp on the stand slid to the floor and exploded in a sea of broken glass. Sean didn't wait to see if the intruder would stay down. She hurdled his moaning figure on the ground and jumped onto the bed. Her movements were slowed by the plush mattress and down comforter, and she threw herself across the bed to reach the night table on the other side of the bed. She had placed her off-duty gun in the bottom drawer.

"Logan!" she screamed at the top of her lungs as she ripped open the drawer.

Sean heard the man run across the room toward the windows. She reached for her gun as he ripped open the curtains, revealing a wide-open window. A rope was tied to the window and dangled to the ground.

"Logan!" Sean cried again, as her hand wrapped around the gun handle. She whipped the gun around just as the man went over the windowsill.

Sean ran to the window just as the bedroom door flew open with a crushing boom that yanked the door off the hinges. The door crashed to the hardwood floor with a slap that could have awakened the dead. Sean screamed; then she saw Logan standing in the door frame. She couldn't see his face but she heard his uneven breaths, and she could feel the panic radiate from his body as he stormed into the room, looking around. With a gun in his hands, Chancy followed Logan into the room.

Sean couldn't make her mouth work, and she realized with surprise that she shook.

"What happened?" Logan roughly demanded.

She pointed out the window at the man who sprinted past the tennis courts toward the thicket of trees behind the mansion. Logan ran toward the window and saw the man. He cursed viciously and, without pausing, grabbed the rope and swung out the window. Sean started to follow him but Chancy placed an arm on her shoulder.

"Stay with Terri and your family," he ordered, then followed Logan down the rope.

Sean helplessly watched the two men race across the grass and disappear into the darkness of the trees.

"Sean," came her father's strangled voice. She turned to see her father, Tina, and Terri outlined in the bright light of the hallway. Tina walked into the room and turned on the light. They all gasped at the broken furniture and broken glass littered across the room. Besides the damage from their struggle, the intruder had been thorough in ripping apart Sean's belongings, throwing clothes in every direction.

"What happened?" Terri gasped as she placed a hand over her stomach.

Sean tried to speak again, but before she could open her mouth she fell to the floor. The weakness of her legs surprised her more than it did her family, who instantly raced to her side and formed a circle around her. Sean meant to tell them that she was supposed to protect them, but she doubted any of them would listen to her as they watched over her.

Fifteen

"Where the hell is Tracie?" Logan demanded as he glared at the men and women gathered in front of him.

Logan had to hit something or someone. When he had heard Sean's voice, the fear . . . He couldn't remember running up the stairs or even kicking in her door that had been jammed closed; Logan only remembered seeing Sean standing near the window with the gun in her hands. Her eyes had been huge in the moonlight—huge with anger and fear. It was the fear that drove Logan crazy. Sean wasn't scared of anything, and someone had scared her.

After running almost two miles through the thick forest behind the mansion, Logan and Chancy hadn't found the intruder. Logan's anger had partially receded by the time they returned to the mansion and saw that it was lit as brightly as a Christmas tree. He thought that his anger had disappeared until he had walked into the living room, where the family waited for them and he saw the palm-sized purple-and-maroon bruise above Sean's right eyebrow that stood out like a neon sign on her otherwise unmarred brown skin.

Logan became angrier than he thought he had the capability to be. He had always thought that Cary and Maggie had inherited their mother's legendary temper, while he had inherited their father's charm. Now Logan realized that he had his fair share of Eileen Riley's temper. He could have torn the intruder apart with his bare hands for scaring Sean, and when Logan saw the bruise on her forehead, he decided to first torture the man for a day or two, then to tear him apart.

"Tracie is spending the night with Sheldon," Terri responded weakly from her position in an armchair. With dazed expressions, Banning and Tina sat on an overstuffed sofa next to Terri. Like a sentry, Chancy stood behind Terri's chair and seemed prepared to spring at Logan if he made one move toward her. Logan almost met Chancy's challenge. He didn't care whose ass he kicked, as long as it was someone, and Chancy could substitute for the intruder.

"Call Tracie and tell her to come home now. And tell her to bring that excuse for a man who's with her. I have a few answers that I want to beat out of him," Logan bit out.

"Logan, you're scaring everyone and you're annoying me," Sean said sharply from her position behind him. She stood next to the entrance of the living room. She had changed into dull-colored cargo pants and an oversize sweatshirt. Logan knew that her gun—maybe even a few guns—was underneath the sweatshirt. And he wouldn't have been surprised if the numerous bulging pockets on her pants held ammunition. "Chancy called several of his trusted associates to guard the perimeter of the house. For now, there is nothing else any of us can do. There is no reason to call Tracie at two in the morning."

"I think there's a hell of a reason," Logan exploded. "You were almost killed, and we both know it's related to Carl Madison."

"What is going on?" Banning asked, finally recovering his voice.

"Carl Madison is a weapons dealer wanted by the FBI, the SFPD, and local police across the country—"

"Logan," Sean warned.

Logan glared at her as he snapped, "There are more secrets in this family than even the Pentagon could contain. Carl Madison is one that needs to be let out of the bag."

Sean narrowed her eyes at him, then addressed her family. "Carl Madison is a weapons dealer who operates across the country. I thought I saw him at the dinner party."

"Is that the man whose picture you showed me?" Terri asked.

"We showed all of you," Logan said. "And Sean thought that Sheldon and Tracie were holding something back from her when she showed them the picture, which makes sense since she saw those two with Carl Madison at the dinner party. Sheldon obviously knows something, which is the exact reason why I should go to Sheldon's house, wherever it is, and beat him silly."

"Logan, please."

Logan turned on Sean, momentarily forgetting their audience as his fear curled into anger in the pit of his stomach. "Some man was in your room. He attacked you. It was obviously Carl Madison, tipped off by Sheldon and Tracie that you were asking questions about him. He wants to know what you know or worse."

"Are you saying that Tracie was involved in the attack on Sean?" Tina asked in disbelief. "Tracie would never hurt her sister."

"By not telling Sean about Madison, she did hurt her," Logan exploded, causing Tina to flinch at the volume of his voice. With a confused expression on his face, Banning stared from his wife to Sean. Logan bitterly said, "That's right, Banning. You may have to choose between your wife and her daughters or your own daughter. To a real father, it wouldn't be a choice."

Banning recoiled as if Logan had hit him while Terri gasped. Tina buried her face in her hands, and her shoulders began to shake as she silently sobbed. Logan knew that he should feel ashamed. He did feel ashamed, but Sean had been attacked. No matter how much he told himself that he shouldn't be as angry as he was or care as much as he did, it didn't stop the need to lash out and make everyone hurt the way he did.

Sean stalked across the room and grabbed Logan's arm, forcing him to look at her. Logan welcomed the outrage in her eyes. He would rather have her never speak to him again than to see her looking scared and bruised.

"You need to calm down, Logan," Sean ordered. "Having a temper tantrum and bullying us is not going to solve anything."

"You can stay as calm as you want, but I'm going to find this bastard. I'm going to beat the crap out of him and then I'm going to drag him back to San Francisco—alone." Logan pulled his arm from her grip, then stormed from the room.

Logan walked across the foyer and out the front door, slamming it behind him. His car still sat at the front of the house, reminding him of the desire-filled moments he had shared with Sean. All the anger drained from his body and the fear returned tenfold, causing him to sag against the car. Sean could have been killed. She was the only woman in America who, instead of looking at him as if he were an alien when he told her about his five years of no sex, equated him to a swan and meant it as a compliment.

"Are you all right, Logan?"

Banning's gruff voice surprised Logan as the older man walked out of the house.

"I'm fine," Logan lied, then quickly opened the car door. "Tell Sean that she can do whatever she wants with my clothes in the room—"

"You're not going anywhere."

Logan saw the certainty in the man's eyes and demanded, "How do you know that?"

"Because Sean was attacked tonight. She needs you."

"Sean doesn't need anyone. Didn't you see her in there? She doesn't care that some idiot just tried to kill her—"

Logan cursed and decided to keep his mouth closed, since talking only made him angrier.

"You don't buy her Sean-against-the-world routine any more than I do, which is exactly why you're so angry at my family and me. You blame Tracie for not telling Sean about this Madison person. You blame me for not choosing my daughter—"

"I was out of line," Logan interrupted, chancing a glance at Banning.

"But you think that I should be doing more for her," Banning guessed.

Logan thought about sparing the older man's feelings, but it was only a thought before he said, "She may not express it, but Sean needs you just as much as Terri and Tracie do. I doubt Sean even knows that's what she wants, but I can tell when she watches how you interact with them that it hurts. The only reason Sean has been resistant to the Three Ts all of these years is because she thinks—deep down inside—that they took you away from her, and you never told her that no one could do that."

"You're right, Logan; I should be more of a father to Sean."

"That's not what I meant, sir—"

"It should be. I wouldn't tell her about the shooting because I didn't want her to worry or do something foolish to put herself in danger, but then I allowed her to deal with a new stepmother and new stepsisters without ever taking the time to talk to her and tell her that she's my first love no matter what." Banning sighed, then leaned against the car next to Logan. He said in a choked voice, "Please don't leave."

Logan stared at the man, surprised. He could tell that *please* was one word Banning did not say often. Just like his daughter. "After that scene I just caused, I would think that you would want to kick me out of your house."

"I remember how I reacted the first time Sandra got hurt

on the job. I'm certain I said some regretful things in the heat of the moment to her partner, to her, to anyone who would listen. I threw a pot of boiling pasta out of our third-floor apartment window. . . ." Banning's voice trailed off as he smiled at the memory. He placed a hand on Logan's shoulder and said, "Whether you noticed or not, you calm Sean. You give her the security to be angry and not scared. I don't like seeing my baby scared."

Logan slowly nodded, then closed the car door and followed Banning into the house. Logan instantly noticed that most of the lights in the house had been turned off and the place once more seemed quiet, almost as if the mansion wanted to forget the unpleasantness of Sean's attack. Everyone had left the living room except Sean, who arranged sheets and blankets on the foldout sofa. Banning gave Logan an encouraging pat on the shoulder, then walked up the stairs.

Logan walked into the room, and Sean momentarily paused in her motions when she saw him. She snorted in disgust, then continued spreading sheets on the sofa.

"There are three empty bedrooms around this mansion. Why are you sleeping on the sofa?"

"As soon as that man steps foot in this house, I'm going to blow his head off," Sean said simply, then threw a pillow on the sofa.

She took off the sweatshirt, revealing a tank top underneath and two guns in holsters. She unstrapped one holster, then the other, and placed them on the floor next to the sofa. Then she pulled out a tiny pistol from an ankle holster. Logan didn't know that he was smiling until Sean glared at him.

"What is so funny?" she demanded.

"Where did you have room in your suitcase to pack all of those guns?"

"I only brought one with me. I have a small collection here that Dad keeps locked in one of his safes. He doesn't like to see them, though. He hates them, if you can imagine that." Sean abruptly stopped chattering as she glared at him, then said through clenched teeth, "I thought that you were leaving. I thought that you were going to catch Madison and take all the credit."

"The best chance that I have to catch Madison is to stay right here. He has some connection with Sheldon and I'm going to find out what it is."

Sean appeared thoughtful before she murmured, "A few things confuse me. First, why would Madison shoot at Sheldon and Tracie? When I saw him—if that was him—standing behind them at the dinner party, he seemed happy. He didn't seem angry or vengeful. Second, Madison is not considered dangerous. There was no report in his file of any physical violence. It seems out of character for him to attack me."

"I don't know, but when we find him, I'll be certain to ask." His thoughts quickly changed from Madison and other criminals as he noticed the tired slump of Sean's shoulders. He crossed the room and placed one finger on the bruise on her forehead. She winced, then sighed as Logan softly pressed his lips against the spot. When he looked at her again, she had tears in her eyes. The tears tore his heart apart, but he forced a teasing note into his voice as he said, "And I wanted to stick around to see what creative things you'll do to Madison once you get your hands on him."

Sean smiled through her unshed tears. "You have a lot of faith in me, Riley."

"I know who to bet on," he said. He pulled off his shoes, then lay on the sofa with a satisfied sigh. He smiled at the disbelieving expression on Sean's face. He was relieved to see the healthy glow return to her face.

"What do you think you're doing?"

"Unless you have another gun hidden somewhere else on your body, I'm sleeping with you."

"No, you're not."

"You and me are glued at the hip, Sean," Logan said simply. "No one gets to spar with you except me."

"I don't need you as a bodyguard, Logan. I can take care of myself."

"What if Madison comes after me? Who's going to take care of me?" Logan asked with a mock expression of fear on his face. Sean rolled her eyes in annoyance at his bad acting. "I'm hiring you as my bodyguard. Can we go to sleep now? It's been a long day."

Logan thought that Sean would protest more, but instead she turned off the lamp, plunging the room into darkness. The fact that she didn't put up a fight told Logan more than anything else how much the attack had affected her. He clamped a lid on his rising anger at Madison and instead watched Sean cross the room toward him.

She crawled onto the sofa, and even though there was plenty of space for them to lie side by side, she entwined her body with his and laid her head on his chest. Logan smiled to himself, feeling surprisingly content and . . . and happy. All he needed was Sean in his arms and he suddenly felt satisfied. Logan had never felt like this around another woman, and he wondered if that was the number one reason why none of his previous relationships had worked.

"I was scared, Logan," Sean confessed in a whisper. "I've been trained for situations like that, but that didn't stop me from being scared."

"I was scared, too," Logan admitted as he wrapped his arms around her. "When I heard you scream, I . . . My heart stopped beating, Sean. If anything had happened to you . . ."

"Nothing happened," Sean assured him, then surprised him by placing a soft kiss on his lips.

"This has been a wild night, hasn't it?" Logan grinned as she laughed against his lips. He loved her laughter. He smoothed her hair from her face and saw the amusement dancing in her eyes in the moonlight through the windows.

"No one can say that things are ever boring when the Westons are around."

Sean laughed again, then kissed him as an answer. Logan felt the uncontrollable desire that raced over him like a burst dam when Sean touched him. He met her lips in one chaste kiss even though he could tell from her questing lips that she wanted more. Logan sweated with the feeling of how much more he wanted, but he remembered their situation and Banning's trust. Banning had asked him into his home because Banning loved his daughter, not because he wanted Logan to sleep with her.

It took all of Logan's strength to draw his lips from the addictive taste of hers. He placed a gentle hand on her head until she lowered it onto his chest again. She sighed in contentment and was asleep almost instantly. Logan was not so lucky. He spent the next hour remembering every torturous second from their time in the car. He realized in the darkness that he could never make love to Sean, because if he did and she hurt him like every other woman in his life had, Logan knew that he would never be able to recover.

Sean finished the last touches to her makeup in the early morning sunlight that brightened the guest room. She realized with an amused smile to herself in the mirror that with each day she had worn less and less makeup, although she had been heavy on the foundation that morning to cover the purple bruise on her forehead.

She tightened the sash on her robe and stared at the various outfits on the bed. Early that morning while she had been asleep—hard at work, guarding her family from Carl Madison—Tina and Terri had moved Sean's belongings to the guest bedroom near Logan's. Sean had awoken alone on the sofa to fresh-squeezed orange juice and croissants. The whole family had been overly bright and energetic, shining brighter than the morning sun, and naturally annoying Sean.

Banning hadn't even mentioned the guns on the floor beside the sofa. She had wolfed down the breakfast, taken her guns, and run to the guest bedroom as fast as possible to take a shower and change.

She wished that Logan had still been there. She felt a familiar tumble in her stomach when she thought about last night. She had been stunned by his outburst and prepared to skin him alive when he stormed out of the house after the attack. And without even wanting an explanation, she had been overjoyed to see him when he returned to the living room. She loved him. And Logan liked her. Nothing had changed, no matter how many short skirts she wore. Logan was her friend and that was it.

There was a knock on the door and Sean prayed that it was Logan. Instead her father walked into the room, holding a stack of papers. Sean forced a smile at her father as he watched her with the same concerned expression that Terri and Tina had worn during breakfast.

"How are you feeling, sweetheart?" Banning asked.

"The same way I was feeling thirty minutes ago, Dad. I'm fine."

"We're just worried about you, Sean. When I heard your scream, I think I aged about ten years."

"I'm sorry." She glanced out the bedroom windows that overlooked the front of the house instead of the back, as her old room had. "Have Logan and Chancy returned from scouring the area for clues?"

"Not yet. I asked our neighbors downhill if they saw or heard anything last night, and no one had."

"Madison is a professional, Dad; I'm not surprised that no one heard anything. Has Tracie returned?"

"She called and she's on her way home. She should be here in about ten minutes."

Sean turned to the dresser and began to brush her hair. She noticed that her father remained in the room and she smiled at him in the dresser mirror. "What's wrong?"

"A fax came for you this morning from Special Agent Eddie Morton. I didn't notice the cover page addressed to you and I started to read it. . . ." His voice trailed off and he stared at the papers in his hand.

Sean placed the brush on the dresser and hesitantly said, "I know Sheldon's background is none of my business, but Carl Madison is a dangerous man, and if Tracie is somehow caught up in whatever is going on, we need to know. She could be in danger."

"This report says that Carl Madison is Sheldon's uncle. His mother's brother," Banning spoke in a quiet voice. "I looked on the computer through the address labels that Tracie made for the wedding invitations. There was a label for Carl Madison, but there was no address with it. She or Sheldon must have hand-delivered it to Madison herself."

Sean wordlessly took the report from him and scanned the information on the pages. She briefly closed her eyes, then looked at her father.

"We have to talk to Tracie, and I have to contact the Bureau."

"Go easy on her, Sean. She loves Sheldon."

"I know, but if he's knowingly putting her in danger, he's going to have to answer to me."

Banning visibly hesitated, then asked softly, "What if you're wrong? What if that wasn't Madison at the party? What if the attack last night has nothing to do with Madison? We could potentially be ruining Tracie's wedding."

"Her wedding is already in danger of being ruined," Sean said. "She and Sheldon were shot at; I was attacked in this house . . . It's too much of a coincidence to not relate those events to Sheldon and Carl Madison."

Banning rubbed a hand down his face, then quietly asked, "What if none of this relates to Carl Madison? What if there's a faceless monster out there trying to hurt my girls?"

Sean crossed the room to wrap her arms around her father. Banning returned her embrace, and she was surprised to realize that tears floated in her eyes. For the first time in her life, her father had asked for her advice and he wanted to know the answer.

"If it isn't Madison, we'll find whoever it is. We'll get to the bottom of this." Sean pressed a kiss to her father's stubble-covered cheek. He hadn't shaved. She couldn't remember the last time she had seen her father unshaven. "Don't worry, Dad."

"You do what's best." He turned to the door, then hesitated for a second before he turned to face her again. "And, Sean, Sheldon's background is your business. Everything that goes on in this family is your business. Understand?"

Sean swallowed the sudden lump in her throat, then croaked out, "Yes."

"After the wedding, when you and Logan catch the bad guys, maybe we can go skydiving."

"Skydiving?" Sean repeated, laughing in the middle of her amazement.

"I do that every once in a while," Banning said dismissively, as if he discussed the weather. "I've been bungee jumping, and I was in a drag race—"

"Dad," Sean admonished.

"It's all safe—except the drag racing, but that was only once."

Sean had so many questions, but didn't know where to start. Instead she grinned and said, "I would love to go skydiving. And I bet Tina would love to go more than me."

"Tina wouldn't go skydiving in a million years," Banning said.

"You should ask her. I bet she'll surprise you," Sean said, then laughed at his confused expression. "Trust me."

"I do," he whispered, then abruptly laughed and asked, "Do you know something about my wife that I don't know?"

"Talk to her, and I'm sure that she'll tell you anything you want to know." Sean pointedly glanced at her watch and said, "I have to get dressed."

Banning threw his hands up in surrender, then winked at her and walked out of the room, closing the door behind him.

Sixteen

Half an hour later, Sean walked onto the patio. She blinked at the bright sunlight but her eyes quickly adjusted and she spotted Terri, who sat on a patio chair. With a hand resting on her stomach, Terri watched Tracie stroke through the swimming pool. Sean momentarily watched Tracie. Tracie had always been a powerful swimmer. Sean had taught her how to swim when Tracie was nine years old.

Banning and Tina walked onto the patio behind Sean. The three exchanged glances, then walked across the patio to the end of the pool. Tracie rose from the water when she saw the group. She removed her swimming goggles and smiled at her family. When no one smiled back, Tracie's smile dripped off her face like the water.

"Is something wrong?" Tracie asked.

"Get out the water, Tracie," Sean said tonelessly. She didn't wait for a response but walked to the patio table where Terri already sat. Banning and Tina followed Sean and the three took their chairs. Sean looked at each person at the table. They looked like the bench in an appellate court— somber faces and blank eyes. Tracie climbed out the pool and wrapped a white terry-cloth robe around her body.

"What's going on?" she asked nervously as she sat in the chair in between her mother and Banning.

Sean unfolded the paper that she held in her hands and

set it on the table. It was the picture of Carl Madison. Tracie's eyes widened as she looked from the paper to Sean.

"I'm going to ask you one last time, Tracie. Have you seen this man?"

"I already told you that I haven't," Tracie firmly said.

"Tell Sean the truth, Tracie," Tina ordered.

"We know that he's Sheldon's uncle," Banning said.

Tears filled Tracie's eyes and she took a deep breath before she said, "Sheldon wanted his uncle at our wedding. He's not a bad man."

"He sells weapons to criminals, Tracie," Banning said, his disbelief in her proclamation apparent in his voice. "Those weapons kill people. He is a bad man, and he's wanted by the law."

"Tell Sean where he is," Tina said gently.

"I can't."

"Are you protecting Sheldon?" Banning demanded. "He's not worth it, if he would involve you in this."

"Sheldon doesn't know where Carl is and neither do I. He won't tell us after the . . . the shooting." Tracie wiped away her tears, then admitted, "There was more to the shooting that I didn't tell you. The other car didn't initially shoot at us; it forced us off the road. A man got out of the car and demanded that Sheldon tell him where Carl was. Sheldon didn't know. The man pulled out a gun and Sheldon took off, but the first bullet still pierced the side of the car. We wouldn't have told you, except Dad saw the bullet in the car before I could get it fixed."

"You and Sheldon both could have been killed protecting this man," Terri cried, grabbing her sister's hands across the table.

"We're not protecting him," Tracie protested. "You don't understand. Sheldon is closer to his uncle than he is to his parents. His uncle is the world to him. He wants him at our wedding. We were both surprised when Carl showed up at the dinner party. We expected him at the wedding, but not before. I knew Sean had seen him."

"Why did you lie to Sean?" Banning asked gently.

"Because Carl said that he was going to be at the wedding. People are trying to kill him and he has to leave the country, but he promised Sheldon that he would see him be married first. We didn't want Sean to alert the authorities. Word would get out and then the people who are trying to kill him would know where he was, too." Tracie turned to Sean and pleaded, "Sean, Carl is not the man you think he is."

"Carl attacked me last night, Tracie," Sean said, trying not to allow her anger to show.

"No, he couldn't have," Tracie cried in disbelief.

Sean moved aside the hair that hung in her eyes and, when Tracie covered her mouth with one hand, she knew that Tracie saw the bruise. "Someone did. If it wasn't Carl, then who was it?"

"Carl wouldn't do that," Tracie insisted. "I met him. I talked to him. He's kind, just like Sheldon. He wouldn't hurt a fly. Whoever attacked you last night must have been with the same people who shot at Sheldon and me."

"Does Sheldon know what his uncle does for a living?" Sean asked.

"He only knows that whatever Carl does, it's illegal. His parents forbade Carl from entering their house when Sheldon was in junior high school."

Banning tiredly sighed, then looked at Sean and asked, "What are you going to do, Sean?"

"Don't ruin our wedding, Sean," Tracie cried.

"Sean won't be ruining anything, Tracie. You and Sheldon did that all by yourselves when you lied to her and to us," Tina corrected.

"I have to call the Bureau, Tracie," Sean said softly.

Tears rolled down Tracie's face and she buried her face in her hands. She shook her head. Sean glanced at her father, but his expression was blank. Tina laid a comforting hand on Tracie's back but encouragingly nodded at Sean. Terri squeezed Sean's hand. Sean knew what she should do. She should call her supervisors and have an undercover team waiting to apprehend Carl as soon as he stepped foot inside the Weston house for the wedding. She should personally want Madison's head on a chopping block for attacking her.

But Sean could still remember Tracie as a five-year-old little girl with two cottonballs as pigtails. Sean hadn't admitted it to herself then, but she had fallen in love with that little girl, and even when Sean told herself that she dreaded being at the mansion, she always looked forward to seeing Tracie. Sean knew that Logan would be angry and point out the fact that Madison had attacked her, but Sean knew that whoever attacked her had not meant to kill her or else she would be dead now. And a small part of her believed Tracie's faith in the man.

Sean couldn't believe it herself, but she said, "I guess it won't hurt to wait and contact the Bureau after the wedding."

Tracie looked up with a watery smile, while the rest of her family looked at her with surprised expressions. "Really?"

"As soon as I spot him at the wedding, he'll gain me as another shadow. He's not leaving Santa Barbara a free man, but I won't stop Sheldon from having his uncle at the wedding."

"Sean—"

"You can't tell Sheldon or Carl," Sean cut off Tracie's gratitude. "The only reason I'm doing this is because it means so much to you to have him there, but you should consider him FBI property from this moment on."

Tracie wordlessly nodded in agreement, then reached across the table to hug Sean. Sean squeezed her in return and smiled at her father, who watched her with tear-filled eyes.

"You won't regret this, Sean, I promise," Tracie whispered.

"We have to leave for the rehearsal at church soon, Tracie," Terri said, standing and offering her hand to her sister.

Tracie smiled one last time at Sean, then allowed Terri to lead her into the house.

"Do you think that she'll tell Sheldon?" Tina uncertainly asked Sean.

"She won't tell him. It'll eat her alive for the next two days, but she won't tell him," Sean said somberly.

"Thank you, Sean," Tina said with a grateful smile.

"For what?"

"For giving Tracie these two days."

"She's my sister. It's the least I could do; besides, if she and Sheldon don't know where Madison is, there's no point in calling the Bureau," Sean muttered with a casual shrug. Although, judging from Banning and Tina's expressions, they were not fooled by her act.

"We make a good team, don't we?" Banning asked cheerfully.

"I should bring you, Tina, and Terri to the interrogation room at the Bureau. You three cracked Tracie in about three seconds flat."

"Sean!" The part-time housekeeper, Estelle, called her name from the open living room doors. She held up the telephone and called, "It's your mother."

Sean glared at her father and said through clenched teeth, "Tell me that you did not call Mom and tell her what happened last night."

"I called her," Tina said defensively. "We made a pact a long time ago to keep each other informed about this family."

"Thanks, Tina," Sean muttered, trying not to show her surprise at the news that Sandra and Tina had any sort of agreement. Sean wasn't aware that her mother had ever spoken to Tina.

"You're welcome," Tina said with a sweet smile.

"You have the right to have a lawyer present when you

speak with Sheriff Weston," Banning teased Sean, which caused Tina to giggle. The two shared a look filled with revealed secrets and truths, and Sean bet that Tina would not be bored any longer.

Sean groaned in frustration, then jumped from the chair and stalked across the patio. She knew that her mother would eventually find out about the attack, because her mother always knew everything, but Sean had hoped that she would have Carl behind bars before Sandra knew. She restrained her anger long enough to smile at Estelle, who always seemed petrified whenever Sean stood within ten feet of her. Sean took the telephone and walked into the hallway so that Banning and Tina could not eavesdrop on the conversation.

"Mom, I'm all right," Sean said into the telephone.

"Tell me what happened."

"An intruder dressed in all black with his face covered was in my room. We fought; he escaped. That's the short version."

"And the long version?" Sandra asked coolly.

"The long version includes me screaming Logan's name like a little girl."

"Logan is there?"

"Didn't your spy tell you that?" Sean dryly asked while rolling her eyes.

"I'm glad Tina called me. At least someone is thinking of me in the middle of all this."

"Guilt trips are not your style, Mom."

"Thank you for reminding me," Sandra said in that expressionless tone that Sean never could determine whether it was sarcasm or just her normal voice. "Deputy Howell and I will be there early tomorrow morning before the wedding, unless you need me to come now."

"I'm all right."

"Do you have any idea who the intruder was or what he wanted?"

"No," Sean lied.

"I'm going to have to look over your father's security system when I get there," Sandra said more to herself than to Sean. She cleared her throat, then said, "At least Logan is there."

"And if he weren't?" Sean demanded.

"Then I would be there this afternoon."

"You don't think that I can take care of myself?"

"I know that you can, but I like the idea of having Logan around. May I ask why is he around?"

"Only if you'll tell me why Deputy Howell is coming with you to the wedding."

Sandra didn't respond, and Sean sighed in relief. Sean knew that some women considered their mothers their best friends and they talked about everything—men, careers, cooking tips. Sean and Sandra did not have that relationship. They were best friends and they talked about everything— except men. Sean didn't know if she could suddenly change her entire view of her interaction with her mother to talk about Logan.

"If everything is all right then I will see you tomorrow morning," Sandra said, returning to the business at hand.

"Wait . . . Tina told me that you . . . you and she have a pact. . . ." Sean's voice trailed off as she tried to get her mother to share her emotions. In a way it was easier to open up to her father than to her mother.

"The first summer that I drove you to stay with your father and Tina, I didn't leave when you thought I did. I spied on you," Sandra answered Sean's unspoken question.

"You didn't." Sean gasped in shock.

"Do you really think that I would allow my only child to spend the entire summer with a woman whom I didn't know?"

"You didn't trust Dad?"

"At that point in his career, your father didn't have much control over the hours he worked. He usually was at the office twelve to fourteen hours a day. Even though he married the owner's daughter, I knew that Banning would never allow that to positively or negatively influence his career. Everything he did at that company, he did on his own. So who do you think took care of you while he was at work?"

Sandra didn't wait for an answer but continued, "The second night that I sneaked onto the grounds, Tina was waiting for me at the gate. We talked and we made a pact to keep each other informed about our daughters, about our lives, about the man we had in common. If I had to have another woman assist in raising my daughter, I'm glad it was Tina Harrison-Weston."

"I never knew," Sean whispered, gripping the telephone.

"There are a lot of things that you don't know about me, Sean." Sandra audibly hesitated, then abruptly said, "I love you."

Before she had time to react, Sean heard the dial tone in her ear. Her mother had hung up, either to run to an emergency or, more likely, to avoid any displays of emotion.

Sean smiled as she whispered into the receiver, "I love you, too, Mom."

"What?" Logan exploded, whirling around to face Sean. He had spent half the morning traipsing through the hillsides around the Weston manor, searching for clues about the intruder. While he had sweated through a shirt and a pair of shorts, Sean apparently had been lounging by the swimming pool selling him down the river. Logan still hadn't taken a shower, but had been on his way to the bathroom when Sean knocked on the door.

He forgot the towel wrapped around his waist and quickly grabbed for it as it almost fell from his sudden movement. Sean's eyes momentarily grew wide and she quickly moved across his room far from him to sit on the window seat. Logan felt that part of him that grew exponentially whenever she was around begin to swell as he watched Sean's hips sway beneath the simple black dress that she wore before she sat. He forced himself to take several deep breaths. They were just friends. He had promised her that he would not attack her anymore. He suddenly cursed himself for his big mouth.

"I promised Tracie that I wouldn't call the Bureau until I could confirm that Madison was at the wedding," Sean repeated simply, meeting Logan's eyes.

"Are you insane, Sean? I knew we should have taken you to the hospital about that bump to your head."

"This is not about the bump to my head or . . . It's about Tracie. She's never asked me for anything in her life except this. I have to give it to her."

Logan rolled his eyes in disbelief, then fell on the bed, not caring that the towel split dangerously on his right thigh. He did notice that Sean's eyes were glued to the spot where the most skin was visible. No sex. He had promised her. He had promised himself. No more broken hearts, no more five-weekers. With a snap he closed the two sides of the towel.

"If you aren't going to think about yourself and the fact that this man tried to kill you, then think about me. What about my career? Bringing in Carl Madison could be the step I need to my next promotion." Sean didn't answer as she stared at the floor, and Logan groaned in disbelief. "I cannot believe this! You're going to allow a wanted criminal like Carl Madison to disappear to give your spoiled sister a Cinderella wedding."

"When I was a freshmen in college at UC Santa Cruz, Tracie came to visit me for one weekend," Sean began in a quiet voice that made Logan pause in his ranting. "She was thirteen or fourteen, too young to be in a college dorm for the weekend. We had so much fun, Logan. For one weekend I talked about boys, I complained about my weight. I didn't go target shooting once. Tracie always has looked up to me. No matter how withdrawn I was, she's always loved me.

When I would crawl on the roof to cry or to scream, sometimes when I'd crawl back into my room, Tracie would be asleep on my bed, waiting for me. And I never told her how much it meant to me. I owe her for that."

Logan knew that he would give in. He always did where Sean was concerned, and he had a feeling that he always would.

"Fine," he reluctantly muttered. "We won't tell anyone about Madison, but at the wedding tomorrow I'm in on the capture."

Sean stood and began to wander around the room, but she didn't leave. Logan watched her, enjoying the way the silk material of the dress clung to her body in all the spots that he had dreamed about kissing and touching while she lay in his arms the night before. He had spent five years without it; now he couldn't go more than thirty seconds in Sean's company without thinking about it.

"I have to take a shower now," Logan grumbled, trying to rush her from his room.

Sean didn't head for the door but stopped at the dresser, where she picked up his watch and studied it as if it were the most interesting object she had ever seen. He caught her darting occasional glances at his bare chest, and Logan grinned. Sean Weston was trying to discreetly ogle him. Logan's face burned, and he wondered if he was blushing for the first time in his life.

"What are you going to do until the rehearsal dinner?"

"I haven't decided," he lied.

"No skydiving with my father?" She quickly turned to him to catch his first, unguarded reaction.

Logan laughed at her antics, then said, "I'm glad that he told you."

"He didn't tell me everything, but I know that you two did not go golfing yesterday morning."

"We went hang gliding."

"You? Logan Riley, the only man I know afraid of heights, went hang gliding?"

"Yesterday your father needed a friend. I was there, He's a good person."

"They all are," she said, sounding surprised. "I guess I was so busy making fun of them that I never realized how good they are."

"I'm glad that you realize it now," Logan said sincerely.

Sean laughed, then leaned against the dresser to stare at him as she said, "You could come to the rehearsal. I can't adequately protect you if I can't see you."

Logan suspiciously watched her, wondering why she wanted him at the rehearsal. She continued to lean against the dresser and not move one muscle. He finally admitted, "I'm going to Sheldon's house while you all are at rehearsal."

"I knew it," she shouted, clapping her hands together. "You just agreed that we wouldn't apprehend Madison until after the wedding."

"That's because we don't know where he is," Logan pointed out. "You promised Tracie that you wouldn't call the Bureau until you spotted him at the wedding. You didn't say anything about if we found him on our own."

"Logan—"

"If I find him, I won't take him. We'll rotate twenty-four-hour surveillance on him. How's that?" He relented so fast that it made his own head spin.

"I can't stop you, so it'll have to do." Sean appeared suddenly nervous as she set his watch on the dresser with a loud bang and said, "I guess I should leave you alone so that you can take your shower."

"You don't have to leave," Logan said with a grin as he stood and walked across the room toward her. His "no sex" mantra was completely forgotten as he watched Sean's chest rise and fall underneath the black dress. "You could join me."

Sean appeared flustered and stared at his bare toes, and Logan silently cursed himself. "I didn't mean that," he muttered.

Sean shook her head as she laughed and said, "You can't help yourself, can you? You see a woman and you have to flirt, whether you want to or not."

Logan shrugged in response, not bothering to correct her. She could believe that he flirted with every woman who crossed his path, because Logan found the truth more difficult to explain to himself. He wasn't flirting with Sean; he was begging her.

Sean continued to smile as she studied him. "I guess this means that you've recovered from your confession last night."

"I'm a swan," Logan said bluntly.

"You'll find her, Logan, I promise." Sean comfortingly patted his arm, then turned and walked from the room.

Logan stared at the closed door and wondered if he already had found her.

Seventeen

Logan stared over the Santa Barbara beach below the small white church that sat on a hilltop and overlooked the wealthy, the poor, and everyone in between. It was another picture-perfect day in southern California. The sun shimmered on the ocean waves that crashed onto the beach with relaxing regularity. Men and women strolled across the beach, even as the sun's magnitude dimmed in the sky.

It was a gorgeous day, when a man should have been frolicking in the ocean with his woman, if the man were the type who could frolic without caring what anyone else thought. Logan would have loved to frolic anywhere with Sean, except that he had a feeling she would throw him into the ocean if she had any clue about his thoughts. Logan was in love with Sean. The truth had hit him like a balled fist in the gut about an hour ago.

After his fruitless search in Sheldon's home, where Logan hadn't found any clues on Sheldon or Madison, Logan had planned to drive to the beach and spend the rest of his afternoon actually having that vacation that he claimed to be in Santa Barbara for. Then he had spotted a picture of Sean and her stepsisters in Sheldon's house and Logan had stared at Sean's image for ten minutes before he could admit it to himself: he was in love with Sean Weston. The impossible had happened: Logan had found someone to love. Someone who would never love him back because she would never believe that he was sincere.

Logan didn't even know when it had happened, when he had fallen in love with Sean. He knew that it had happened long before they drove to Santa Barbara. Maybe the first day he saw her, when she knocked on his apartment door and demanded—not asked—for him to untie her boxing gloves.

Logan groaned in frustration, then pulled the cellular telephone from his shirt pocket. He dialed the number to his brother's cellular phone.

"This is Riley," Cary's gruff voice greeted.

"This is Riley," Logan said in an identical rough, manly-man voice.

"No, this is Riley." Cary suddenly laughed, then muttered, "Why do I fall for that every time?"

"Where are you?"

"Where am I every day at six-oh-seven? Fighting traffic on Market Street, trying to reach the Two-eighty."

Logan laughed to himself. He would bet that if he asked his brother, Cary could tell Logan the details of his day down to the nearest second. Cary was a control freak. Logan was almost a control freak, which was better than being a straight-out control freak like Cary.

"As you're stuck in your car in traffic like every other mindless robot in the Bay Area, I'm sitting on the steps of a beautiful church that overlooks the Pacific Ocean," Logan teased. "It's a balmy seventy-six-degrees, and I haven't heard a phone ring or a computer beep all day."

"It sounds like you're having fun on your vacation," Cary noted. "What else have you done?"

"What else have I done," Logan murmured to himself as he rubbed his chin. "I've gone hang gliding, someone attacked Sean, and I think that I'm in love with Sean. All in all, this vacation has been just what I expected."

Logan laughed at the silence from the other end of the phone. Cary finally said one word, "What?!"

"I know, I know, I hate heights, but Banning—Sean's father—wanted to go hang gliding, and he's about thirty years older than me. How would I have looked if I had sat in the car?"

Cary abruptly asked, "Someone attacked Sean? When did this happen? Is she all right? Do you need backup?"

"She's fine," Logan responded. "We do not need backup. Repeat. We do not need backup."

Logan knew that if he told Cary about the possibility of Madison appearing at the wedding, Cary would catch the first flight to Santa Barbara, ostensibly to "supervise," but more likely because he didn't trust Logan or Sean to catch Madison.

"Are you certain, Logan? I can have a team down there in half an hour—"

"Sean and I have the situation under control."

"I don't know if I like the sound of that—"

Logan finally lost patience with his brother's interest in violence and snapped, "Did you hear the other part, Cary? About me being in love? That's a big deal!"

"It is?" Cary asked uncertainly.

"Yes, it is," Logan retorted angrily. "Don't you even care?"

"Of course I care; I just don't know why your loving Sean is supposed to be earth-stopping news," Cary said hesitantly.

Logan threw up his hands in frustration and tried to be patient as he said, "I'm in love with Sean, Cary. Sean Weston, my next-door neighbor. It sure as hell surprised me, so it should be a surprise to you."

"Logan, you spend more time with Sean than you do with the women you're so-called dating. You have more fun with her than you ever have had with any of your five-weekers. You went with her to Santa Barbara just because she asked.

And you talk about her all the time," Cary explained patiently. "I've known that you were in love with her for the last two years. The real surprise is that you're just now realizing it."

Logan opened his mouth but no sound came out. He wanted to be outraged, to tell his brother that he was completely wrong, but he could only gape like an idiot. When he did speak, he could manage only, "You're the one who told me to come to Santa Barbara for vacation, not because of Sean."

"I threw you that excuse so you would stop feeling tormented about it and just go with her," Cary said simply.

"This big-brother thing has gone to your head," Logan muttered.

Cary ignored the remark and asked, "Does Sean know how you feel?"

"No," Logan muttered. He groaned, then ran a hand through his hair and said, "What's wrong with me, Cary? Why do I want to ruin the only friendship with a woman that I've ever had?"

"Maybe that's why you do love her. You and Sean are friends. Could you say that about any of the five-weekers?"

"No," Logan answered. "Maybe I shouldn't say anything to her. I don't want to end the one relationship in my life with a woman that lasted longer than five weeks."

"I don't— There it is!" Through the receiver, Logan heard a squeal of tires, then a string of Cary's colorful curses.

"What are you doing?" Logan asked, laughing as he imagined the traffic maneuvers Cary was executing in the middle of San Francisco traffic.

"I have spent the last month launching a full-scale search-and-acquire mission encompassing the West Coast. I saw this baby crib on the Lifetime channel that I must obtain and I can't find it anywhere. But I just saw it in a window of a store on Market Street. That crib is mine."

"Since when do you watch the Lifetime channel?"

"It was late and I couldn't sleep," Cary muttered. "Shit, Logan, a woman—five-foot-four, Caucasian, about a hundred and forty pounds—is looking at my crib. I have to go."

"Please remember that she is a civilian and this is not a war."

"As long as the civilian doesn't get in my way and I get the crib, everything will be fine," Cary muttered.

Logan laughed, then said, "Good luck, brother. I'll be certain to tell my niece or nephew about the Crib Battle one day."

Logan heard Cary's hesitation before he softly asked, "Are you all right, Logan, about Sean?"

"What can I do? I can't force her to love me. I know that she's attracted to me, I know that I can seduce her into sleeping with me, but I want more than that."

"Somehow I have a feeling that it will all work out. If you need any help, call me." Cary suddenly groaned, then said, "The subject is calling over a salesperson and pointing to my crib. I'll call you in the morning."

Logan listened to the dial tone for a moment, then pressed the disconnect button. He stared at the ocean and had just convinced himself to find a beach bunny to spend the rest of the weekend with and forget this love idea, because Cary was wrong and he had not loved Sean for two years, when he heard voices coming from inside the church. The double doors opened and the wedding party spilled out of the church. For a wedding with over two hundred guests, the wedding party was small. Tracie had four bridesmaids—her two sisters and her two roommates from college. In return, Sheldon had four matching groomsmen. Of course, the small size of the wedding party did nothing to diminish the price tag. Logan didn't know how much weddings went for every day, but he knew that not all of them had cakes priced at five thousand dollars as he had seen on the bill in Sheldon's house.

Logan stood, feeling strangely nervous as he searched the

familiar faces for Sean. Now that he knew he loved her, he didn't know how to act around her. His palms grew wet and his stomach rumbled. For a frightening moment, Logan thought that he would fall down unconscious. He could imagine Sean's laughter when she found him facedown on the steps of the church. Logan could not tell her how he felt. He would not ruin their friendship with his ridiculous vows of love that Sean would not believe and would respond to with laughter.

"Hi, Logan," Terri said when she noticed him standing to the side of the entrance. "I thought that we were going to meet you at the restaurant for dinner?"

"I got through with my errands a little early."

"You spent the day looking for Carl Madison, didn't you?" Terri said with a suspicious gleam in her eyes.

"I'm on vacation, Terri."

"You didn't answer my question."

"How are you feeling?" Logan asked, switching the subject.

Terri's smile disappeared as she glanced around to make certain that none of the others listened to their conversation. "Didn't Sean tell you?"

"Tell me what?"

Terri heavily sighed, then whispered, "I'm pregnant." Logan examined Terri's apprehensive expression and figured that the only safe response was not to respond. Terri said, "I haven't told anyone but Sean . . . and now you."

"When are you planning to tell Chancy?"

Terri's eyes grew wide and she recoiled from Logan as if he had struck her. "How did you know that Chancy was the father?"

"I didn't know it was a secret that you two were together."

"It's a secret, Logan. It's a big secret. . . . Besides, we aren't together anymore."

"Why?"

Terri said through clenched teeth, "I don't like men who are after me only for my family's money."

"Are we talking about the same man who looks at you like a giant, slobbering puppy dog?"

Terri bashfully laughed, then said, "He does not. Does he?"

"If you love him, you should tell him, Terri."

"I've known him for only three months."

"What does that have to do with anything? A relationship can last two days or two years and none of that matters, except if you truly love the other person." Logan smiled at the wisdom in his own words that he should listen to. Maybe Sean was right: he was a swan. There was no five-week curse. His past relationships hadn't lasted because he hadn't been in love with the other women. Logan turned his attention back to Terri and asked her, "Do you love Chancy?"

"Yes," Terri said without hesitation.

"And he loves you."

"Are you sure?" Terri asked doubtfully.

"He's in love with you," Logan answered. "He'll want you and the baby. And if he doesn't, you can always have Sean break a few of his limbs until he changes his mind."

"There's something about you, Logan, that makes me believe everything you say."

"Really? I have some beachfront property in Florida that I can sell you too."

Terri laughed, then said, "Sean is still in the church with Mom."

"What are they doing in there?"

"Sean is a great tango dancer, but she can't walk down the aisle without tripping herself and her escort. Elton said that he wouldn't walk with her unless she learned how to walk."

"Please tell me that Sean hurt him," Logan pleaded.

"I'm sorry to disappoint you, Logan, but Sean was concentrating too hard on the steps to pay attention to Elton's insults," Tracie said, while patting his shoulders. "Mom is working with her in the church. They should be only a few more minutes. I'll see you at the restaurant."

Logan nodded in acknowledgment, then forced himself to walk into the church. The cool, calm interior framed the gleaming oak pews and ornate altar at the front. His parents had taken him and his siblings to church every week when they were alive. Logan hadn't been in a church since their deaths, and he was glad to return. It had been a long time, and he welcomed the familiar scent of wood polish and ancient books.

Sean and Tina stood at the front of the church. Sean's head was bent as she concentrated on Tina's feet, while Tina counted out loud in time to the music the organist played, filling the sanctuary with the powerful, deep sound.

Logan found himself smiling as he watched Sean. He had never seen her look more beautiful. With her face scrunched in concentration and her full attention on Tina, Logan could watch her without fear that she would notice. His heart beat faster. His palms grew more damp. Maybe he could tell her that he loved her. Maybe this time he had found the right woman, who could love him in return.

Sean finally threw up her hands in helplessness and Tina laughed, then motioned for the organist to stop playing. The organist shook her tightly curled gray head in disbelief at Sean, then walked out of the church. Sean laughed until she turned and saw Logan standing near the entrance of the sanctuary. Logan grinned as the smile faded from her face. His nerves instantly disappeared. All he needed was to see Sean annoyed with him and he felt calm and back to his normal self. Tina's reception was more welcoming as she waved at him and began to walk toward him.

"How was the first real day of your vacation?" Tina asked cheerfully.

"Uninspiring," Logan murmured, then glanced at Sean, who continued to stand as far from him as possible. She didn't seem on the verge of moving toward him anytime soon. He turned to Tina and nervously smiled when he caught her watching him. "Tina, I want to apologize for what I said last night, or, I mean, early this morning. After Sean's attack, I was angry and out of control. I'm sorry, Tina; I didn't mean to hurt you."

"I understand, Logan," Tina said with a sweet smile as she squeezed his hand.

"I hope that one day I can make it up to you."

"You love Sean, and you make her happy. You've already made it up to me." Logan was surprised that Tina knew the truth before he had. She squeezed his arm, then glanced at her watch and said, "Banning went to the office for a few hours today. I'm going to pick him up; then I'll see you both at the dinner." Tina waved to Sean, then walked from the church.

The door closed and it echoed against the high ceilings. Logan glanced around the church, at the colorful stained-glass windows, the painting of Jesus on the cross behind the altar. Standing in the church for the first time Logan accepted his love for Sean. He accepted that he was a rare species of man who loved once and loved truly. He had never loved those other women. He had never felt as at peace and happy with any of them as he did with Sean. Now he just needed to find the courage to tell Sean how he felt.

"Are you all right?" Sean asked as she finally approached him. "You have a goofy smile on your face."

"I'm fine." Logan took her hand and pressed a kiss in the palm. He was encouraged when Sean didn't pull her hand away. Logan smiled and caressed the soft skin on her face. He could see hesitation begin to creep into her eyes, and he quickly withdrew his hand from her face and led her from the church.

They walked out of the church. Logan inhaled the sea breeze that circled across the hilltop. All the members of the wedding party and their cars had disappeared, leaving

Logan's car alone at the bottom of the hill. If Logan hadn't seen a few people far below on the beach, he would have thought that he and Sean were the only people in the world.

"Did you find anything out at Sheldon's?" Sean asked, as she tried to pull her hand from his grip.

"Nothing, except that he has about ten pairs of Dockers."

"That's not a crime."

"It should be."

"I was watching Tracie and Sheldon. . . ." Sean's voice trailed off as she once more tried to yank free from his hand. She glared at him and ordered, "Let go of my hand, Logan."

"Why?"

"You promised," she reminded him.

"Promised what?"

"You promised there would be no more kisses, no more . . . no more challenges. Remember our talk last night? You're searching for that swan, remember?"

Logan smiled slightly at her description of their talk; then he softly asked, "Do you really not like my kisses, Sean?"

He saw the truth in her eyes. She liked his touch. She liked his kisses, but that was probably all she liked. No matter how long he had not slept with another woman, Sean still saw him as an insincere playboy. For the first time in five years, Logan wished that he hadn't been so careful in charming every woman who crossed his path and that he had waited for just one—Sean.

She ignored his question and said, "I watched Tracie and Sheldon during the rehearsal. I don't know if we can trust her."

"You want to call the Bureau now and I'll call SFPD?"

"No, but tonight you're going to have to forgo your beauty sleep." At the mention of sleep, Logan resisted the urge to touch her, to place his lips against hers and to feel those strange sensations race through his body. "You and I are doing a stakeout."

"Stakeout?"

"Sheldon is not leaving our sight until he and Tracie get on the plane for their honeymoon in the Bahamas."

"Why? Tracie told you that Madison promised to be at the wedding."

"Maybe I'm paranoid, but I don't trust the word of the biggest contraband dealer in the United States," Sean said, with sarcasm dripping from her voice.

"I see your point," Logan murmured.

"If Sheldon and Madison are as close as Tracie thinks, then Madison may not come to the wedding, but he will say good-bye to his nephew. If he does we'll be there."

"Sheldon likes me. I could talk my way into spending the day with him. Some people actually like my company."

Sean glanced at him but didn't respond as she opened the unlocked passenger door of his car. "We don't want to scare off Madison. He can smell a cop a mile away, and I doubt that he'll contact Sheldon if another person besides Tracie is around."

Logan walked around the car to the driver's-side door, then stared at Sean over the hood. "Basically you're saying that we're doing a fruitless stakeout to satisfy your paranoia."

"You don't have to join me," Sean practically challenged him.

"Do you really think that I'm going to miss the chance to be alone with you in a car in a private spot with no one around to hear you scream?" Logan grinned as she shook her head; then he got into the car and gunned the motor. He was only human.

Eighteen

As Sean sat across the table from Logan at the rehearsal dinner, it was becoming more and more difficult for her to keep her mouth closed. She had wanted to convince Logan that she was his matching swan. Then she realized how foolish she was being. If she told him that she loved him and that she always had loved him, he would get that pitying look in his eyes, as he had when she first asked him to come with her to Santa Barbara. Sean could not bear to see that look in his eyes again.

She gulped down the contents of her wineglass, then stared across the table at Logan, who was in the middle of an animated conversation with Damming and Chancy. He was so gorgeous. His dimple winked in the candlelight, his brown skin glowed, and his smile should have been declared illegal, because it made women do unthinkable things. Sean shook her head. She didn't have a chance with him. He was her friend and that was all the two would ever be. Logan had never even been remotely interested in her until she donned her Toni Braxton dresses. She told herself that she didn't want a man who wanted her only if she wore a dress that was the size of a small plastic bag, but Sean couldn't fool herself: she wanted Logan.

"You've been quiet tonight, Sean. Are you all right?" Terri asked softly. She sat to the right of Sean at the long table that seated twelve. The occupants of the table created the most noise in the large Greek restaurant, which was a considerable feat with the number of other diners and the Greek musicians who blasted toe-tapping music at the front of the room.

"I'm fine," Sean said, drawing her attention from Logan to smile at Terri. "How are you and . . . and the rest of you?"

"We're fine," Terri whispered, then smiled across the table. Sean followed Terri's gaze and gasped when she saw Chancy, with the same smile that Logan used on Sean when he thought no one watched, staring back at Terri.

Sean grabbed Terri's arm and Terri reluctantly drew her gaze from Chancy. "Chancy? Chancy is the father?"

"We're going to tell Mom and Dad the day after the wedding. I don't want to detract from Tracie's big day. Even though it's been only three months, it's for real, Sean. I think it'll last like Mom and Dad." The loving expression in Terri's eyes disappeared as she stared at Sean with wide eyes. "I'm sorry, Sean, I meant my mom and your dad. . . . Your parents are divorced. I can't believe I said that."

Sean realized that two days ago, Terri's comment probably would have made her angry, would have made her add another strike against the Three Ts. But, two days ago, Sean realized, she would have been immature. She was a part of Weston family number two, and that was for better or for worse.

"It's all right, Terri," Sean said, squeezing Terri's hand.

"I guess sometimes I forget that you're not my real sister. . . . I mean, I think your real mom is a wonderful woman but . . . I'm making this worse."

"I heard the compliment buried in there somewhere," Sean assured her as the two embraced.

From the corner of her eye, Sean saw Logan watching her with a strange smile on his face. When she pulled away from Terri, she returned his smile with a shy one of her own. Logan winked at her, causing her treacherous heart to flutter at the flirtatious action. As usual, completely oblivious to her feelings, Logan happily resumed devouring his food.

Banning suddenly stood and tapped a knife against his water glass. The talking at the table gradually subsided until everyone stared at him, including a few other patrons in the restaurant. The musicians stopped playing their instruments and filed into the kitchen, leaving only a low murmur of noise in the restaurant.

"This is the part of the dinner that Tracie begged me to not to do, but I have to, sweetheart. I have to tell Sheldon in front of all these people what a wonderful woman he will marry tomorrow," Banning announced as he winked at Tracie, whose chocolate skin flushed as she shook her head in embarrassment. Banning's face sobered and he reached for Tina, who sat next to him. She placed her hand in his and they both looked at Tracie and Sheldon. "Tracie, I've watched you grow from a little girl into the inspiring woman you are today. And I'm just . . ." Banning's voice trailed off as he visibly struggled to control his emotions.

People around the table *ahh*ed as Banning shook his head, unable to continue. Sean felt her own throat clog with emotions. Later she would blame that as the reason she stood. Banning looked across the table at her, surprised. When she smiled at him, Banning gratefully nodded, then sat down. Sean didn't even mind that the ball of emotions in her throat made it difficult for her to talk or that the image of Tracie was slightly blurred by her tears.

Her voice sounded soft and shaky to her own ears as she said, "I think what Dad is trying to say is that he and I both feel blessed and grateful for having the chance to know and love you, and to have you love us in return. When we were little, you, Terri, and I didn't get the chance to choose each other as sisters. No one can choose who they're related to, but we can choose who our family is. And because my father was smart enough to marry your mother, we became a family. And the truth is, Tracie, if I had the chance to choose, I wouldn't want anything to be different. I don't think I've ever said it, but I love you."

Tracie smiled as tears rolled down her cheeks. Sheldon wrapped an arm around Tracie and handed her a handkerchief. Sean laughed through her own tears as she noticed other people at the table with tears shining in the candlelight. Sean glanced at Logan, who watched her with that same strange expression that he had worn in the church. Sean grabbed her refilled wineglass off the table and raised it to the engaged couple.

"Here's to my little sister and to the man who won her heart. Love her, Sheldon, because, speaking from experience, having Tracie's love makes you one of the luckiest people in the world." Sean quickly covered her mouth as she felt a sob on the verge of escaping. She blamed it on the hectic events of the past forty-eight hours, but Sean knew the truth was that she had waited so long to tell her family how she felt that her heart wanted to rejoice.

"To the bride and groom," Logan toasted loudly, filling the heavy silence as everyone at the table waited for Sean to finish.

Cheers followed, then laughter as they all noticed one another's tears. Sean slowly took her seat and forced herself to exhale. She wiped the tears from her face with the napkin and tried not to feel embarrassed by her near breakdown, even as Tracie's blond roommate from college stood and began her own speech about her relationship with Tracie. With a shaky hand, Sean took a sip of wine, then looked across the table at Logan.

While everyone else's attention was on Bonnie, Logan watched Sean. When she met his eyes he didn't turn away or smile; he just continued to watch her. And Sean realized at that moment that she would never love another man the way she loved Logan Riley. And she was so scared of that love, because if he knew how much she loved him he would probably run from her, screaming his head off.

* * *

An hour later, Sean realized another disturbing fact about herself: once she started crying, she couldn't stop. While everyone else in the rehearsal dinner had laughed their way from the strong emotions that Sean had inspired, Sean still felt as if she heard and saw everything from underwater. She watched her family—Banning, Tina, Terri, and Tracie—and she realized how fortunate she had been, how fortunate she presently was to have such amazing people in her life, who wanted to be in her life. And she had spent the majority of her childhood doing everything in her power to place as much distance between them as she could.

Sean finally stood from the table, mumbling to a concerned Terri about the bathroom, and she escaped the festive mood at the dinner table. She walked out the back of the restaurant, which had a lovely view of the parking lot and traffic on the busy downtown street. She sat on an overturned crate and tried to gather her thoughts. Maybe this was the reason she always kept a lid on her emotions, because once she unleashed them, she would never be able to close the lid again. Maybe beneath the hard-nosed exterior that she tried to portray to the world, she was more weak and fragile and emotional inside than she thought the Three Ts were combined.

Sean sighed in disappointment at herself, then opened her purse for the Snickers that she had stashed for such an emergency situation as this.

"You're going to eat that when inside we're being served the kind of chocolate cake that melts in your mouth?"

It surprised Sean that she wasn't surprised to hear Logan's voice behind her. She couldn't look at him now. He would see the love in her eyes. She didn't know if she wanted him to know. If he left her, she would never recover. She could face a den of drug dealers without sweating, but the possibility of admitting her love to one man made her tremble in fear.

Logan held a plate in her face. Her eyes widened when she saw the moist chocolate cake and swirls of chocolate icing. She grinned at him, then placed the still-closed candy bar into her purse. She grabbed the plate from his hands and used the fork to take a bite. She sighed in contentment as the rich burst of sweetness slid down her throat. Sometimes she seriously believed that chocolate was better than sex. She watched Logan grab an empty crate against the building, bending at the waist, his pants molding against his behind. She quickly revised her previous thought. Nothing would be better than sex with Logan.

"Thanks," she finally said.

Logan sat on the crate next to her and watched her eat the cake. He was silent for a moment, which made Sean nervous, and she cursed as the cake she had been expecting in her mouth landed on her dress, icing side down. Logan seemed oblivious to her mess as he said, "That was a nice toast in there."

"Besides the blubbering," she muttered dryly.

"You weren't the only one blubbering," Logan responded softly.

"I just thought it was time I grew up and told at least one member of my family how I felt."

"I'm proud of you." Logan grunted in comfort as he leaned his head against the restaurant wall and stretched his legs out in front of him. "Everyone is about to leave," he said, breaking the silence between them.

"Did you catch Sheldon's plans for the night?"

"He's going straight home to rest for tomorrow."

"I like stakeout targets who go home and rest."

"His parents are flying in early tomorrow morning from Paris, so we can count out seeing Madison then. Madison will show up either tonight or tomorrow at the wedding."

Sean licked icing off the fork, then said, "We can take

shifts. We don't have to do it together. You can go to sleep first, then drive your car over and relieve me of duty. I'm sure Dad wouldn't mind if I took one of the cars."

"Is that what you want, Sean?" Sean heard the edge in his voice, and she concentrated on the cake. "Do you not want to be in the car with me?"

"Strange things happen when we're in the car alone."

"Those strange things happen with you, and with no other woman, because . . ." Logan's voice trailed off and Sean watched him, not realizing that she held her breath until she had to gasp for air. She didn't know what she waited to hear, but she did know that her heart pounded against her chest and she was sweating underneath her dress. Logan appeared oblivious to her breathing problems, especially since he only stared at her hands. Logan finally looked at her and blurted out, "I'm in love with you, Sean."

Sean was speechless for several seconds. She felt her mouth moving but no sound came out. She didn't know what she had expected to hear from him, but a proclamation of love . . . This should have been the happiest moment in her life, but instead she wanted to cry.

His smile of relief and expectation quickly faded and he impatiently demanded, "Say something."

"Do you really love me, Logan?" Sean whispered, digging her nails into the palms of her hands to hold back her tears.

He appeared insulted as he said, "I don't take those words lightly."

"Neither do I."

"What are you saying, Sean? I tell you that I love you and you sound suspicious."

"I'm saying that I don't give my love that freely. It takes more than one weekend of tight clothes to make me love someone."

Sean saw the temper flare in Logan's eyes. She had seen him angry plenty of times over the last year, over the last twenty-four hours, but he had never been angry with her. She had always thought their friendship involved arguments and teasing, but she had never hurt his feelings, and she had a feeling that she just had. But she had to protect herself. Logan loved her now, but when they returned to San Francisco and she went back to the real Sean, Logan would realize his mistake. Sean could not survive the pain when he did.

Logan's jaw clenched as he said through his teeth, "I've known you for two years, Sean. I take seriously everything that has happened between us this weekend."

"I don't know what to think, Logan," she told him truthfully. "You haven't had sex in five years. And when you finally decide that you're ready to open yourself up to someone, it's in one of the most beautiful cities in California during a wedding, when I look about as different from myself as possible. How do you even know how you really feel?"

"This all goes back to your thinking I'm attracted only to your supposedly irresistible clothes and exterior appearance, doesn't it?" Logan exploded angrily. He shook his head and suddenly began to laugh, except that Sean had never heard him laugh like that. He sounded cold and foreign. She hadn't known that he was capable of laughing like that. "I thought the reason all of my other relationships failed was because I didn't know the women, and I thought that couldn't happen with you. After two years of living next door to you, I thought there were no surprises left, but there are. You're the superficial one. You'll kiss me, you'll sleep with me, but when it comes to giving your heart I'm not good enough."

Sean bit her bottom lip to prevent her automatic protest. She avoided his eyes but felt the anger and tension in his body as he jumped to his feet. She knew it was for the best. He could believe what he wanted to believe about her. The truth was, she knew a man like Logan Riley could never love her for herself, and as invincible as she liked to believe she was, even she could not survive a broken heart.

"Just admit the truth, Sean, and stop blaming me."

"The truth is that we would return to San Francisco and you would realize your mistake, except it would be too late and you're too nice. You'd stay with me for a few weeks out of guilt; then I'd be in the pile with the other five-weekers. And the worst part is that we wouldn't even be friends anymore."

"No, Sean, the worst part is that I actually thought telling you that I loved you would mean something to you. But I should have known. I'm wasting my breath on the great Special Agent Sean Weston, who doesn't need anyone, least of all a player like me. Right?" he roared angrily. He laughed, that strange laugh that left her heart cold, then muttered, "I'll take the first shift tonight."

In a burst of violence, he kicked the crate that he had sat on. The crate smashed against the wall and clattered to the ground. Logan glared at her one last time, then stormed into the restaurant.

Sean flinched as she heard the restaurant door slam. She told herself that it was what she wanted. She wouldn't suffocate Logan with her love. She didn't have to worry about his reasons for supposedly loving her. She could sit with her gun and her chocolate and be as happy as one woman could be. Except that Sean couldn't eat the rest of the cake, and, for some reason, she was crying again.

Sean slowly opened the door to the mansion and groaned when she heard the television in the living room. That meant that whoever watched television would see her and probably be able to tell that she had spent the last two hours crying and cursing herself—crying because she was too scared, and cursing herself because she was too scared. By the time she had walked into the restaurant, her family had been long gone. Sean wanted to stay in the city, but after washing her face in the restaurant bathroom and seeing her bloodshot eyes, the dark circles around her eyes, and her flyaway hair, she decided not to frighten people and head home.

As she entered the mansion, Sean forced herself to smile, then walked toward the stairs. She momentarily peered into the living room to make her presence known. Maybe if she took the initiative to be courteous, the family would then ignore her for the rest of the evening while she cried herself to sleep.

Tracie and Sheldon cuddled together on the living room sofa, watching the large-screen television. The picture of domestic bliss almost made Sean cry all over again. She didn't even know that she had wanted to cuddle on a sofa with a man until she saw Tracie and Sheldon. Sean had never thought of herself as a cuddler, but she had spent all night on the sofa with Logan. And she had loved every second.

"Hi, Sean," Tracie said, noticing her standing in the door frame.

"Thanks for the toast at dinner, Sean. It was beautiful," Sheldon said.

Sean forced herself to sound upbeat as she asked, "The big day is tomorrow. Are you two ready?"

"I was ready the first time I saw Tracie across campus," Sheldon answered as he pressed a kiss on Tracie's forehead, which made Tracie giggle.

"I'll leave you two alone. . . ." Sean heard footsteps echo on the hallway floor and she knew, without a doubt, that it was Logan. He didn't wear heavy cologne. He didn't wear clothes that made noise when he moved. Sean knew it was him because the air around her seemed to change. She changed.

Sean looked over her shoulder to find Logan standing directly behind her. He wore all black and he looked formidable and intimidating. She knew Logan's brother, Cary, and while she didn't scare easily, Cary Riley scared her. But, standing in front of her with an expression as blank as a canvas, Logan scared her more than anyone at that moment.

"Are you going somewhere, Logan?" Tracie asked from her position on the sofa. Sean inhaled air into her suffering lungs when Logan's eyes finally moved from her to Tracie.

"I thought I'd check out the Friday nightlife in Santa Barbara," Logan said, his tone emotionless, like a movie robot.

"You're coming to the wedding and reception tomorrow, right?" Tracie asked hopefully.

Logan smiled, but Sean noticed that the smile never reached his eyes as he said, "Of course I'll be there."

"We'll see you tomorrow," Sheldon said.

Without looking at Sean, Logan turned and walked out the front door. Sean ran after him, closing the door behind her, then she grabbed his arm. Logan yanked his arm from her grip so fast that Sean stumbled. She could feel the tears rushing to her eyes and throat hot and fast when she saw the coldness in his eyes when he finally looked at her.

Sean took several deep breaths before her heart stopped racing long enough for her to ask, "Where are you going?"

"I'm going to park at the end of the hill and wait for Sheldon to drive by so I can follow him. I heard him and Tracie talking earlier, and he said that he would leave in about half an hour," Logan answered. Whatever emotion he felt was covered by the blank mask he wore. He didn't sound angry; he didn't sound upset. He just sounded . . . as if he talked with a stranger. That wasn't exactly true. Logan was nice to strangers. He smiled at little old ladies and he winked at children. He hated her because she was honest.

When Sean didn't respond, Logan asked, "Is there anything else?"

"What time do you want me to relieve you?"

"I'll call you," he said, then walked toward his car.

Sean didn't want him to leave. She had a feeling that if he did, she would never have her friend back. She thought that loving Logan had been the best thing about knowing him, but being his friend had.

"The only reason I asked is because I thought you were really going to a club," she called after him, hoping that he would turn to her.

As if he never heard her, Logan yanked open the car door. "You were wrong," he finally said, then sat in his car and sped down the drive.

Sean waited until the car disappeared down the road; then she sat on one of the steps that led toward the door. If she were a smoker, she would have pulled out a cigarette at that moment. Instead she raked her hands through her hair, then rubbed her eyes. She was being noble. She was giving Logan a chance to find his real true love, and he repaid her with anger and snootiness. Sean figured that she had the right to be angry with him, but she couldn't do it. She loved him too much.

Sean buried her face in her hands when she heard the front door open. The problem with having a family who loved her was that they never left her alone. Sean looked over her shoulder and found herself smiling through sudden tears when she saw Tina, surprised by the hopeful feelings she felt just seeing Tina's kind face. The benefit of having a family who loved her was that they never left her alone.

In her perfectly arranged cream-colored linen suit, Tina sat next to Sean on the step. Sean laid her head on Tina's delicate shoulder and Tina wrapped an arm around Sean's shoulders.

"Are you and Logan having an argument?" Tina asked in a gentle voice that made more tears fall.

"Why am I so bad at this?" Sean wailed. She forced herself to move from the comfort of Tina's arms and wiped at her tears.

"Bad at what, Sean?"

"I'm a freak," Sean announced, then wiped her dripping nose with the back of her hand, which she then rubbed on her dress. "I don't know how to be a daughter; I can't even talk to my mother about her boyfriend. And I was a horror to you and Dad all these years—"

"No, you weren't."

"And I don't have any girlfriends because I don't know how to be a friend. I try, but I just can't handle talking about clothes and beauty stuff and weight problems. And I . . . and I love Logan, Tina, and he claims that he loves me. I know that he doesn't because he hasn't had sex in five years and . . . even if he did love me, it wouldn't have worked because I don't even know how to be a girlfriend. Someone has to be the woman in the relationship and I can't ever do that and that's why it never works. I'm a freak."

Tina smiled slightly as she pulled a handkerchief from somewhere and began to gently dab at Sean's face. "Calm down, Sean."

Sean nodded even as she cried louder. Tina wiped the tears from her face, then smoothed her hair. Sean slowly gained control over her tears, and she sniffled as she looked at Tina.

"You are not a freak," Tina said softly.

"Yes, I am. I'm not like normal women."

"There is no normal woman," Tina said firmly. "We're just who we are. If we were all alike, this would be a very boring world to live in."

"There is a normal woman," Sean insisted. "And my mom and me . . . we don't fit. That's why we'll always be alone."

"Is that what this is about? Did you ever ask your parents why they divorced?"

"I know why. Because Mom is a cop and Dad isn't."

"Your father loved your mother because she was so different. I don't think they would mind my telling you that they divorced because they drifted apart like normal married people do. For your father, it had nothing to do with your mother's job."

"Mom is just more normal than me."

Tina smiled as she said, "You have an answer for everything."

Sean nodded in response, then said, "That's why I'm not normal. I always know the answers."

"I'm going to say this once; then I don't ever want to hear you call yourself a freak again." Sean took a deep breath, then reluctantly nodded as she stared into Tina's calm eyes. "You are different, Sean. There aren't many black female FBI agents. There aren't many black women who get more excited about a brand-new gun than about a piece of jewelry. There aren't many black women who could have fought off that attacker last night. Logan Riley loves you because you are who you are, not in spite of that."

"How do you know?"

"I know that I look like Tracie's and Terri's sister, but I'm actually quite old and I have witnessed a lot in my lifetime." Sean started at Tina for a moment, and when she noticed her serious expression, Sean decided not to contradict her. Tina burst into laughter and Sean stared at her, surprised. "You must be feeling really bad if you allow that sister comment to go by without one word."

Sean laughed, then abruptly kissed Tina on the cheek. Tina's laughter turned into a soft smile as Sean said, "Thanks for listening."

"Anytime." Tina and Sean stood, both dusting dirt from their outfits. "What are you going to do about Logan?"

"Nothing." Sean stared down the road where Logan's car had disappeared. "I've loved Logan for two years. He loves me after he sees me in clothes and makeup that I've never worn in those two years. If I allowed myself to love him back, once we return to the city and he remembers who I really am . . . I couldn't go back to just being friends."

Tina stared at Sean for a moment, and Sean slowly became self-conscious as the silence lingered. Tina said in a gentle voice, "There is one thing I can point to about what's wrong with you: you're so busy protecting your heart from what other people could do to it that you never give them a chance. You cut anyone off before they can get too close. You can't go through life scared to love because you're scared of being hurt. It's not a good way to live, Sean, and it's not very fun either. Now come inside; I made those chocolate–peanut butter cookies that you love."

At the mention of her favorite cookies, Sean almost forgot that Tina had just called her a scaredy-cat. Almost.

Nineteen

Logan was so bored that he thought about knocking on Sheldon's door and asking if he could watch television instead of sitting in his car under the few trees behind Sheldon's house. He glanced at his watch. It was just eleven o'clock—five minutes after the last time he looked at his watch.

He had been sitting outside of Sheldon's house for the last four hours since Sheldon had left the mansion and had headed directly home. Logan had seen the glow from the television through the living room windows for about two hours; then Sheldon had gone to sleep at exactly ten o'clock. Logan could have gone for a car chase, a fistfight, anything but sitting in his car bored out of his mind.

Because sitting in his car made him think about Sean. Everything made him think about Sean. Logan had thought that Sean was different from other women. He couldn't have picked a more different woman from his usual dates if he had planned it. Sean never hid her feelings. When she was angry, he knew it. When she was happy, he knew it. Sean didn't care if Logan made a million dollars a year or his lousy cop's salary. Sean was the last woman Logan thought that he would fall in love with, but he had, and he was the fool for it, because Sean was like every other woman he had dated in one way—she had crushed him. Whereas the other women had trampled his pride or self-confidence, only Sean had the distinct pleasure of having crushed his heart.

Logan cursed, then pulled out his cellular telephone. He quickly dialed his brother's home phone number and kept his eyes on Sheldon's house as he heard the phone ring.

"Hello," Jessica greeted in a sleepy murmur.

"I'm sorry to wake you, Jess. Is Cary there?"

Logan heard her hesitation before she murmured, "No."

"What's going on?" Logan asked suspiciously.

"Nothing is going on," Jessica said, the nervous pitch of her voice hinting at the exact opposite answer.

"You're lying."

"I am not."

Logan laughed at her attempt to sound indignant. "You're not a good liar, Jess."

"I think it's against the law to abuse a pregnant woman like this."

Logan ignored her protests and bluntly asked, "What is Cary doing that he doesn't want me to know about?"

"Cary is going to kill me."

"Talk."

"Cary is picking up Maggie from the airport right now."

Logan almost dropped the telephone as he gasped in disbelief. "What?!"

"Maggie was concerned about you. She and Cary talked this morning and they . . . they're flying to Santa Barbara tomorrow morning."

"Both of them? Why?"

"I'm sorry, Logan. I tried to talk sense into them but they wouldn't listen to me."

Logan moaned into the telephone. "Please tell me this is a joke."

"Unfortunately, it's not. I told Maggie to come to San Francisco for a vacation, but that she and Cary should leave you alone."

"Why do they treat me like a child? I am a grown man.

I work every day, I pay taxes, I qualified for an American Express. The American Express membership letter said that not everyone can claim that privilege."

"I know, Logan; I agree with you. I told them to let you work out your own problems, but they're worried about you. Cary said someone attacked one of his agents and he has to get to the bottom of it, and Maggie said that it's time you stopped having all of these women problems."

"I'm looking forward to seeing them . . . so I can drag them back to San Francisco by their ears."

Jessica laughed; then her tone gentled as she asked, "How are you, Logan? We both know how protective Cary and Maggie can be, but tell me if I should be worried about you?"

Logan sighed, then raked a hand through his tangled curls. He admitted, "Probably."

"Oh, Logan."

"I told Sean that I love her and she told me that I didn't love her, that I was only attracted to her new look."

"Is that true?"

"Of course it's not true," Logan snapped. "I don't care about her clothes. The first time I realized that I did love her, she was wearing a typical Sean outfit. And when I thought about it, I realized that I've probably loved her since the first moment I saw her. You have to believe me, Jess. Someone has to believe me."

"I believe you, Logan," she reassured him. "So Sean never said that she didn't love you? She just said that you don't love her, right?"

"She didn't have to say it. I could tell."

"Then there's hope."

"I've been hoping for five years. Maybe it's time I stopped hoping and started living like the rest of the human race." He didn't wait for Jessica to respond and said, "I'll be home tomorrow evening after the wedding."

"Maybe you should talk to Sean again. I can't imagine

that she doesn't feel something for you. Why else would she ask you to go with her to meet her family?"

"I'll never know what goes on in Sean's head. And I've given up trying to figure it out." Logan rubbed his eyes, suddenly tired. "As soon as I get home, I'm looking for a new place to live."

"It took you almost a year to find that place. You love that apartment."

"I can't live next door to her. I can't see her every day. I can't hear her screaming as she beats the punching bag. I can't see her at the shooting range—"

"I see your point."

Logan smiled as he heard the concern in Jessica's voice. "Thanks for warning me about the Terrible Two."

"Go easy on them, Logan. Everything they do is because they love you."

"I know." Logan punched the disconnect button, then leaned back in his seat as he stared at Sheldon's still house. He should call Sean, since it was her turn. It was her bright idea to do a stakeout, but every time Logan thought about calling, he would picture Sean in the large bed in the guest room reaching for the telephone. He would picture her caramel brown skin glistening in the moonlight, the look in her eyes when she wanted him to kiss her.

Logan groaned, then threw his cellular phone into the backseat. He would rather sit in his car all night than hear her voice. Not for the first time, Logan wondered why he didn't turn on the car engine and start the drive to San Francisco. He knew why: he loved Sean.

An hour later Logan saw headlights shine in his rearview mirror as an indistinguishable car parked behind him, blocking any chance for Logan to drive away. Logan grabbed his gun from the passenger seat and clicked off the safety as a dark figure stepped from the car and slammed closed the

car door. As the person came closer and closer to his car
window and finally came into view, Logan's heart began to
pound, but he engaged the safety on his gun. It was Sean.
Logan would have welcomed Madison. He would have welcomed Hannibal "the Cannibal" Lecter over Sean at that
moment.

Logan got out of the car as Sean opened his door. He
could not distinguish her face in the darkness because the
trees that hid their cars also hid the moonlight, but he could
tell that she was angry—the anger rolled off her in waves.
He almost smiled; then he remembered that she had thrown
his love in his face. The best way to end things with Sean
was simply and cleanly. He could not be her friend, her acquaintance, or anything. Then a breeze riffled through the
waves of her hair and Logan caught the scent of raspberries.
He wished that she would give him a chance. He wished it
with all of his soul.

"You were supposed to call me to relieve you," Sean
snapped as her greeting.

Logan forced himself to sound nonchalant. "I don't mind
staying here all night."

"You can't stay awake all night."

"I said that I don't mind staying here. Go home, Sean."
He waited for her to leave but she didn't move.

"Don't you understand why it has to be this way?" she
pleaded, stepping closer to him.

"This is not the proper time or place." Logan glanced
around the dark trees, then muttered, "With all the noise
we're making, we'll scare Madison off."

"When else can we talk, Logan?" The softness in her
voice tore more holes in his soul as she whispered, "I have
a feeling that you'll leave as soon as the ceremony is over
tomorrow and I'll never see you again."

"We're next-door neighbors, Sean."

"And I bet that you're working to rectify that situation.
How long will it take before you move out?" Logan tried

not to express his surprise that she knew him that well. He leaned against his car and stuffed his hands into his pants pockets. "I don't want to lose you as a friend, Logan."

"That's not my problem," he snapped, forcing himself to stop relaxing. It was not easy to grow comfortable when Sean was around, even when they argued. He didn't have to constantly amuse her or make conversation. She didn't always yammer his ear off. Logan realized that he had missed her. In the last five hours since he hadn't seen her he had missed her. Logan cursed to himself, then said to her, "Both of us shouldn't have to stand out here all night. If you're not going to leave then I will."

"You're starting to piss me off," she snapped. She had obviously lost patience with him. He knew it would happen sooner or later, but he thought he at least deserved a few more encounters where he could give her the cold shoulder. She had completely shot him down. "Will you get over it, Logan? A few kisses should not destroy a two-year friendship."

"A few kisses did not destroy the friendship. You'd rather believe that I'm a liar and a superficial jerk, and that's the reason why we can't be friends," Logan retorted.

"What do you mean? Of the two of us, I'm the only one being real."

"Keep telling yourself that, Weston, and maybe you'll start to believe it. I thought that we were friends, but we were never friends. I don't know what we were."

"We were neighbors, you big baby," Sean retorted. "We were neighbors and we were friends until you allowed your five-year hyperdrive libido to take over because I showed a little leg."

Logan felt the anger cover his face in a heated rush. He didn't trust himself to stay alone in the trees with her any longer. He would either throw her on the ground and make love for the rest of the night or he would shake some sense into her. He tightly asked, "Are you going to leave or am I?"

"You haven't slept with a woman in five years. All of the kisses between us have obviously affected you," she said as if she spoke to a small child. "You almost broke your vow to not sleep with a woman unless she was your soul mate, and somehow you have to justify why you want to sleep with me, so you decide that you're in love with me. But you're not. You just found out that you're a normal man and not a celibate monk. Can't we move pass this?"

"When did you find the time to become a psychiatrist, in addition to your FBI duties?" Logan mused, then snorted at her explanation.

"If you were thinking clearly, you would see that I'm right," Sean said, ignoring his sarcasm. "I just don't want anything to be said between us that we'll want to take back when we get home."

" 'I love you, Sean' definitely qualifies as something I want to take back," Logan snapped.

She seemed to deflate in the night air as she whispered, "Your love faded that quickly?"

"Not yet, but it will." Logan brushed past her and sat in the driver's seat of Banning's Lexus. In the darkness inside the car, he felt the car keys dangling from the ignition.

"What are you doing?" Sean demanded as she ran to the driver's door.

"Since you don't seem ready to move the car anytime soon, I'll have to drive this car back to the mansion. I'll be back in three hours to relieve you."

"Don't bother," Sean spat out.

"Do you think I'm going to allow you to take all the credit for catching Madison?" Logan slammed the car door and reversed the car before Sean could answer.

He shook his head as he sped down the road. If Carl Madison was smart, he wouldn't come anywhere near his nephew's house that night, or he would have two very pissed-off law enforcement officers to deal with.

Wearing only his briefs, Logan cursed as an hour later he paced the length of the bedroom. He tried to sleep. He normally could squeeze a lot of sleep into three hours, but he couldn't sleep thinking about Sean alone in the darkness behind Sheldon's house. Every time he closed his eyes, he saw a faceless man dressed in black emerging from the shadows, reaching for her. He should call her. He knew that she carried her cellular telephone with her. He wouldn't even have to speak. He just wanted to hear her voice and make certain that she was all right.

Logan reminded himself that he was supposed to be getting her out of his system, not spending every spare second thinking about her. But she was his partner on this investigation—however unofficial the investigation was. He looked out for his partners even if they were women who broke his heart as if it were a game.

Logan had just reached for the telephone on the nightstand next to his bed to call Sean when there was a quiet tap on his door. Logan cautiously crept across the room, then opened the door. His stomach tumbled and his groin twitched when Sean brushed past him and walked into the room. She placed a hand against her lips to signal quiet, then motioned for him to close the door. Logan obeyed, then turned to her for an explanation.

"Sheldon left his house twenty minutes ago and I followed him here." Sean laughed as she said, "Tracie was waiting for him at the front door."

Logan couldn't help but return her smile. "I guess they couldn't spend the last night apart before their wedding."

"It's bad luck."

"Don't tell me that you believe in that stuff."

"Of course I do. And Tracie should, too. They're even

taking the wedding pictures before the ceremony. I have half a mind to burst into her bedroom right now and drag Sheldon out by his shirt collar."

Logan's eyes were involuntarily drawn to his large, empty bed. He shut his eyes against the image of Sean's nude body entwined with his in the middle of the white sheets. That didn't help. With his eyes closed, he now saw in more detail her wicked smile as she beckoned to him with one finger. He finally trusted himself to look at her again, and whatever she was about to say fell from her lips as she took one step from him. He didn't want to scare her, but he couldn't control himself any longer. Not around her.

He clenched his fists at his sides, wishing that he had the right to touch her, wanting to touch her. His body reacted to the memory of kissing her petal-soft skin. His hands ached to touch her. Never the fool, she slowly began to move toward the door.

"I parked directly next to Sheldon's car. He can't get in his car without setting off your alarm." Her voice sounded thick as her eyes touched on his bare chest, then moved lower and lower. Logan wanted to tell her that looking at him as though he were her next meal was not the way to ensure a safe escape from the room.

He had never responded to any woman so fast. He knew that Sean would say that it was because it had been such a long time since he had had sex, but he knew it was more than that. His body wanted Sean Weston, not any other woman. His heart wanted her, too. She wasn't wearing her sexy Sean clothes, but the real Sean clothes, and his heart beat just as fast, his palms were just as damp, and his body ached just as much.

"Good job," he murmured as he moved across the room to stand directly in front of her.

"I just wanted to tell you because I saw the light on and I thought that you were waiting for your shift . . ." Her voice trailed off and she finally tore her gaze from his chest to meet his eyes. She tried to turn to leave, but he placed a hand on her arm. She looked at him, a mixture of emotions playing across her face, as he brushed his index finger over her smooth dark eyebrow.

"I'm scared, Logan," she whispered. "What's going to happen when we return to the city and you see all of your girlfriends, and you're no longer celibate?"

"You're no longer celibate either. What's going to happen?" he whispered. "Are we just two friends who fulfill a need for each other, or do we have something more? You know what I think, Sean. I'll give you a little longer to think about it. But in the mean time . . ." Logan placed soft kisses along the edge of her jaw.

Sean always seemed so hard and untouchable, but she was so soft. He wrapped his arms around her, pulling her close to him, drinking in her warmth and softness. Her breasts underneath her sweater were cradled against his chest, creating an erotic cushion. Logan had dreamed about this moment so much, about how slowly he would go, about each inch of her body that he would lick, that he had never actually thought about what Sean would do. He definitely did not imagine her spinning them around until she had him backed against a wall. And then—there was no other word for it—she attacked him. With her tongue, her teeth, her hands, she launched a sensual attack that momentarily stunned Logan until his body shook with an unquenchable desire and his frantic hands were on her, too.

Logan tore the sweatshirt over her head and threw it to one side of the room. He stared at the black lace that confined her breasts; then his hands were on the full mounds as his mouth slammed over hers once more. She moaned low in her throat as she met each challenging stroke of his tongue with her own. Her hands squeezed his arms and moved lower and lower on his body until one hand cupped him. Logan almost jumped from his skin as she caressed him through his briefs. Through the thick material, he could feel the heat of her hand that sent shocks through his body as her tongue sent similar sparks of intensity through his mouth.

Sean reached for the waistband of his shorts at the same time that Logan popped the button on her jeans. Their frantic movements became even more frenzied as they kicked off their clothes. She wrapped her arms around his neck as his hands raced over his skin that sang at the contact. His hands moved everywhere at once, hitting every peak and valley that called for him. She heard her bra rip but didn't care, especially when Logan placed one open mouth on a soft, dark peak.

She gasped at the contact as she unconsciously rubbed her thigh against his strong, hair-covered ones. She inhaled his natural scent and slowed for the first time as she leaned her head on the wall and concentrated on the overwhelming feelings that Logan inspired with a simple flick of his tongue. It was anything but simple the way her body nearly trembled as he lavishly lapped one breast, then moved to the other. His hands skimmed down her body and rounded her behind, molding and massaging the skin.

Sean grabbed his head and lifted his face to meet her eyes. For one brief moment they just looked at each other. It was as if a light went off, because the two suddenly began to move more slowly, to take time, to realize that neither was going anywhere. One of his hands slowly traveled from her neck to between her breasts and down her stomach to settle between her thighs, to play with her other curls. Sean tried to speak, to tell him that she loved him, but then she felt his fingers on the hidden knob nestled amid her curls, and she could only bite her bottom lip to keep from screaming down the house.

Logan increased the pressure, then dragged his other hand through the thickness of her hair, brushing it from her face, seeming to memorize the texture and feel of it. She would later mull over his fascination with her hair, almost as if he thought it was beautiful and not a big mess, as she had always thought.

His mouth lowered onto hers and his tongue aggressively swept inside, matching the intensity of his hand. Her entire body moved in natural response as she clutched both of his shoulders. She was incapable of doing anything but responding to the attention he bestowed on her. She wanted to give as good as she got, but with powerful emotions beginning to wash over her and heat every inch of her skin, the only thing she could do was hold on for the ride.

His tongue in her mouth grew more intense, more erotic, as he made love to her mouth just as his hand made love to her. She could feel his hard length against her stomach, but he made no move to enter her. She wanted to cry in frustration, but the wandering rainbows in her body suddenly focused in one point and she realized that Logan Riley knew exactly what he was doing. As her completion tore through her body, she arched against his hand and moaned into his mouth.

She didn't have time to recover or attempt to calm her beating heart before Logan swept her into his arms and began to walk across the room toward the bed.

"Are you really carrying me, Riley?" she murmured, staring at him through a haze of fulfilled pleasure. "Put me down before you pull a muscle."

"You don't weigh that much," Logan said through clenched teeth, pretending to strain underneath her weight.

Logan smiled—the smile that would have turned her knees to jelly if they weren't already liquefied—as he laid her on the bed and hovered above her, staring at the feast that her body presented. Sean unself-consciously stretched under his intense scrutiny. She felt sated, warm, and loved. He moved on top of her, and her arms, of their own accord, moved around his body.

"I can't believe you carried me," Sean whispered, smiling as he stared at her breasts as if he had just won a prize.

Sean shivered slightly as cool air rushed around her breasts, but Logan's heated gaze instantly made her feel hot. She could feel her blood began to flow again; her entire body flowed as she felt that emptiness deep inside that she wanted only Logan to fill. She had been dwelling on the fact that he hadn't slept with a woman in five years, but he didn't seem in much of a hurry, while she could barely contain her struggles to be closer to him.

His hand began to slowly and carefully massage her breasts as his tongue moved around her navel in lazy circles.

"Why can't you believe it?" he murmured, then dragged his tongue to lightly touch one nipple.

Sean sighed in pleasure as her nipples beaded for more of his attention. "Why can't I believe what?" She moaned just before his mouth covered the other nipple and his tongue did wicked things that made her legs open a little wider in anticipation.

Logan grinned, then nipped her bottom lip. He moved away from her long enough to retrieve a package from a bag in the nightstand drawer. Sean momentarily forgot his question as she started at the entire naked length of Logan from head to toe. He was beautiful. From his long toes to his flat, defined stomach to his winking dimple, he was a work of art that belonged in a museum. But he was all hers.

The mattress sank under his weight as he moved on top of her, instantly warming every inch of her skin. "Why can't you believe that I carried you?"

"I'm not the carrying type of woman."

"You're my woman," he said in a growl, then claimed her mouth with his at the same time that he plunged into her. Sean screamed from the intensity of feeling the thickness of him inside her. He moved and then she screamed from the sheer spirals of pleasure that threatened to destroy her ability to dare compare sex to something as trivial as chocolate ever again. Logan laughed as he said against her mouth, "You're going to have the whole house running in here thinking that the intruder is back."

Sean bit her bottom lip as her hips matched his in their own special rhythm. Her hands squeezed his sweat-slick arms, then ran down the chiseled hardness to link fingers with his, which rested on the bed next to her face. Like lapping waves on the beach, bliss rolled inside her. And like the incoming tide, the waves became stronger and faster.

"You were worth the wait, Weston," Logan panted through clenched teeth. "Every night, every hour of waiting, was all for you."

His words sent her into a warm, contented abyss. She realized, before Logan smothered her scream of completion with a wet kiss, that if Logan didn't really love her, he did a damn good job pretending. A few moments later he cried out . . . louder than she would have, she thought with satisfaction.

Twenty

Sean felt herself smiling before she opened her eyes. She stretched her arms over her head as her eyes adjusted to the sunlight that streamed through the open curtains of the bedroom window. She had never felt so relaxed or so well rested. Considering that she and Logan had spent almost the entire night until the sun rose making love, she didn't understand why she wasn't tired. In fact, she felt downright giddy.

Sean brushed her hair from her eyes and turned to wake Logan. The smile instantly disappeared when she saw his empty side of the bed. She caressed the pillow, noticing that it was cold, as if no one had slept there at all. She glanced toward the open door of the bathroom. Both rooms were completely silent except for the panicky voice that screamed in her head about what she had done. She knew that she should be berating herself about sleeping with him, but she couldn't. She felt too good.

Sean wrapped the sheet underneath her arms and stood from the bed just as Terri, wearing the bridesmaid uniform of flowing pink from armpit to toes, burst into the room. Sean momentarily admired how beautiful Terri's petite frame looked in the sleeveless dress that draped to the floor, while Sean imagined herself looking like a giant pink balloon.

Sean quickly dismissed thoughts of the disastrous brides-maid dress and tried to rack her brain for a valid reason to explain her presence in Logan's bedroom in the morning, but Terri didn't appear to want or need answers as she rushed toward Sean. Without speaking, Terri began to arrange Sean's hair in a knot on top of Sean's head. Terri held a pink clip next to Sean's face, then nodded to herself.

"You're finally awake," Terri said as she grabbed Sean's hand. "We're already running late. Come on." Terri dragged Sean toward the open door, toward the numerous voices that Sean could hear in the hallway. She yanked her hand from Terri's iron grip and tightened the knot of sheet that rested between her breasts. Terri expectantly stared at her.

"It sounds like people are in the hallway. I can't go out there wearing a sheet."

"It's only the hairdresser and makeup artist," Terri said dismissively, then grabbed Sean's hand again. Sean once more pulled her hand from Terri's grip and Terri sighed in frustration. "We don't have time for this, Sean. You have to take a shower and change into your dress within the next fifteen minutes. Then Franco and Renee have to work their magic, and then we have to be at the church in one hour for the pictures."

"One hour . . . What time is it?"

Terri glanced at her watch, then said, "Ten-oh-three."

"Ten o'clock?" Sean asked, surprised. "I slept until ten? The wedding starts at twelve-thirty."

"Before he left, Logan told us not to wake you," Terri said, then reached for the sheet that Sean clutched around her body.

"What are you doing?" Sean demanded, amazed.

"There is no time for modesty, Sean. If you want to talk while you undress, fine, but we don't have time for you to talk and then undress and then—"

Terri's voice ended in a squeak as Sean grabbed her hand with just enough pressure for Terri to know that she shouldn't touch the sheet again. "The sheet stays."

"At least hurry, Sean," Terri pleaded. "Franco and Renee

have been doing hair and makeup all morning. They're tired."

"Why didn't anyone wake me up sooner?"

"And risk the wrath of Logan Riley?" Terri asked with a laugh. "He left explicit instructions for no one to touch this door upon threat of being shot."

Sean allowed the report of his concern about her to wrap around her body. It had to have meant something that he had threatened her family with bodily harm to allow her to sleep. Logan didn't issue threats for just any reason.

She grinned like a clown, then sighed. "Logan would never shoot any of you."

"You weren't awake to tell us any of us that," Terri responded dryly.

Sean didn't know if Terri would allow her the time to laugh, so instead she asked, "Where is Riley?"

"He left early this morning to drive Sheldon home. Sheldon was too nervous to drive. You'll see him at the church."

Sean hesitated, then cringed as she asked, "Does Dad know where I am?"

Terri's eyes narrowed as she crossed her arms over her chest. "No, but he can know if you aren't in the shower by the time I count to twenty."

Sean thought about challenging Terri, but as soon as Terri reached five in her count, Sean ran toward the bedroom door.

"Sean," Terri called, laughter in her voice as she stopped her count. Sean paused in the hallway door frame and looked at Terri. Terri grinned as she said, "I'm glad that you and Logan worked out whatever happened at the rehearsal dinner. He's a good man."

"He is," Sean said, then added, "So is Chancy. You should tell Dad and Tina about him. They like him."

Terri beamed, then glanced at her watch again and said loudly, "Six, seven, eight . . ."

Sean laughed but ran out of the room.

* * *

Sean's gasp of amazement mingled with the sighs from Terri and Tina as Tracie glided down the stairs. Sean had always known that Tracie was gorgeous, but she looked like a chocolate angel surrounded by a white silk cloud in the flowing, shimmering wedding dress. Sean clapped her hands as Tracie whirled around for the three women, showing every angle of the dress and gauzy veil that trailed past her waist.

Sean had never thought about her wedding. She longed for the stability and love that marriage supposedly came with, but she had never seen herself walking down the aisle in a big, white dress. In fact, Sean had thought that the whole idea of a woman being "given" to a man by her father was an insult to her intelligence. But as Tracie stood beaming in front of her, Sean could think only about how happy her sister looked and how she hoped to one day be standing in her own white cloud of a dress. And Sean vowed that she wouldn't make her bridesmaids wear a pink dress that itched and wrapped around their legs, with each step threatening to trip them.

"Mom, don't cry," Tracie said in a moan while rolling her eyes.

"My baby is getting married. I can cry if I want to." Tina dabbed at her moist eyes with a soft pink handkerchief that matched her beaded dress. She wrapped her arms around Tracie. "You are so beautiful."

"I can't wait to marry Sheldon," Tracie whispered while clutching her mother's hands.

"I know, sweetie."

"Oh, Trace." Terri gasped as she threw her arms around her sister. Tracie giggled, then stretched her other arm to Sean, who happily joined the circle.

Banning's busy steps sounded on the hardwood floor as he walked into the foyer saying, "We need to get moving. . . ." His voice trailed off when he saw Tracie. His mouth comically dropped open and he shook his head with a bemused smile. "You look breathtaking, princess."

He placed a soft kiss on her forehead, then glanced at the other three women. "What a lucky man I am."

"You'll be a hunted man by Sheldon if you don't get Tracie to the church," Terri sang out.

The doorbell echoed through the house, and Tracie said with a gasp, "That's the limo!"

Sean ran to open the door, stumbling on the three-inch thin heel of the shoes that Terri had thrust at her to wear with the dress. Sean forgot about her feet when she saw her mother's familiar profile through the frosted window of the door.

"Is it the limo?" Tina asked anxiously as she arranged Tracie's veil.

"No, it's my mother," Sean said, perplexed, then opened the door. As usual, Sandra was a unique mixture of sensual femininity and cop arrogance in a pale blue linen pantsuit. Her short brown hair glowed around her head in a halo effect, offset by pearl earrings and a pearl necklace that accentuated her outfit. Sandra Weston was the only woman Sean knew who found absolutely nothing wrong with wearing pearls and a shoulder holster at the same time.

Sandra walked into the house and shocked Sean by hugging her with a strong embrace that had Sean gasping for air. Sean couldn't remember the last time that she and her mother had embraced. She had never realized how much she missed touching her mother until that moment.

"Are you all right?" Sandra asked. Her voice was calm, but Sean felt the trembling in Sandra's hands as she touched her face.

Sean was slightly unnerved to see her mother express emotion. She had never doubted her mother's love, but Sandra was not the type of mother who proclaimed her love easily and frequently. Sandra's eyes narrowed slightly as she examined Sean's bruise, and Sean wondered if her mother also saw the fact that she and Logan had made love last night.

"She's fine, Sandy. We're taking good care of her," Banning said as he walked across the foyer to stand beside Sean. Banning was the only man Sean ever heard call her mother Sandy and live to tell about it.

"Sandra, I'm so glad that you could come," Tina said as she brushed a kiss on Sandra's left cheek.

Sean had been wondering if an alien had inhabited her mother's body, but when she saw the discomfort flitter across Sandra's face at the exuberant embraces from Tina, then Tracie, and finally Terri, Sean sighed in relief.

"Tracie, you are a gorgeous bride," Sandra complimented. Tracie smiled in gratitude, but Sean saw her nervous glance at the antique grandfather clock in the living room that was visible from the foyer.

"I'll go call the limo service and see where they . . ." Banning smiled in relief when a large, gleaming black limousine cruised to a stop in front of the open door. Tracie grinned her relief as well, then wordlessly picked up the front of her gown and ran out the door.

"Do you think she'll remember that she's not wearing any shoes?" Tina asked with a sigh as she waved a pair of white satin pumps. She shook her head in amusement, then walked out of the house and disappeared into the limousine with Tracie.

Sandra placed a large, firm hand on Sean's shoulder and told Banning, "Sean can direct me to the church. We'll be right behind you."

"We want both of you to come with us in the limousine," Banning protested.

Sandra didn't remove her hand as she squeezed Sean's shoulder—hard—then sweetly said to Banning, "Mother and daughter need alone time."

Banning nodded in understanding, then offered his arm

to Terri, who kept casting glances over her shoulder at the staircase behind them.

"Are you ready, sweetheart?" Banning asked Terri.

"Isn't Chancy going to ride with us?" Terri asked, then raised her chin in defiance when Banning's eyes narrowed in suspicion.

"Why would he?"

"He's practically family since he's been living here for so long. It would seem rude to just leave without him," Terri said weakly.

"Practically family—"

Sean interrupted her father's answer. "Don't you want to help the environment, Dad? The fewer cars that we drive, the less auto emissions pollute the air. Chancy should ride with you."

Banning stared from Sean to Terri, then back to Sean before he muttered, "Of course I want to help the environment."

Chancy walked down the stairs, looking uncomfortable and slightly nervous in a dark suit. Sean hid her laugh as she realized that Chancy would rather do anything but ride in the limousine with Banning. Terri grabbed Chancy's hand as soon as he walked into the foyer. Chancy nervously glanced at Banning, then followed Terri out of the house and into the limousine.

Banning glared at Sean and demanded, "What is going on?"

"Enjoy Tracie's wedding, Dad," Sean ordered.

"You've been in this house for seventy-two hours and you already know more about what's going on here than I do," Banning grumbled, but Sean saw the twinkle in his eyes. "Does Chancy have anything to do with the reason Terri has been spending more time here than at her apartment for the last three months?"

"Dad! Come on!" Tracie screeched from inside the limousine.

"She's nervous, Banning. Don't make her wait," Sandra encouraged.

"You two are not the only investigators around here. I'll find out what's going on with Terri and Chancy." Banning brushed a kiss on Sandra's cheek and murmured, "I'm glad you could make it, Sandy. Mother will be glad to see you."

"I haven't seen Naomi since Sean's college graduation," Sandra said with a grin that Sean knew was so like her own.

"My brother is bringing her. She asks about you all the time. She'll be happy to see you." He glanced at Sean once more and said, "Your grandma can't wait to see you either. She said that she wants to examine your fingers and make certain that they're broken, since that must be the reason she hasn't heard from you in the last month."

Sean grimaced at the silent scolding, then murmured, "I can't wait to see her either."

Banning walked out of the house and climbed into the limousine. The driver closed the door, then hurried to sit behind the steering wheel. Sean watched the limousine sail down the long drive toward the road. She could feel her mother's eyes on her, and Sean wondered how she could avoid the impending discussion. Somehow she knew that the intruder and Logan would be mentioned. And she wasn't certain if she could handle a heart-to-heart with her mother when she still hadn't found the courage to have a heart-to-heart with Logan.

"Let's go," Sandra said, then walked out of the house toward her blue Jeep. Sean locked the front door, then climbed into the passenger seat of her mother's Jeep. Sean watched the scenery speed by as Sandra drove to the church.

"Where's Deputy Howell?" Sean asked, deciding the best defense was a good offense.

"He's at his daughter's house. I'm going to pick him up after I drop you at the church."

"I didn't know that Phil had a daughter."

"He has two daughters. The older one lives in Santa Barbara and the younger one lives in Chicago. Both are married with children."

The two rode in silence for several moments before Sean blurted out accusingly, "Why didn't you tell me that you're seeing Phil?"

"Why didn't you tell me that you're seeing Logan?" Sandra calmly said in response.

"Logan and I . . . I don't know if I'm seeing him or not."

"Have you two slept together?"

"Mom." Sean knew that she sounded like an embarrassed teenager, but she still rolled her eyes in exasperation.

"Have you?" Sandra prodded, undeterred by Sean's resistance.

"Yes," Sean admitted in a small voice.

"Then you're seeing him."

Sean cringed as she said, "If you admit that you're seeing Phil that means that you're sleeping with him. . . . I didn't want to know that."

"I love Deputy Howell, Sean," Sandra said softly.

"That's great," Sean replied for lack of a better response, since she wasn't exactly certain how she should feel. The few times that she had met Deputy Howell she had liked him, but she had never pictured him as her mother's boyfriend before. She forced herself to sound neutral as she asked, "Do you think that you two will get married?"

Sandra laughed, then said, "I don't know if I'll ever do that again." Sean briefly smiled, then directed her mother to turn onto the highway that led to the church. "Tell me about Logan."

"There's not much to tell. I shellacked on some makeup, squeezed into a few tight dresses, and Logan suddenly decided that he was interested in me, that he loves me."

"Are you in love with him?"

"I've had a crush—if that's what you want to call it—on Logan for a long time, but love . . ."

"He's a good man."

"He makes me laugh. He knows when I need to be angry and when I need to be sad. . . . I sound like a greeting card." Sean abruptly sighed then blurted out, "I do love him, Mom."

She glared at Sandra for a contradiction, but when Sandra continued to keep her gaze on the road, Sean continued in a small voice, "Logan says all the right words, but I can't help but think that he only means them now . . . here . . . with me looking like this. I couldn't handle it if he woke up one day and realized with disappointment who I really am. If I ever do fall in love, I want it to last forever, and I don't think Logan knows what forever is."

"I told your father to stop playing so many Nat King Cole records when you were a baby," Sandra said with an amused smile.

Sean smiled at her mother's words, then admitted, "I love him so much, and that scares me more than staring down the barrel of a sawed-off shotgun. I couldn't even get his attention when I looked like the normal me. How am I supposed to believe him when he says that he loves me now?"

"What does that mean? When you looked like you? What's wrong with how you normally look?"

"Nothing . . . if the man you love isn't Logan Riley. You've seen Logan, Mom. Most days he looks like a model from the pages of *GQ*. On his casual days he looks like a model from Polo. What does he want with me?"

Sandra shot her an enraged look as she demanded, "Where is this low self-esteem coming from? Did Logan say something to make you doubt—"

"Of course not," Sean said, shaking her head. "I just meant that Logan can have any woman in the city. I, on the other hand, have to find a man who doesn't mind that I could probably break his arm if I wanted to, who doesn't mind that half of my meal may wind up on my clothes, and who doesn't mind that—"

"In other words, a man who doesn't mind that you're

you," Sandra finished. "And all of your faults, as you apparently see them, bother Logan? That surprises me. I never imagined Logan as such a jerk."

"He's not a jerk. He wouldn't care if I bathed in a bottle of ketchup," Sean hotly protested. She fumed while her mother pulled into the sparsely populated church parking lot at the bottom of the hill. The black limousine containing the rest of her family drove up the hill toward the narrow driveway behind the church. Sean yanked the lever and pushed open the door. "I'll see you at the wedding."

"Sean." Sandra's soft voice stopped her and she turned to her mother. She didn't like the smile that lifted the corners of Sandra's mouth. It was too knowing and . . . smug. "If you know that Logan doesn't care about all of those things, why can't he love you the way he says he does?"

"I'm like you, Mom; I'm a difficult woman to love. Logan is like Dad. He needs someone perfect and feminine like Tina. I couldn't handle the pain I would feel once Logan found her."

Sean wondered if her mother actually smiled before she asked, "What exactly are you talking about?"

"I know why you and Dad divorced. He couldn't accept you," Sean muttered, surprised by the burst of anger she felt toward her father. "Why are men so intimidated by a powerful woman?"

"I couldn't accept your father."

"Strong, independent women want a man to love just like . . ." Sean's thoughts trailed off as her mother's admission finally registered. She stared at her mother and gasped. "What? You couldn't accept Dad?"

"At first our differences drew me to your father, but then . . . Banning's idea of a fun Saturday night when we were married was sitting in front of the television or going to a country club to talk to the same people he talked to all week at work," Sandra said, the frustration in her voice still evident after all the years. "Guns scared him. My job scared him. He tried to belong in my world. In fact, I think he would have willingly done more of the type of things that I wanted if I had just asked him. He didn't care that I could outshoot him and outfight him . . . but I did." Sean saw the regret on her mother's face as Sandra whispered, "I really hurt him."

"I always thought that Dad left you."

"I was offered a position in the Santa Cruz Sheriff's Department at the same time Banning was offered a position in the Santa Barbara office of Harrison and Harrison. He wanted to discuss his offer with me; I accepted my job without discussing the move with him. He saw the writing on the wall. He helped you and me move to Santa Cruz and then he drove to Santa Barbara. I can't tell you how relieved I was when he fell in love with Tina. She's who he always needed, who I always saw him with."

Sean leaned back in the seat, uncertain whether to feel hurt or angry. She had never blamed her father for leaving, but for years Sean thought that she would never find love, just like her mother, because no man could accept them. The other cops didn't want them because they saw the females as colleagues and nothing more, while civilian men thought of them as too masculine. After wrapping herself in a blanket of misunderstood superiority for so long, Sean didn't like realizing that she was completely wrong about everything.

"I don't think that you really loved Dad, Mom," Sean finally said, without anger or sadness. "If Logan suddenly lost the ability to be a cop, and if he became the weakest man on Earth—weaker than Dad—I would still love him. Always."

Sandra smiled as she placed a hand on Sean's head. "Exactly, baby. I now know that's how I should have felt. I'm glad that you do feel that way about Logan."

Sean grinned at her mother, suddenly understanding what her mother wanted to tell her. She did love Logan, and if he loved her even a fraction as much as she loved him, their love could survive an eternity. She had completely given her love to someone. And for once, the thought didn't make her fear him. It made her want to throw her arms around him and risk it all to tell him.

Twenty-one

Grinning like a maniac, Sean burst into the church to find Logan. She inhaled the smell of wood mixed with slightly musty carpet, and wondered if she had ever smelled anything so wonderful in her life. She ran down the aisle toward the private chambers to the side of the altar and pushed open the door that led to the hallway. She tripped over her dress but didn't curse or even become angry; she just raised the front of the dress, then ran toward the bridal chamber.

Sean threw open the door, expecting to see Logan with her family, since she knew that Sheldon had to be at church for the photographs as well. Tina and Terri fussed around Sheldon, who looked more comfortable in the traditional black tuxedo that he wore than he had in the khakis and T-shirt he had worn to the rehearsal. The wedding photographer stood in the corner of the room loading film into the large, intricate camera he held in his hands. However, there was no Logan.

Sean's question about Logan's location died on her lips when she saw the tears in Tracie's eyes. Sheldon looked equally as downcast, but at least he pouted rather than cried.

"Stop crying," Terri ordered as she fanned Tracie's face with a piece of paper. "You're going to ruin your makeup."

"What's wrong?" Sean asked, surprised by the dark mood in the room compared to the happiness at the mansion.

"You mean besides the fact that the rest of the bridal party will not be here in time to take pictures before the ceremony because after the rehearsal dinner they went to one too many bars and were arrested for public drunkenness?" Tracie cried.

Sean tried not to laugh at the image of Walter Simmons of the Boston Simmonses, as he had informed everyone at the wedding rehearsal, in jail. "What?"

"Walter called us on Banning's cellular phone from the police station. Since my father and mother were on their way to the church, they detoured to the police station to pay bail," Tina said in a moan. Sean nodded sympathetically even as she bit her bottom lip to keep the laughter from tumbling out.

"Who cares about them?" Sheldon spat out angrily. Sean almost thought she saw his eyes water as he said, "Our photographer broke his arm last night. He sent a replacement."

Sean glanced at Tina, who looked more distraught than did the couple. "We pushed back the wedding two weeks to accommodate our photographer's schedule," Tina said in a disbelieving whisper. "He's the best wedding photographer on the West Coast, and now . . ."

Sean exchanged concerned glances with Terri, who shrugged in response. Sean cleared her throat, then said, "I'm certain that this man . . . What's your name?" she asked the photographer.

The photographer stared at her, seeming surprised that she addressed him. She noticed the bulging muscles underneath his charcoal gray suit. Sean hadn't known many photographers, but she never pictured them as being able to compete with professional bodybuilders. The man's dark brown face was partially hidden by a thick beard and mustache that, although neatly trimmed, gave him a slightly dangerous look. It was his eyes that made Sean pause and assess him longer. His eyes were dark and cold, and, for an insane moment, Sean thought about the gun in her purse and whether she needed it.

"My name is Harrick," the man finally answered.

"Harrick what?" Sean demanded, turning her full attention to the photographer. There was something about him that made the little hairs on the back of her neck stand up.

"Harrick the photographer," he answered with a smirk. Sean studied Harrick the photographer's face. There was nothing that made him distinguishable in a crowd. He was attractive, but not noticeably so. Harrick could blend into any crowd that he wanted to, but Sean also knew that a photographer would not return her stare with the same amount of apathetic distaste that Harrick was giving her now.

"Sean is right," Terri told Tracie and Sheldon as Sean and Harrick engaged in a silent staring contest. "Harrick will take beautiful pictures. Maurice wouldn't have sent him if he didn't believe in his abilities."

"You two can look at my portfolio if you want," Harrick chimed in, finally turning from Sean. "I could run to the office and get it."

"We don't have time for that," Tina reluctantly dismissed the idea.

"I'm sorry for doubting you, Harrick; I just want everything to be perfect," Tracie said, sniffling.

"With the way you and your soon-to-be-husband look, I won't have to do anything but point and shoot for a beautiful picture," Harrick assured Tracie with a comforting smile.

Sean shook her head at her overactive imagination as Tracie visibly relaxed at Harrick's words. Harrick was a simple photographer, and she was creating drama where none existed. Sean set her purse on a table, then walked across the room to arrange the veil that hung around Tracie's face. Tracie smiled gratefully at Sean, then dabbed at her eyes with a tissue.

"Where's Logan?" Sean asked Sheldon.

"I forgot something at my house and he went back for me."

"What did you forget?" Sean asked.

"My parents," Sheldon muttered in a long-suffering tone that made Sean laugh. "When I got home early this morning, they were there . . . angry and waiting outside the house in their rental car. I thought that we were supposed to meet at the church this morning."

"Speaking of angry parents, where're Dad and Chancy?" Terri asked nervously, glancing at Sean.

"Your father wanted to speak to Chancy. They took a walk," Tina said, then narrowed her eyes at her older daughter. "What is going on? Your father glared at Chancy during the entire ride to the church."

"Why? I thought Daddy liked Chancy," Tracie said, confused.

"I'm pregnant and Chancy is the father," Terri blurted out. She quickly crossed the room to stand behind Sean, as if for protection.

"Nice timing, Terri, very nice," Sean muttered sarcastically as she stared at the three identical stunned expressions. Only Harrick seemed oblivious to the tension in the room as he continued to load film into his camera.

"You're what?" Tracie exclaimed.

"You've known Chancy for only three months," Tina said in a gasp.

Terri looked at Sean for courage, then said to her mother. "We love each other, Mom. Would I have chosen to be pregnant right now? No. Am I happy that I'm carrying Chancy's child? Yes."

"You don't even know him well enough to love him," Tina protested.

"How long did it take you and Dad to fall in love? How long did it take you and Sheldon, Tracie?"

Tina and Tracie were suspiciously silent, and neither

could meet Terri's eyes. Everyone in the room flinched as a loud crash resounded through the church.

"That sounded like pews crashing to the ground," Sean said, not believing her own ears.

"Dad and Chancy." Terri gasped, then ran from the room calling Chancy's name.

"I'll handle this one, Sean," Tina said as Sean turned to follow Terri. "Stay with Tracie and keep her calm. I'll beat up those two idiots myself if they ruin this wedding."

Sean watched Tina run out of the room, then turned to Tracie and Sheldon. The three looked at one another, then began to laugh.

"Do you really think Dad is fighting with Chancy?" Tracie asked, amazed.

"Maybe you should go help Banning, Sean. Chancy is a big guy," Sheldon remarked, laughing.

"Terri and Chancy may be in love, but if Chancy seriously hurts Dad, Terri won't go near him ever again," Tracie said confidently.

"I think that we should take pictures of the bride and groom with family first, then pictures with just the couple," Harrick said, seemingly oblivious to the fact that two grown men were potentially fighting in a church.

"My dad is kind of preoccupied at the moment," Tracie said, laughing.

The door suddenly opened and Sean gasped when Carl Madison himself walked into the room. As if in slow motion, Carl looked around the room and smiled when he saw his nephew. Sean hadn't known what to expect from Carl Madison. Maybe she thought that he would pull out a gun and shoot them all. She had spent so much time thinking about him that maybe she had expected him to have a tail and two horns.

Instead he wore an expensive dark suit and polished black shoes. Carl Madison wasn't going to kill them. He just wanted to congratulate his nephew, then disappear from

America with millions of dollars that came from the blood of innocent men and women on the streets. Sean began to breathe again.

Carl instantly dismissed the others in the room as his gaze focused on Sheldon. Sheldon grinned and the two men crossed the room to embrace each other in a manly hug with lots of backslapping and laughter. Sean glanced at her purse—with her gun and handcuffs inside—on the table across the room. Since Carl had paid virtually no attention to her when he walked into the room, Sean doubted if Sheldon had told his uncle that his future stepsister-in-law was a federal agent.

"I can't stay long, but I had to see my boy on his big day," Carl said.

"It's too dangerous for you to be here," Sheldon responded. "Mom and Dad will be here in a few minutes."

"I know, I know, but I told you that I'd be here, and I've never lied to you." Carl smiled at Tracie, who nervously darted a glance in Sean's direction. Sean slowly inched across the room toward her purse. "Are you ready to make my boy happy, Tracie?"

"Whether she is or not, you'll never find out, Madison." At the sound of Harrick's bitter tone, Sean turned to see Harrick holding a very real, very dangerous nine-millimeter Smith & Wesson, equipped with a silencer, pointed at Carl. Sean's blood ran cold when she realized that Tracie stood directly in the line of fire between Carl and Harrick's lethal weapon.

Sean didn't think but acted. She moved to kick the gun from Harrick's hand, but instead of connecting with any point on Harrick's body, her right foot tangled with the long hem of the dress at the same time as her left foot stepped on the back hem of the dress. There was a loud rip of fabric; then Sean lost her balance as she was suddenly free of her pink prison. In a heap of curses and pink material, Sean tumbled to the ground.

Harrick immediately moved to stand over her, pointing his gun at her. He smirked as he said, "You're not so big and bad now, are you? Not like in your bedroom."

"That was you who attacked me?" Sean asked, not surprised when he nodded.

"I knew the bride had a stepsister who was an FBI agent. I wanted to make certain that you didn't know who I was or that I was in town. I only wanted to search your room, but you interrupted me."

"Now that you know who I am and I know who you are, you're under arrest," Sean said with as much confidence as she could muster, considering the fact that a pink dress was twisted around her body and hair fell in her eyes. "Put down your gun and raise your hands. Now."

Harrick snorted in disbelief, then said with a snarl, "Get up and move over there with the others."

Sean slowly complied, yanking down the cursed dress in the process. She glared at Tracie as she walked to stand next to her.

"I told Mom the bridesmaids' dresses should be shorter," Tracie said defensively.

"Shut up!" Harrick screamed at Tracie. Tracie flinched and turned in to the protective circle of Sheldon's arms.

"Harrick Wagner," Carl finally spoke in a resigned voice. "I never pictured you working for the Donalds."

"I work for whoever can meet my price. The Donalds are paying me top dollar to make certain that you disappear. Then they'll fill the void left by your untimely disappearance and take over your operations."

"Testify against Madison and the Donalds in court and I can guarantee that you'll serve only a few months," Sean said to Harrick.

"You are really starting to annoy me," Harrick snapped at her. "Madison, you're coming with me. And just to make certain that our little FBI agent doesn't do anything stupid, the happy bride is coming with us, too, until we get away from here."

Tracie whimpered and Sheldon clung to her. Sean stepped in front of her sister, keeping an eye on the gun now directed at her chest.

"Tracie will only slow you down, Harrick," Sean said, proud of herself for not sounding nervous. "She'll cry and beg and complain about her feet. You won't get far. Why deal with her when you can have an FBI agent? No one will shoot you with a federal agent shielding you."

"Tracie Harrison is worth a lot of money. No cop will shoot me with her around either," Harrick retorted.

"Do you want to take that chance? A cop could rationalize shooting a Harrison to make certain that two known criminals don't escape. Some might even think that Tracie was involved, since she knew that Madison would be here and didn't warn the authorities. There won't be much sympathy for her. However, any cop would hesitate knowing that one of their own was involved," Sean quickly said.

Harrick didn't respond, but instead he snapped, "Where are your handcuffs?"

"In my purse." Sean turned to reach for her purse, her hands itching to wrap around her gun.

"I'll get them," Harrick demanded, glaring at Sean and raising the gun once more at her.

Sean quickly stopped in her tracks, and Harrick ran across the room and ripped open her strapless clutch purse. He winked at Sean when he saw the gun and immediately tucked it into the waistband of his pants. He found the handcuffs and snapped one end on Carl's left wrist, then roughly grabbed Sean and snapped the other end on her right wrist. Sean sighed in relief that he didn't grab Tracie, who now sobbed against Sheldon's shoulder.

"Give me your suspenders and ties," Harrick demanded of Sheldon and Madison. He forced Sheldon and Tracie to sit on the floor near the table, then tied both of their wrists to one of the table legs with the suspenders. Tracie winced in pain while Sheldon stared at Carl, fear for his uncle evident on his face.

Sheldon looked at Harrick and pleaded, "Don't kill him. Please."

He tied the ties around Sheldon's mouth, then Tracie's, then motioned with his gun for Carl and Sean to walk out of the room. Carl glanced at Sheldon, and Sean actually felt sympathy for him. She could tell that he loved his nephew. She had never even entertained the thought that Carl could truly love Sheldon. She had never entertained the thought that he was capable of love.

"Walk," Harrick ordered, digging the muzzle of the gun into Carl's back. Sean nodded encouragingly at Tracie, then yanked on the handcuffs, causing Carl to stumble after her as she walked out of the room and into the hallway. She stiffened when she heard her father's angry voice on the other side of the hallway in the sanctuary.

"One word, Agent Weston, and I'll kill your entire family," Harrick said in a lethal whisper. "I won't even charge the Donalds extra. I'll consider it a bonus."

Sean kept her mouth closed and walked down the hallway. She noticed that Carl walked slowly, very slowly, as if he took his time to leave the church to frustrate Harrick. Sean silently glared at Carl and yanked at the handcuffs again to make him walk faster. She wouldn't entertain the idea of escaping until they were free and clear of any danger to her family. Carl rolled his eyes, then painfully grunted when Sean yanked at the handcuffs again, jerking his arm in the process.

The three walked out of the church's side entrance. The bright sunlight and crystal blue sky contrasted with the fear that lodged in Sean's throat. The heel of her right shoe caught on one of the porch steps and she stumbled to the bottom, dragging Carl with her. She cursed when one of her shoes slipped off.

"Keep moving," Harrick commanded.

"My shoe," Sean protested.

"It'll just slow you down," Harrick snapped, then added matter-of-factly, "I don't know why you women wear those things. Did you know that high heels are really bad for your feet?"

Sean glared at Harrick, then Carl when he nodded in agreement. If she didn't want to beat the two men senseless before, she definitely did at that moment. She took off the other shoe and held it in her hand. She planned to slam the high heel into Harrick's head if he came close enough, just to show him how bad high heels were for his big head. She refused to tell the truth—that women wore high heels for stupid men like them.

Carl abruptly stiffened as he glanced around the side of the building to the entrance. Sean followed his gaze and her heart thumped against her chest. Logan. She wanted to jump up and down and wave. She still had never told him that she loved him. It would be a shame to die without telling him that. Carl abruptly yanked Sean's arm and she glared at him, but his eyes were trained on the older couple who walked in front of Logan up the hill steps.

"Aren't you supposed to be kidnapping us?" Carl demanded, glaring at Harrick. "We should really get moving."

"Who are they?" Sean asked, taking a second to stare more closely at the older couple.

"Sheldon's parents." Carl groaned. "My sister and her husband. If I'm going to die today, I'd rather die without having to deal with those two."

"Don't worry, Madison; you'll get your wish." Harrick motioned with his gun for Sean and Carl to walk down the hill toward the beach below. He commanded, "Keep walking."

Twenty-two

"Why is the church so damn small?" Edward Cameron demanded as he and his wife waited for Logan to open the doors of the church.

"I don't think you can say 'damn' in church, dear," Beatrice absently responded as she blankly stared at the doors as if she had never seen how to operate one before. She glanced at Logan.

"We're not in the church," Edward snapped. "Of all the magnificent churches and missions in the area, I should have known that they would pick something like this."

"This is the church they attend, dear," Beatrice told him.

"Or they could have married in our church in Los Angeles," Edward continued as if Beatrice had not spoken. "Instead Sheldon wants to make our guests climb up a hill, then sit in this." Pure irritation entered his eyes as he pointedly glanced at Logan, then at the door.

Logan dramatically bowed, then opened the doors. After spending fifteen minutes in the car on the drive from Sheldon's house to the church with the Camerons, Logan understood why Sheldon had turned to a criminal like Carl Madison for affection instead of to his parents. Logan had never met two people who could irritate him so quickly. He could admit that it wasn't exactly their fault. He was impatient to see Sean. It felt like a lifetime since he had been pulled from her warm, luscious body to help Sheldon, since his best man and fellow groomsmen were nowhere to be found.

Logan had taken his unofficial groomsmen duties very seriously, or as seriously as he could, considering that he spent every thirty seconds smiling to himself as he remembered some moment of the night before with Sean. And every second with her had been worth every cold shower, every torturous second that he had endured over the last five years. He knew that his five-week curse was officially over. He would never be able to have enough of Sean after five weeks, five months, five hundred years. Maybe that was real love. No matter what happened, he would do whatever he could to be with her. Five weeks would never be enough.

Logan walked into the church, then stopped in his tracks when he noticed Chancy and Banning standing in the middle of the aisle. Both of their faces gleamed with sweat and anger that radiated off them in waves. Chancy's suit sleeve was partially torn off and his tie haphazardly dangled around his neck, while Banning looked equally as rumpled, but unhurt, besides a cracked lens in his glasses. Tina stood in the middle of the two men, looking angrier than either man ever could, while Terri cried into her hands as she stood next to Chancy.

"What the hell is going on?" Edward's voice boomed throughout the church, but no one paid attention to him.

"I don't think you can say 'hell' in a church, dear," Beatrice automatically responded. Edward glared at Beatrice, then turned back to the group.

Logan rolled his eyes in frustration at the older couple, then stalked down the aisle to glare at the two men.

"What's going on?" Logan demanded.

"I invited this man into my house. He abused my trust—"

"I love Terri," Chancy screamed over Banning's roar.

"This is not the time or the place for this," Logan snapped, glaring from one man to the other. Both men had the decency to look ashamed. "Tracie is getting married. If you two have a problem with each other, like grown men you wait until the beer starts flowing so you won't feel the pain from the other man's fists; then you take it outside."

Logan didn't know when Banning or the Weston family had become so important to him, but they had. Logan wanted Tracie to be happy on her wedding day. He didn't want Banning to do something that he regretted. And he wanted Terri to find the same love that Logan had with Sean. He was acting as if these people were his real family, and it felt good.

Banning glared at Chancy but reluctantly held out his hand. Chancy smiled in relief, then quickly shook the offered hand. Terri smiled through her tears and wrapped her hands around one of Chancy's arms.

"We should have told you sooner, Mr. Weston," Chancy said. "I'm sorry about that, but I'm not sorry about loving Terri or about our baby. I'll never apologize for that. I know I'm not good enough for Terri—I'm not like Sheldon or Logan—but I promise you that I'll make her as happy as I can."

While Logan wondered if he should feel insulted that Chancy placed him in the same category as Sheldon, Banning rolled his eyes, then glanced at Tina, who smiled at Chancy. Banning finally muttered, "I guess that's all I can ask."

Chancy grinned, then kissed Terri, who threw her arms around Chancy's neck. Logan laughed to himself as Banning cringed in distaste. Banning suddenly noticed the Camerons standing behind Logan and he straightened his tie.

"Edward, Beatrice," Banning greeted with an embarrassed smile. Tina whirled around and saw the Camerons for the first time. Her embarrassment matched Banning's.

"Your unmarried daughter is pregnant?" Beatrice asked as she raised one eyebrow. She whispered to her husband in a dry tone that carried across the Church, "Lovely family that Sheldon picked."

Logan barely restrained the urge to grab the two by their collars and throw them out of the church. The wedding was already disastrous enough without having to deal with their condescension.

"Where's my son?" Edward demanded.

"With Tracie, Sean, and the photographer in the dressing room," Tina quickly answered.

Edward spun on his heel and walked toward the dressing room. Beatrice quickly followed. Logan stared at his family, who all looked on the verge of collapsing into laughter. Logan winked at Banning, which made him smile; then he followed the Camerons.

Without knocking on the door, Edward pushed it open. "What the hell . . ." Edward demanded, sounding more perplexed than angry.

Logan recognized the slight panic in his voice, and he pushed past Edward's broad shoulders to see a bound and gagged Sheldon and Tracie on the floor of the dressing room. The table they had been tied to had tumbled to the floor, and the two breathed heavily through the rags stuffed in their mouths as they wriggled on the floor to try to loosen their ties.

Logan ran into the room and immediately untied the gags around their mouths.

"They have Sean," Tracie said as soon as her gag was removed.

Logan's hands stilled on the tie around Tracie's wrists. His entire body stilled. Sean. If he ever doubted his own love for her, he knew it was real now. And he had never told her how much he loved her or even why he loved her. No wonder she didn't believe him.

"Logan, untie us," Sheldon ordered in a loud voice, snapping Logan from his fears.

"Who has Sean?" Logan demanded as he quickly untied

their wrists. He helped Tracie stand, and Sheldon brushed dust off Tracie's white dress, which now had several rips and tears.

"Uncle Carl was here," Sheldon finally said, his eyes downcast.

"Carl was here?" Edward asked in a strangled voice. "What kind of strange wedding is this?"

"Madison took Sean?" Logan asked, ignoring Edward's confusion.

"No, the photographer took Carl and Sean a few minutes ago," Tracie said. "His name was Harrick, except he wasn't a photographer. He was hired by the Donalds to kill Carl because they want to take over his operations."

"The Donalds must have hired whoever tried to drive us off the road," Sheldon announced.

"Someone wants to kill Carl?" Beatrice gasped. For the first time Logan actually heard emotion in her voice and not bored superiority.

"Harrick wanted to take me but Sean talked him into taking her," Tracie said, her tears starting over. She grabbed Logan's arm and pleaded, "You have to help Sean. If anything happens to her, I'll never be able to forgive myself."

"I'll never be able to forgive myself," Sheldon muttered. "I never should have invited Uncle Carl to the wedding. I put everyone in danger."

"You love your uncle, Sheldon. He shouldn't have come," Edward said in a soft voice that Logan didn't know the man was capable of.

"Everyone will forgive him- or herself because nothing is going to happen to Sean or Uncle Carl," Logan said impatiently. "Go tell the family what happened. Tell Banning to call the police and to get in touch with Sandra. Understand?"

"Where are you going?" Sheldon asked.

"I'm going after Sean," Logan said, then ran out of the room. He heard Tracie yell a warning to be careful after him, but Logan only increased his pace. He burst out of the church and scanned the hillside running along all four sides of the church. He hoped that he was not too late. He could not be too late.

Logan spotted a flash of pink on the empty beach and he began to run. Even though they were far below, Logan could see Sean, her hair trailing in the wind after her, handcuffed to a man who trudged after her through the sand. A tall man dressed in a dark gray suit walked behind them. A glint of silver from the man's hand reflected in the sunlight, and Logan knew that it was a gun.

Logan's fear and anger combined to pump his legs faster as he sprinted down the hill toward the three. His only rational thought was that a man pointed a gun at his woman—his woman, whether she wanted to admit it or not. And by the time he was through with her, she would have no choice but to admit it, because Logan wasn't going to release her until she said it.

"Let's make a deal," Carl screamed over the pounding surf to Harrick as he tugged on the handcuffs, and Sean winced as pain radiated through her shoulder.

"Do that again and you'll be missing an arm," Sean warned Carl through clenched teeth.

"I don't make deals," Harrick told Carl.

"Whatever the Donalds are paying you to kill me, I'll triple it," Carl continued.

"What kind of businessman would I be if I allowed my targets to bribe me out of my mission?" Harrick said, genuinely confused. "No one would hire me again."

"I'll quadruple it," Carl answered.

"I can't offer you money, but I can offer you freedom, Harrick," Sean chimed in. "Testify against them all, and you'll be free from this life."

"One hundred thousand dollars or life in the witness protection program with a promising career as a fast-food cashier? That's not much of a choice to make," Harrick said dryly.

"Release me now, Harrick, and I'll put in a good word for you. I promise," Sean tried again, while pushing the hair wildly blowing in her face from her eyes.

"You've outlived your usefulness, Agent Weston, and you're really starting to annoy me," Harrick said, forcing them to stop. He pointed the gun at Sean's head. Sean refused to close her eyes. She refused to show fear and give Harrick the satisfaction, but her knees shook. Her entire body shook. She started directly into Harrick's cold eyes.

"Don't do this, Harrick. You'll just make things worse for yourself," Sean said, her voice firm and strong as every moment of her life played before her eyes. She didn't have any complaints, except that she had never told Logan about her love. Hopefully he knew.

"At least unhook me from her first," Carl said with a shudder of distaste.

One second Sean stared down the barrel of a gun; the next second she saw a whir of black. Logan leaped onto Harrick, tackling him to the ground, sending the gun flying into the sand. The two men rolled around the sand, clutching and grabbing at each other, occasionally landing punches and jabs.

Sean recovered from her shock and spotted the gun that had flown from Harrick's hand at the impact of Logan's tackle—lying twenty feet from her in the sand. She tried to run to it and was instantly stopped when Carl remained rooted to his spot.

"Move," Sean ordered, tugging on his arm. His arm jerked at her pull but he didn't move, and she only hurt her own arm.

"What do I get in return for helping your friend?" Carl asked simply, as he watched the two men splash into the water. Carl cringed as he muttered, "That's gotta hurt."

"You get to not have your face smashed in by me," Sean impatiently snapped. "Move. Right now."

"That's not good enough. I want a deal."

Sean was too afraid for Logan to rationalize with Carl. She was too angry with Logan for jumping into her fight with Harrick to have patience with Carl. And she was too in love with Logan to attempt to have a reasonable conversation while he was being hurt.

She glared at Carl and said through clenched teeth, "I'm going to tell you one last time, Madison: move!"

"You didn't seem surprised to see me. You knew that I would be at the wedding. Didn't you call your fellow agents? They should be right around the corner sitting in their vans eating doughnuts. Every cop deserves to have his butt kicked once in a while, which is exactly what Harrick is doing to your boy."

"I didn't call anyone," Sean reluctantly muttered.

"Oww," Carl said, then laughed in sympathy. "Your boyfriend just took a right to the kidneys."

Sean turned to see Harrick land a fist in Logan's stomach. He swung toward Logan's face, but Logan blocked the blow, then in a quick combination landed two solid fists in Harrick's face and stomach. Harrick fell into the water, but in a quick motion grabbed sand and threw it toward Logan's eyes, momentarily blinding him. Logan covered his eyes with his hands, trying to clear the sand, but Harrick didn't give him time as he punched him in the face, causing Logan to fall into the water.

Sean screamed in anger. She had to get the gun and stop Harrick from hurting Logan, and she didn't have time to negotiate a deal with Madison. In a rapid-fire motion, she used Carl's own weight to steady herself and whirled around to kick him in the face. Carl instantly dropped to the sand in an unconscious heap. Sean cursed as she stared at his large, unmoving form. She had meant only to knock a warning into him, not knock him unconscious.

She gritted her teeth, then attempted to drag the six-foot-two, 230-pound man across the sand toward the gun that winked in the sunlight at her. Sean's arm muscles and leg muscles burned with exhaustion under the motionless weight when she realized that she had traveled only about five feet. Her breath came in ragged gasps for air as she plopped down and dug her bare heels into the sand to attempt to pull Carl.

She looked over her shoulder to see Logan tackle Harrick into the small crashing waves. Logan slammed his fist into Harrick's face and blood spewed from Harrick's nose. Logan slammed another fist into Harrick and the photographer/assassin fell backward, unconscious on the wet sand, the surf lazily rolling over his legs and waist.

"Logan," Sean screamed, concerned, holding her untethered hand out to him.

He momentarily stopped to pick up an object from the sand; then, with his chest heaving for air, he trudged across the sand toward her. Water sluiced from his ruined suit and dripped from his face, mixing with blood that streamed from his nose and a cut on his bottom lip. Sean felt every cut and bruise that showed on his face. He half fell and half sat next to her, and Sean threw her arms around him, causing Carl's limp hand to slap Logan in the face. Logan winced in pain but his arms wrapped around her and painfully tightened.

Sean's smile of relief mixed with her own tears and the water from Logan's face as she pressed kisses on every inch of his face. She finally settled on his lips, and she groaned in pleasure and hunger when Logan responded, his tongue drifting into her mouth. His hands clutched her shoulders, and Sean welcomed the pressure to ground her in reality.

Logan finally broke free from her mouth and held up two wet sand-covered objects: her shoes. Sean could barely stand the burst of love that shot through her body. He was the only man in the world who could listen to her blab about guns one second, then fulfill her own private fairy tale the next second. And he did it all because he loved her. Sean accepted the love that she saw on his face, and it made tears fill her eyes. Logan Riley loved her. For some reason it didn't sound as out-of-this-world as she always thought it would.

Since she could share none of the emotions that clogged her throat, she warned, "If you mention Cinderella, I'll hurt you."

Logan laughed, then threw the shoes over his shoulders and wrapped his arms around her waist, pulling her into his lap. Sean didn't even mind the fact that her right arm couldn't follow the rest of her body, which meant that she had to uncomfortably twist to move as close as possible to him. All she cared about was being with Logan.

"I love you, Logan," Sean whispered against his lips.

"Do you really mean that or are you just saying that because I saved your life?" Logan asked with his familiar grin. His wet hands brushed her now-damp hair from her face as his eyes searched hers for a sign.

"You didn't exactly save my life; I was working on a way to disarm him," Sean felt compelled to say.

Logan laughed, then abruptly sobered as he uncertainly asked, "Do you really love me?"

Sean rolled her eyes in disbelief, then said, "Did you notice that I always have a six-pack of beer in the refrigerator?" When he nodded, she said, "I don't like beer that much, Logan."

"Did you notice that I always nursed one bottle of beer whenever I came to your apartment?" Sean felt a smile cross her face as she shook her head in confusion. He grinned like the playboy he never was and said, "I don't like beer either, Sean."

Sean laughed, then slowly sobered when she noticed the searching expression on his face. He softly asked "Why didn't you believe me at the restaurant? I've never told a woman that I love her, and when you didn't believe me that hurt."

"I was scared."

"Of what?"

"Have you looked in the mirror, Logan? You're sophisticated, gorgeous—"

"So are you," he interrupted in a firm voice that made her laugh.

"You're one of the few intelligent men who recognize that," Sean teased as she placed a soft kiss on his bruised cheek. "I just couldn't believe that someone like you could truly love someone like me."

"What changed your mind?"

"Nothing," Sean confessed, which caused Logan to protest, but she placed a gentle hand on his lips and said, "I know that I love you, Logan, and if you're giving me this chance then I'm going to take it. Whether you love me or not now doesn't matter, because when I'm finished with you you're not going to remember a time when you didn't love me."

"Is that a threat?" Logan asked, a smile lurking in his eyes as he raised one eyebrow.

"That's a guarantee," Sean answered with a confirming nod. Logan grinned in response and she saw the truth in his eyes. She wouldn't need threats. He loved her, and he was the rare type of man who believed love meant forever.

A suddenly conscious Carl said, "I hate to interrupt this touching moment but we still have a problem."

Sean glanced at Carl, surprised to find him awake, then she followed his pointed finger. Harrick had climbed to his feet in the surf and was reaching behind his back into the waistband of his pants. Sean's eyes widened as her gun appeared in his hands. He smiled as he pointed the gun at them. In a move so quick that Sean didn't have time to react, Logan slammed her to the ground and covered her with every inch of his body to protect her from a bullet. Sean screamed as she heard the sound of a single bullet rip through the air.

Seconds of eternity passed as Logan laid on top of her, unmoving. Silence weighed in the air. Sean couldn't hear the surf or Carl's uncomprehending screams. All of her senses seemed to completely stop as she fought the images of Logan dead on top of her. Then Logan moved. She stared in amazement as Logan slowly stood to his feet, no new spots of blood on him. He looked above her head and suddenly grinned. She scrambled to her feet, her arm weighed down as Carl remained on the sand. Harrick lay in the water, screaming in pain, as he held his bloody hand.

Like a vision emerging from the ocean, a tall, honey-colored woman with streaming brown hair strode through the water toward Harrick and picked up Sean's gun, which lay near his hand. With the appearance of the woman, Sean's senses all slammed into place as she suddenly heard the sound of excited voices and shouts. She followed Logan's gaze and saw her mother in a shooting stance on one end of the beach, still directing her gun at Harrick. In an identical position with his gun, Deputy Howell stood a few feet away from her. Logan's brother, Cary, stood on the other side of Sean, with a gun also directed at Harrick. And Sean could guess that the woman who slammed Harrick facedown into the sand, then slapped handcuffs on his wrists was Maggie, Logan's little sister.

"I thought that you didn't call the cops," Carl said as he slowly got to his feet.

Sean grinned as she took Logan's hand with her free one. "We didn't call the cops," she told Carl. "This is family."

"And I thought that my family had problems," Carl muttered while shaking his head. Sean and Logan looked at their family members, who all stood like statues prepared to blow several holes in Harrick if he breathed too hard, and Sean had never felt so loved in her entire life.

Twenty-three

An hour later, Logan's entire body painfully ached as the arriving wedding guests stared at the bruises that angrily blossomed across his right cheek. Actually, Logan wasn't certain if guests stared at his swelling lower lip and right eye, or at the dark slacks and dress shirt he wore when all the other male guests wore suits and ties. His Armani suit and tie had been ruined from the combination of sand, water, and blood.

While Logan normally would have been heartbroken at the idea, he could only smile because Sean was safe, her family was safe, and his brother and sister sat beside him on the front pew of the church. He had never known such rage as that which had filled his body when he saw the gun pointed at Sean. Even now his hands shook slightly at the thought, but he tried not to think about Harrick holding a gun on Sean. Instead he concentrated on the fact that the church was once more peaceful, the beach was free of guns and fighting men, and Sean loved him. She loved him so much that she threatened him, and he knew from experience that she used threats only when she cared.

The murmuring in the church grew louder as Logan heard guests complain about the now-fifteen-minute wedding delay. He could only laugh to himself, which caused a shot of pain in his bruised ribs. Only he and the rest of the family knew that Sean had to shower and change into clothes that

Sandra had brought from the mansion, that a seamstress was quickly trying to repair the damage to Tracie's dress caused by her attempt to escape from the ropes, and that the wedding had almost ended before it began. Only fifteen minutes late for the wedding was a miracle.

Logan glanced at his sister, who sat next to him, and at Cary, who sat on the other side of her. They looked like angels underneath the sunlight streaming into the church through the stained-glass windows. Looks could definitely be deceiving.

"Don't think you two are off the hook for stalking me to Santa Barbara on my vacation," Logan told them in a quiet whisper. Both turned to him with identical expressions of disbelief.

"Vacation? You were about to be killed! Cary had to shoot the gun from that man's hand. We saved your life," Maggie protested, her eyes wide at his lack of gratitude.

Logan muttered to Maggie, "I was working on a way to get out of it."

"At least admit that without us, you and Sean never would have stopped playing junior high school and told each other how you truly felt," Maggie prodded.

"I was handling that, too, little sister," Logan told her.

Maggie threw her hands up in frustration, then crossed her arms over her chest. Cary winked at Logan over Maggie's head, and Logan laughed in response just as Banning ran over to Logan. Through his new pair of eyeglasses, Banning shot a nervous smile at the more than two hundred pairs of eyes that were trained on the father of the bride when he bent next to Logan.

"Could you tell the pastor that we're almost ready to begin?" Banning asked Logan.

"Of course. How is everything coming along?"

"There's a handcuffed man in the back of the church surrounded by federal agents," Banning said in a harsh whisper, while glancing over his shoulder at Carl Madison, who sat in the last pew looking pained as he spoke to Sheldon's parents. Banning looked back at Logan as he continued, "I can't stop shaking, and I don't know if it's because my daughter was almost killed by the photographer or because my youngest daughter is getting married. My wife is crying because the wedding dress that she loves more than the bride is probably damaged beyond repair. We have no photographer to take pictures of the wedding, since our original photographer was found by the police tied up in his studio and he refuses to come near this family now, and the replacement photographer was a hired killer. How do you think everything is coming along, Logan?"

"I think that everything is going great," Logan immediately responded, grinning from ear to ear.

Banning grinned and clapped a hand on his shoulder as he said, "You must have read my mind."

"Mr. Weston, I may not be able to help with Tracie's dress or your nerves, but I can help with the pictures," Cary whispered. "Did Harrick bring the photographer's equipment to the church?"

Banning looked confused as he said, "All of the equipment is still in the dressing room. You can take the pictures? I thought you worked for the FBI."

"I do now, but in the past I was kind of a jack-of-all-trades. A few years ago I operated a photography studio for a few months," Cary said. Logan was impressed by Cary's ability to keep a straight face, because Logan knew that Cary actually meant that during one of his undercover assignments for the Group he had operated a photography studio. Logan exchanged a look with Maggie, who failed at looking innocent as she stared at Cary.

Banning glanced uncertainly at Logan, and Logan reassured him. "Trust him, Banning. I bet that he'll take beautiful pictures, as if his life depends on it."

Banning nodded, then motioned for Cary to follow him.

Cary stood and not-so-gently pushed Logan's legs out of his way before he followed Banning down the aisle.

Maggie sobered as she held Logan's hand. "They seem like good people."

"You trust my judgment now?"

"No," she flatly answered, while shaking her head. "But when we were all running down the hill and I saw you and Sean together, two law enforcement officers completely oblivious to the fact that a hired assassin was aiming a gun at you, I figured that you must have done something right."

"There aren't going to be any more five-weekers," he said softly.

"No more five-weekers." Maggie leaned her head on his shoulder and whispered, "Be happy, Logan. You deserve it."

Logan's response was cut off as organ music sounded loudly. As a group, the guests turned in their seats toward the entrance of the church to watch the procession of the parents of the bride and groom and then the bridal party. Logan was momentarily confused when Elton walked down the aisle by himself, because he knew that Elton was Sean's escort. Then Sean stepped into the aisle, and Logan grinned as he realized why Elton walked by himself: he probably had refused to walk with her.

Sean wore her favorite pair of jeans and a navy blue tank top, while carrying in her hands the same colorful bouquet as the other bridesmaids, as she walked down the aisle in her running shoes. Her head was held high and her hair streamed around her face in a wild profusion of soft curls. Desire and that strange emotion that he now identified as love lit throughout his body. And he couldn't prevent the grin that crossed his face.

"What the hell." Maggie gasped in Logan's ear.

The guests began to whisper loudly at Sean's unconventional outfit, and Logan saw Sean momentarily hesitate. Then, down the aisle, her eyes met his and Logan winked at her. She sent him a blinding smile; then she continued down the aisle. She reached the front of the church and their eyes remained locked on each other even as everyone else *ooh*ed and *aah*ed when Tracie filled the door frame on the arm of Banning. Tracie looked beautiful, but to Logan no one could compete with Sean.

Logan finally tore his eyes from Sean to watch a beaming Tracie walk down the aisle with Banning.

Two hours later, Sheldon held up his arms to silence the clapping and cheering crowd underneath the large white tent set up in the back of the Weston mansion to house the wedding reception. Logan turned his attention from talking with his sister and watched Sheldon as the crowd's applause slowly dimmed to silence. Logan glanced around the reception area to assure himself that at least the reception would continue to be gun- and hostage-free. So far, so good.

With champagne flowing and lobster dinners consumed, Logan had a feeling that everyone was too mellow to cause any trouble. Soft torchlights surrounded the tent, and until Sheldon quieted the crowd, the band onstage had played a mixture of uptempo and classic songs that matched the care-free mood in the room. Looking at Sheldon and Tracie's matching glowing faces, Logan would never have been able to tell that the two had been the center of danger earlier.

Logan thought of guns and immediately searched the area for Sean. For some reason the two had not had a moment alone since she was whisked away from his arms at the beach to change for the wedding. He still hadn't gotten the chance to express how much he loved her and why he loved her. Logan had a feeling that she needed to hear it more than he needed to say it. He finally spotted her standing in a corner of the tent with an older woman who resembled Banning, who, with a pointed finger appeared to be lecturing Sean.

"My wife and I want to thank you all for celebrating this beautiful day with us," Sheldon said into the microphone.

He beamed as he waited for the resulting applause to die down. "The wedding day is traditionally centered around the bride and groom, but I have to take a moment out of our day to recognize someone else."

Sheldon's mood turned sober as he scanned the crowd until his gaze finally rested on Sean. Logan laughed at the uncertainty that crossed Sean's face when she saw Sheldon staring at her.

"When Tracie told me about her sister, Sean, I thought that she exaggerated. I thought to myself that no one could be that selfless or brave. In the future, I'll always trust my wife's opinions, because Sean is all those things and more. She brought this family together. She protected us and listened to us, and I don't think anyone has told her how much we appreciate her. Thank you, Sean." Sheldon smiled as he held up his champagne glass. Tracie immediately followed suit, then Banning and Tina, until every guest underneath the tent held a glass of champagne in the air to salute Sean. "A toast to my wife's sister, Sean. Thank you, Sean, for being you."

There were other murmurs of "To Sean," and Logan grinned as he saw confusion and amazement war on Sean's expression as she looked across the room. Her face flushed; then she burst into a large smile that made several guests laugh.

Sheldon grinned in return, then said into the microphone, "Now let's dance!"

The band started another modern, jazz-infused version of an old classic, and slowly a majority of the guests moved to the dance area. Logan winked at a silently protesting Maggie as the same ancient man who had ogled Sean at the dinner party grabbed Maggie's hand and led her toward the dance floor. Logan made his way through the reception tent, briefly noting his brother arranging a group of women for a picture. Logan smiled at the seriousness with which Cary took any job; then he focused on Sean, who now stood alone, waiting for him. He realized that she had waited for him for a long time. He would remember to thank her every day for the rest of his life.

He didn't speak but simply pulled her into his arms and onto the dance floor. Sean didn't protest, but wrapped her arms around his neck and moved with him in their silent, familiar dance.

"Will this do for a ball, Cinderella?" Logan murmured as he nipped her ear.

He laughed as Sean groaned into his ear. "Remind me never to mention another fairy tale around you again."

Logan only smiled, but didn't promise anything. He mentioned the fairy tale because, despite her protests, Logan knew that Sean was just as much a romantic as whoever wrote *Cinderella*—almost as much as he himself was. She tried to hide it from him, from everyone, but Logan knew that with Sean it would always be true love and happily ever after.

She suddenly became serious as she added, "This outfit doesn't exactly qualify as a Cinderella gown."

"The point of the story wasn't her clothes; it was her," Logan said as his lips grazed across the soft skin of her jaw. "You're the most beautiful woman in the room, Sean, with or without a ball gown."

Sean studied his eyes for a second, and Logan wanted to ask her what she sought. Surprise crossed her face as she finally said, "You really believe that. You're either blind or you really don't care about the truth."

"A Prince Charming is never blind to his own . . ." He comically hesitated, then seriously said, "I won't say her name, but it rhymes with Spinderella."

"Can you really handle me, Logan Riley?" she implored, clutching his shirt. "Not just for five weeks?"

"The five-week curse applies only to women whom I don't love, and you're not in that category. You're stuck with me for much longer. Forever."

Sean nearly melted underneath the sweetness of the kiss

he then placed on her lips. They had shared more passionate kisses, more seductive and loving kisses, but this kiss she would always remember because it held a taste of promise and of a whole bunch of tomorrows.

"I love you so much, Logan." Tears of happiness filled her eyes, but she still gruffly told him, "I hope you don't expect declarations like that all the time. You know how I feel about that touchy-feely stuff."

"Definitely no touchy-feely stuff," Logan said, surprising and disappointing Sean with his quick agreement. He appeared completely apathetic to the fact that they were proclaiming their love to each other. Instead he gingerly touched the bruised spots on his face and winced. "Since we can't talk about touchy-feely stuff, let's talk about my bruises. Have I mentioned to you how much my face hurts?"

Sean felt a smile cross her face that she knew matched Logan's sudden grin. They would never be a couple who walked down the street holding hands or slobbering all over each other in public. But Sean didn't need or want that. She just needed gorgeous, sexy Logan—her own Prince Charming—who understood her better than anyone and who loved her in a way that she had never imagined anyone loving her.

Logan leaned close to her, until only a pucker of lips separated them; then he asked in that deep voice that made her entire body hum with a desire that only he awakened, "Am I ever going to get any sympathy from you, Weston?"

Sean knew that he expected a sharp retort or snort about his lack of toughness. Sean had a surprise for him. She was going to tell him the truth. She linked her arms around his neck and, with a silky whisper in his ear, promised, "Every day for the rest of our lives, Riley."

Logan answered by pulling her against his body, with a manly grunt that didn't annoy her as much as she thought it should have. But she decided that, with the quiet music, soft lights, and the fact that he had saved her life, she would let him get away with it this once.

COMING IN MARCH 2002 FROM ARABESQUE ROMANCES

__WHEN A MAN LOVES A WOMAN
by Bette Ford   1-58314-237-1 $6.99US/$9.99CAN

Successful designer Amanda Daniels is desperately afraid her hasty marriage to rancher Zachary McFadden will lead to nothing but heartbreak. She agrees to give their union a try for one year. To her surprise, Amanda finds the fiery sensuality between them creating a fragile bond that grows stronger every day.

__SURRENDER TO LOVE
by Adrianne Byrd   1-58314-291-6 $6.99US/$9.99CAN

Julia Kelley's abusive husband has been murdered . . . and she's afraid she might be next. Penniless, she hits the road with her six-year-old daughter, only to have her car give out in the middle of a small town. Julia's sure her luck has turned from bad to worse . . . until handsome mechanic Carson Webber comes to her rescue.

__WHAT MATTERS MOST
by Francine Craft   1-58314-195-2 $5.99US/$7.99CAN

If there's one thing that mezzo-soprano Ashley Steele knows, it's that the demands of love and career don't mix. She's already seen her first marriage destroyed by her dream of singing all over the world. So why—just at the moment she's poised to become an international star—is she about to let a gorgeous horse-breeder steal her heart?

__PRICELESS GIFT
by Celeste O. Norfleet 1-58314-330-0 $5.99US/$7.99CAN

Burned by an ex-fiancé, professor Madison Evans has poured her life into her work. The only thing she wants when she arrives at the small Virginia coastal island is peace and quiet to finish her book. But from the moment she encounters antique dealer Antonio Gates, Madison finds herself swept up in sudden, breathtakingly sensual desire.

Call toll free **1-888-345-BOOK** to order by phone or use this coupon to order by mail.

Name_____

Address_____

City_____ State_____ Zip_____

Please send me the books that I checked above.

I am enclosing	$_____
Plus postage and handling*	$_____
Sales tax (in NY, TN, and DC)	$_____
Total amount enclosed	$_____

*Add $2.50 for the first book and $.50 for each additional book.

Send check or money order (no cash or CODs) to: **Arabesque Books, Dept. C.O., 850 Third Avenue 16th Floor, New York, NY 10022**

Prices and numbers subject to change without notice.

All orders subject to availability.

Visit our website at **www.arabesquebooks.com**.

SIZZLING ROMANCE BY
ROCHELLE ALERS

__HIDEAWAY	1-58314-179-0	$5.99US/$7.99CAN
__PRIVATE PASSIONS	1-58314-151-0	$5.99US/$7.99CAN
__JUST BEFORE DAWN	1-58314-103-0	$5.99US/$7.99CAN
__HARVEST MOON	1-58314-056-5	$4.99US/$6.50CAN
__SUMMER MAGIC	1-58314-012-3	$4.99US/$6.50CAN
__HAPPILY EVER AFTER	0-7860-0064-3	$4.99US/$6.50CAN
__HEAVEN SENT	0-7860-0530-0	$4.99US/$6.50CAN
__HIDDEN AGENDA	0-7860-0384-7	$4.99US/$6.50CAN
__HOME SWEET HOME	0-7860-0276-X	$4.99US/$6.50CAN
__VOWS	0-7860-0463-0	$4.99US/$6.50CAN